Grounds
for
Murder

Grounds for Murder

A COFFEE LOVER'S MYSTERY

Tara Lush

CROOKED
LANE

NEW YORK

Copyright © 2020 by Tamara Lush

Published in the United States by Crooked Lane Books, an imprint of The Quick Brown Fox & Company LLC.

Crooked Lane Books and its logo are trademarks of The Quick Brown Fox & Company LLC.

Library of Congress Catalog-in-Publication data available upon request.

ISBN (hardcover): 978-1-64385-618-6
ISBN (ebook): 978-1-64385-619-3

Cover design by Brandon Dorman

Printed in the United States.

www.crookedlanebooks.com

Crooked Lane Books
34 West 27th St., 10th Floor
New York, NY 10001

First Edition: December 2020

10 9 8 7 6 5 4 3 2 1

For my father, who taught me
to always ask questions.

Chapter One

I gripped the bowl-shaped mug in my left hand so hard I thought it might crack, then eased off and took a deep breath. The aroma of rich, heady coffee hit my nose. I almost swooned.

"The espresso's perfect," I murmured, more to myself than anyone else. "Here comes the froth."

In my right hand, I held a stainless-steel pitcher filled with steamed milk. I hesitated for a second, and my café's best barista inched closer. I gave him a side-eye and leaned away, in the direction of the counter.

"Sorry, Lana. Didn't mean to violate your personal space." Fabrizio Bellucci was from Milan. He was something of a coffee celebrity because of his artfully designed lattes, and also for his shirtless selfies snapped on the white Florida sands two blocks from our coffee shop.

"Pour the milk in the center," he said in that velvety Italian accent. "Slow. *Lento.* Slow. I say that to all the women, by the way."

I rolled my eyes. He wasn't hitting on me. That was just Fab. He gently flirted with every woman aged eighteen to eighty. Sometimes it was charming, other times hilarious, and occasionally, like when I practiced my latte art, it was mildly annoying. But I tolerated his quirks because he was a java genius.

"Fab. Focus. I need to learn this if we're going to be a team for the contest."

"We're going to be the perfect team. I promise. You've been doing so well. And there's still a couple of weeks to practice. You've got this." He pointed toward the cup with a smile. I had to hand it to Fab; he was encouraging and loyal, despite his wandering eye.

The jangle of bells erupted over the strains of Fleetwood Mac playing on the Internet radio. Just last weekend, I'd unearthed four tarnished gold bells at a yard sale. After a bit of elbow grease, I attached them to a weathered fisherman's rope, then hung the whole arrangement on the front door so we could hear people coming and going.

Fab moved away, toward the register, while gesturing wildly. "Keep at it. You've got the soul of an artist. Let it out, Lana."

I cracked a grin while drizzling the milk into the espresso. There was a time, not too long ago, that I was a hotshot journalist pursuing a Pulitzer Prize in Miami and married to a handsome network news anchor. Now, I was an aspiring latte artist on the island of Devil's Beach, the princess of Perkatory.

Okay, well, the manager of Perkatory. That's the name of my family's coffee shop, and it's the coziest café on Florida's Gulf Coast. The name might refer to the underworld, but I aimed for a heaven-on-earth vibe.

Or, maybe I'd decorated this way because I was the one in need of salvation. A plausible conclusion after everything I'd been through over the last few years.

Perkatory was decorated in hues of weathered wood, with sky blue accents, and nearly every tourist who stopped by took tons of photos. The regulars smiled the second they walked in. You could see their shoulders lower, the stress ebbing from their bodies.

The coffee shop was a welcome respite on our bustling island, which was jam-packed with festivals, quirky local boutiques, and a plethora of outdoor activities that left both locals and tourists in need of a relaxation station.

And yet despite my interior decorating skills, pretty lattes eluded me. My wrists felt like they were forged from tin and lubed with oil every time I attempted to rotate the mug and drizzle the milk into a heart-shaped pattern.

Today, as I finished, I set the pitcher down and scowled at the design.

"Looks like a poop emoji." I looked up, searching for Fab. He was a few feet away, tending to a customer. I walked over to see him grinning at a woman with short, jet black hair interspersed with deep blue streaks.

"Welcome to Perkatory." I put the warm mug on the counter. "I'm practicing my latte art, so this one's on the house. Just made it. If you're in the mood for coffee, that is."

She glanced down, and to my relief, didn't laugh at my creation. "Sweet!"

I expected her to grab the drink and leave, but instead, she dug around in a black cross-body satchel and pulled out a five-dollar bill. She stuffed it into the tip jar and smiled. "Thanks for the free drink. I know what it's like to be a barista."

"Appreciate the tip. You here on vacation?" That's what I loved about running my family's coffee shop—I could chat with folks all day, every day. People shared the craziest details about their lives, and I loved every conversation and a bit of island gossip. It was like being a reporter, only without the deadlines and the writing. But I tried not to think about that part, because I missed storytelling so much. Heck, I even missed deadlines.

"Nope. Just moved here. Living over at the marina on a sailboat, looking for a job. You know of anything in a restaurant or bar?" The woman took a sip and her dark eyebrows shot up. "Girl, this is some great coffee."

I shrugged modestly. "We buy quality beans from around the world here at Perkatory. My foam art, though, that's the hard part. At least for me. Fabrizio here has been trying to teach me his mad skills."

He crossed his arms and beamed. I suspected he posed like this because it showed off his muscular, tanned biceps that strained the sleeves of his T-shirt. "She's an excellent student."

The woman took another sip. A faint mustache of frothed milk clung to her top lip for a second, until she swiped her tongue to make it disappear. "I could probably explain a few shortcuts. I used to teach foam art to new baristas in Seattle. I ran classes."

She mentioned a well-known coffee chain. My eyes widened. "No way. Really? Could you teach me?"

"Sure. Why's it so important to learn, anyway? Your coffee's great enough as is. You don't need the bells and whistles."

"Well, for one, it's good for business. Customers love latte art. And we're competing in the Sunshine State Barista Championships. It's being held on Devil's Beach in two weeks. I'd really like to win. We need some great publicity for the shop." I didn't say that I also wanted to win because it would prove I was good at something. Ever since I was laid off from the newspaper, I'd felt like a total failure. Coming home seemed like admitting defeat.

"You worry too much, Lana. Of course we'll win," Fab said. "The judges will love me. Er, us."

The bells on the door jangled again, and an older woman walked in. She had short, silver-blonde hair, oversized rose gold sunglasses and wore a zebra-print muumuu. She was trailed by a tall, blonde guy in neon green board shorts and a worn white T-shirt. He looked like he knew his way around a surfboard.

"Excuse me for a moment." Fab moved from behind the counter and went up to the guy. "Lex Bradstreet, what's up, man? You know you're supposed to wear shoes in here." He and the surfer dude gave each other a chummy hug.

Like most of the businesses in downtown Devil's Beach, we had a policy that customers were supposed to wear shoes. Sometimes, people couldn't be bothered. Since we were so close to the public beach, they often tracked sand inside, and I'd sweep up piles of it three and four times a day.

As I was about to say something—*no shoes, no shirt, no caffeine*—the woman pulled a pair of large black flip-flops out of her beach bag and dropped them on the floor. The surfer slipped them onto his tan feet. I turned my attention back to the woman with blue-black hair.

"Fab knows everyone around the island," I explained.

"Is he always so . . ." she waved her hand and we both glanced at Fab. His lips were on the cheek of the woman in the muumuu.

"Flirtatious?"

She nodded.

"Did he ask you to watch the sunset with him from his rooftop lounge?" I winced. That was his usual pickup line with women. He'd tried it with me a couple of times. I'd turned him down. And not just because I hated rooftops and heights.

"No, he stared deeply into my eyes and asked me what I desired. I think he got the message that my answer didn't involve him. He's pretty easy on the eyes, though. But I'm not in the

5

mood to deal with that kind of mess at the moment. You know. A man mess."

A giggle escaped my lips and an image of my ex-husband popped into my mind. "I'm quite familiar with man messes. Fab has a sometime girlfriend, but he's an incorrigible player. Fully admits it, too, so it's not like I'm talking behind his back. He's a hard worker and great barista."

"Sometimes you gotta take the good with the bad." She lifted a muscular shoulder. She had rosy skin, with lots of freckles.

"Exactly. Are you serious about teaching me latte art?"

"Sure. You want me to pull a shot and do a test drink to show you?"

I tilted my head. Hunh. If she was any good, perhaps I could hire her. We'd been slammed lately, and a look at the books last week revealed we had the budget for another barista. Dad told me I should make all the necessary decisions for the café.

"Sure. Why not? Come on back."

She held out her hand. "Erica Penmark. Love the look of this place, by the way."

"Lana Lewis. Good to meet you." Her grip was firm, something I appreciated. Her fingernails were the same hue as the midnight blue in her hair. With her all-black, punk rock aesthetic, she stood out among the café's décor, which was awash in beach shabby chic—right down to the perfectly distressed white wood antique furniture, the inspirational beach slogans painted on one wall and the robin's-egg-blue pillows that graced the wicker furniture nestled next to the floor-to-ceiling windows.

Thanks to the fact that the Devil's Beach main drag was built on a small, barely noticeable incline, the view from one bank of windows meant you could spy a hint of the glittering Gulf of Mexico a couple blocks away.

I gestured to the La Marzocco espresso machine. "There it is. My baby."

Erica let out a low whistle. "That is one sexy coffee maker."

She walked around the stainless steel machine, studying it from several angles. "Does she have a name?"

I grinned. "Fia. It's short for Sophia. As in Sophia Loren. Fia's got independent boilers, auto steam flush and auto brew ratio with drip prediction. My mom picked it out and named her."

With the proper amount of reverence needed to work a machine that cost more than my car, she faced the front. "Nice to meet you, Fia. Mind if I do a few warm-up shots?"

"Be my guest. Here's the grinder and the tamper." I patted the electronic shot tamper that packs the coffee grounds to a fully compressed, even, and level puck of coffee.

"Whoa. I've never used one of those. Always did it by hand."

"Manual tamping isn't consistent," I replied. "But if you'd rather, there's a hand tamper."

Erica became absorbed in the process of pulling a test shot. I stood back and watched her work. She was clearly an expert, with quick, efficient movements. In between watching her, I scanned the front counter for customers. Since it was around two in the afternoon on a Tuesday, it was a slow period.

This was the time of day I loved Perkatory most. In the bright Florida light, with the overstuffed pillows on the sofas and the artfully peeling white paint on the wood tables, it seemed like a soft and ethereal refuge. A waiting room of heaven, even.

She tasted her first shot and shook her head. Then made a second, and a third. By the fourth, she made two from the machine's dual spout and handed me one. I took a sip. "Perfect."

A grin spread on her ruby red lips. "Now for a cappuccino."

Without a word, I took the whole milk, sourced from a farm on the mainland, out of the fridge underneath the counter.

She again made a shot. The robin's-egg-blue mugs were ready and waiting atop the machine, and she plucked one from the nest, then poured the espresso inside. She splashed milk into the stainless steel pitcher and frothed it for twenty seconds (she used the little digital timer next to the machine), the wand making a satisfying hiss.

With the blue cup in her left hand tilted about thirty degrees, and the carafe in her right, she drizzled the milk to mix it with the espresso. A few tightly controlled flicks of her wrist led to perfectly white squiggles in the cup, and then it magically took shape.

"A swan," I gasped. It was one of the more difficult latte art patterns, and, astonishingly, it was better than anything Fab had ever done. "You're incredible."

She smiled, but not in an arrogant way. "And I'm available."

We both laughed. "Listen, I'm actually the owner here. Sort of. My dad technically owns the place but I run it. Let me talk to him. I've only been in charge for a few months, and I want to get his okay. Can you come by at the end of the week? Maybe Friday? I'd like to study the schedule and see where we can fit you in. We've been pretty busy lately, and I'd hoped to bring someone on before the winter tourist season hits."

"Absolutely. Works for me. I'm free any day, any time. Can give you references and everything. I'll bring a resume."

"Perfect. See you then."

Erica walked away and I busied myself with wiping down the counter. When I looked up, Fab was standing there with a sour look on his face.

"What?" I asked.

"We don't need another barista. I don't have time to train another staffer before the competition. You and Barbara and your father are enough to handle." Barbara was our other employee, who worked part time because she also ran an art studio here on the island. My father was, well, my father. Fab was well acquainted with his eccentricities.

"Come on. Erica obviously doesn't need much training. And we've been super busy for weeks. I'd eventually like a day off, you know."

We stared at each other warily. This wasn't the first time that Fab had tried to pull rank on me, even though I was his boss. He'd worked at Perkatory for a year and a half, while I'd technically just started a few months ago. I had a nagging feeling that he'd hoped to manage the place, and was irked when Dad put me in charge. Still, we had a solid working relationship and I'd come to view the café's employees as a little family—not as crass or freewheeling as my old newspaper family, but one that was just as devoted but made better coffee.

Maybe Erica could join our clan.

Fab sniffed. "Working every day isn't a bad thing. Not for you, anyway. You don't do well with downtime."

I straightened my spine. Gah. Dad must have told Fab how depressed I'd been when I first returned to Devil's Beach after the layoff and divorce. Still, why would he care who I hired? Unless he felt threatened by someone who was as good, if not better than him. He'd have to get used to it.

"I'm going to hire her. In fact, I might have her compete in the championship with you, instead of me. We'll evaluate her capabilities this weekend." I grinned. What a brilliant idea. The two of them would be a formidable pair and certainly wow the judges.

"Over my dead body," he muttered.

Chapter Two

Two days later, I was beginning to doubt whether there was enough coffee in the world to drag me through this morning.

"This is weak. Off, somehow." The sound of lips smacking together was as irritating as a steel fork scraping across glass.

I turned to face the guy who was the last straggler of an early morning rush of customers. He was in his fifties, balding, and the Tommy Bahama T-shirt, the white socks, and the tea-colored sandals meant he was likely a tourist. He clutched a cup of coffee in one hand and a copy of the *Devil's Beach Beacon* in the other. Thursday morning's top headlines—Island Gets a Jolt from Upcoming Coffee Contest and Devil's Beach Man Dials 911 to Complain He's Out of Beer—made me fight back a grin because of the clever wording.

Well, at least the irate customer was supporting local journalism.

"Oh really?" I pasted on a smile.

Perhaps the guy didn't like the Ethiopia Aricha roast and its delicate notes of hibiscus, jasmine, and lavender. Why he specifically ordered this blend was beyond me. Just yesterday, I'd spent an hour decorating the menu board in chalk, spelling out the strength of our various brews with the caricatures of coffee beans. The more beans, the stronger the flavor.

Silently cursing Fab, who was supposed to be here an hour ago, I grabbed the customer's drink, dumped it in the sink, and reached for a fresh mug. "Sorry, sir. Let me get you another."

"Stronger. Need it stronger," he barked. "Please."

A cup of bold—and generic—Italian roast would be more his speed, with flavors of dark chocolate and smoke. "Here's something probably more to your liking. Nice and strong. On the house."

As I was wiping my hands on a cloth, the man reached in a glass jar and extracted a baked treat. Before I could say anything, he bit into it. Or tried to. It was hard as granite.

"Disgusting." He tossed the oval-shaped cookie on the counter. It bounced a couple of inches in my direction without crumbling.

"Sorry. Those are for dogs." I tapped the sign on the jar that read PUPPER BAGELS: $1 EACH.

He shot me a dark glance and then lifted the mug to his nose, his mouth turning up at the corners. He took a sip. "At least this cup is excellent."

He stalked away, leaving the dog cookie behind. Jerk. Didn't I deserve a medal for not rolling my eyes or hurling the hard cookie at his face? I swept it into the garbage and prepared to take the next order.

I raked in a deep breath and my eyes landed on a sign I'd put up the other day on the far wall. Our part time barista, Barbara, made and sold the signs, which she cobbled together from four small, weathered planks. There was a word on each perfectly whitewashed piece of wood, and tiny seashells, gathered from the nearby beach, decorated the corners.

COFFEE
COOKIES
BOOKS
GRIND ON

Grind on. My new personal motto.

A woman in a pink bikini top and matching pink shorts shuffled to the counter with her head bowed to her phone. She was one of those former sorority girl types who seemed effortlessly put together and sleek. Maybe the wife of a rich man or a tourist passing through for a bachelorette party.

I, on the other hand, looked like I'd just rolled out of bed to face the morning rush. Okay, I had stumbled out of bed and walked here in the pre-dawn darkness like a zombie. Hadn't even bothered to brush my curly hair before gathering it into a ponytail.

"I'll have a half-caf, pumpkin spice latteccino. With flax milk." She didn't raise her eyes from the screen.

Flax milk. Pumpkin spice. With artisan coffee? What kind of abomination was this? Not here in my cafe. There were five choices: Americano, espresso, cortado, cappuccino, and latte. All those options came iced. We also had a limited and highly curated tea selection, and a single-origin decaf.

I drummed my fingers on the counter and studied the brunette. "Labor Day's a few weeks away. Pumpkin isn't on the menu because it doesn't jive with hella hot temperatures."

"Okay."

"And we don't carry flax milk. We have soy, almond, oat, coconut, and cow. Sorry."

12

She stared at me, slack-jawed and wide-eyed. "Fine. Well then. I'll have a coconut latte with a splash of vanilla. Large."

Still heresy to a coffee buff like me, but it was her palate. "Large coconut latte, splash of vanilla. Coming up. Name for the order?"

A haughty expression crossed her face and she flicked her gleaming blonde hair over one bronze shoulder. "Britt."

Within two minutes, I'd brewed the espresso and frothed the coconut milk. With a shaky hand, I drizzled the milk into the cup, attempting a foam heart.

When I was finished, I let out a little grunt of dissatisfaction. Another slobby looking heart.

"What?" Britt called out. She leaned over the counter, trying to peer around the espresso machine.

"It's nothing. I've been practicing my latte art. When I started, my hearts resembled Jabba the Hut. If Jabba were drawn by a five-year-old. Now they're more like something drawn by a particularly proficient five-year-old." A soft laugh escaped my lips. "It's also not easy due to the coconut milk. Whole cow's milk is preferable for latte art because of its fat content. It yields a creamy, airy froth."

Why was I rambling? She didn't care about the backstory of how her coffee was made. She wanted her caffeine hit. I placed the cup on the counter.

"On the house. It's been a tough morning. I'm usually in a sunnier mood. Lids and sugar are behind you."

"It doesn't look like a child's drawing! It totally looks like a heart." She squealed thanks and pointed her phone at the cup. I must admit, it was probably my best foam heart so far, but that wasn't saying much.

The heart shape had taken me days of practice and still confounded me. An absurd metaphor for my life. But tomorrow was Friday, and I'd be seeing Erica. I planned on scheduling her to work as much as she wanted and asking if she'd represent the café in the barista contest, alongside Fab. Maybe I'd be good enough to compete next year. If I was even here next year. Who knew at this point.

The woman took a sip and moaned. "Yummy."

I beamed, relieved. "Thanks. Hey, we have a coffee cupping coming up next month. I do a full tasting—from light to dark roasts—and throw in some varietals as well. If you're around, come and check it out, it's twenty dollars per person. And our best barista is supposed to teach an Instagram class for coffee lovers soon, too. You know, how to get the perfect shots for social media."

"Really? I love coffee photos. I'm going to Insta this right now," she burbled.

Thank goodness she wasn't going to hold my mediocre latte art skills against me. These days, you couldn't just serve excellent coffee. Every latte had to be the star of a twenty-first century still life: cozy yet modern, hip yet authentic. Tiresome, but necessary for an indie coffeehouse.

I began to slowly spell the café's Instagram handle—PerkatoryInParadise—but she breathlessly interrupted. This was the downside of a service job: absorbing people's microscopic bits of rudeness. Usually I didn't mind, and bad manners rolled off me like water on a duck. Today, though, my irritation simmered because I'd had to handle the morning rush alone.

"I know the name. Love it. Tagging you now. Hey, where's Fab? The guy with the accent? He sometimes keeps a special stash of flax milk for me."

"Excuse me?" I'd have to chat with Fab about this. Flax milk wasn't a big seller, and I hated food waste. It didn't make sense to keep a stash around, no matter how badly he wanted to get in her pink pants.

"You know, the one with all the . . ." she dissolved into a giggle and gestured to her midsection, "Muscles?"

Of course. She was one of Fabrizio Bellucci's groupies.

"You know? Fab? He's always here at this hour." Britt regarded me with hopeful, Bambi-like eyes.

Oh, sweetie, I've seen that look on a half dozen women. He's probably not that into you anymore. I smiled, tight-lipped. *But if you find out where he is, let me know.*

"He's running late." Yet Fab was never late. Where was he? It's not like he had a long commute to work—he lived on the fourth floor of this very building, owned by my family. But he hadn't responded to any of my texts.

Britt responded with a tiny squeaking huff. She also stamped her Barbie-doll-sized foot. "Too bad. He makes the best coffee. I mean, this is nice, too. I guess. Thanks a bunch!" She picked up the cup and shuffled away in her pink flip-flops to a table in the far corner. Probably to wait for Fab to waltz in sporting one of his tight T-shirts and toothpaste-white grins.

Blergh. I turned to wash my hands and wipe down the steamer wand. I had to calm down, Fab or no Fab. A long day stretched ahead of me, and I needed to leave for Miami in a few hours. Which meant I had to solve this staffing problem. This was what managers did. Solve problems; handle a last-minute staffing crisis; try not to alienate customers. A few deep inhales of the roasted coffee aroma grounded me.

As I bent to grab my phone on the shelf so I could again text my late employee, a voice wafted over my beautiful, stainless steel La Marzocco espresso machine.

"You're going to be the death of me with these cookies."

I popped up like a meerkat. That gravelly baritone. Those eyes— the color of Grade A maple syrup hidden behind black-rimmed, almost geeky, glasses. The muscled, bronze forearms. The close-cropped black hair. All signs led to yum.

"Hi, Chief," I chirped. Somehow my voice always went up a half octave whenever Noah Garcia was around.

He was the new top cop in Devil's Beach. Why he chose to come here after working at the Tampa Police Department was a mystery the entire island had speculated about, since his arrival a few months ago. Coincidentally, he'd taken the job not long before I'd returned to town.

Noah was something of a mystery to me and the rest of our gossipy town. The only thing anyone seemed to know about him was that he possessed a mild, laid-back attitude that matched the island's vibe, and that he came from an old Cuban family that founded a cigar factory in Tampa during the turn of the last century.

"Lana Lewis. Good morning. How are things at Perkatory this morning?"

"It's been a rough couple of hours. How's it going with you?"

He furrowed his brow adorably and reached for two cookies stacked on a platter. Real cookies, not a dog bagel, because Noah could read.

"Downright sinful. I mean, the cookies. Not the morning. So far, everything's quiet today." He bit his lip and my insides turned to caramel goo.

"Chewy vanilla coconut." I grinned at him while studying his long, sooty eyelashes.

"They smell incredible. Only five ingredients?"

My cheeks flared with warmth, the earlier irritation of the morning dissolving. "As always." So what if one of the ingredients came from a box mix? A girl could only do so much in the first few months on the job. I was a coffee connoisseur, not a master baker.

"What's up? You seem stressed."

I tucked a wild strand of curls into my loose ponytail. "It's been crazy busy. I'm the only one here, and I need to get on the road to Miami pretty soon. Can't leave the shop unattended."

He quirked his right eyebrow. Adorably. "What's in Miami? Don't tell me you're leaving us."

Would he care if I moved away? A fluttery feeling in my stomach replaced the stress indigestion. "No, I'm going to a journalism thing. It's an award ceremony. A chance to see old friends and all."

I waved my hand dismissively, feeling suddenly defeated. Who was I kidding? Did I really want to hang out with the handful of ex-colleagues who still worked at the paper, the place I missed more than anything? They'd tell me how amazing life was in the city, pity me for losing my job, then urge me to apply for a position at a low-paying blog for the privilege of living in Miami and paying fourteen bucks for a watered-down cocktail. Why was I even bothering? I was setting myself up for humiliation and heartbreak.

"Oh yeah? An award? Congratulations. Which story?"

"Remember that serial killer who was arrested last year? The Miami Ripper?"

He squinted. "Vaguely. Sometimes all that big-city crime blends together."

"He killed women at rest stops on I-95. I wrote a series about the victims and the stories led to his arrest. The articles ran right before I was laid off. But that's how it is in the news business, you know? You can do your best work and then get canned. Que sera, sera and all that. Now I'm back home."

I gestured expansively at the display of whole beans on a painted white shelf, a rack of Devil's Beach postcards, and Perkatory branded travel mugs nestled in a white wicker basket.

"And all this is mine. Thanks to my dad, of course."

It's not that I wasn't proud of the café. I was. But I didn't want to brag that Dad had insisted I take over the business. Partially because he wanted to focus on his yoga classes and real estate, and because I'd basically hid inside my childhood bedroom after the layoff, binge watching reality TV, eating nothing but store-bought donuts and drinking French press coffee for a solid month.

Even in my worst moments, I had coffee standards.

Noah glanced at me for a beat, staring deep into my eyes. I had to give it to him, he had that searching, investigative gaze down pat. He'd get me to confess every one of my sins in under five seconds, that's for sure. Perspiration bloomed on my neck in response to his heated stare.

"Well, I hope you win the award. Sounds like a fascinating series. I'll have to look it up."

I grabbed one of the small, laminated drink menus and fanned my face. Everything about the chief was swoon worthy. "Goodness. It's warm today, isn't it? Summer's never going to end."

He bit into the cookie and chewed with a half-smile. On some men, that would be impossible. Or disgusting. On Noah, it was a combination of sexy and kind. Lord have mercy. I'd never been attracted to cops when I was a police reporter. Most were either too dominant, too cocky, or too power hungry. I'd had a front row seat to all of those qualities during the final years of my marriage.

Noah, though . . . it was a crime how good he looked. That he was also sweet as my cookies, made it even more difficult not to blush and stammer in his presence.

I cleared my throat and broke eye contact, focusing on the ceramic tip jar with the handmade sign that said *TIPS: They're Like Hugs Without the Awkward Body Contact.* "Thanks, Chief. Um, you want your usual?"

"Yes, my usual, please. And you need to start calling me Noah. We see each other almost every day. I think I see more of you than anyone else on the island. Hey, did I tell you about that sci-fi show I binge-watched?" A hot flash rippled through my body. Was he flirting with me? It sure seemed like it. Hard to tell, though. Like me, the chief—excuse me, *Noah*—was a bit geeky around the edges. Or maybe he wasn't, and I was merely projecting that we were secret soul mates. We often discussed our favorite TV shows and books.

"I don't think so. What was it?"

As he described his latest Netflix indulgence, I washed my hands, then grabbed a to-go cup. He was explaining the plot while I imagined us spooning on the sofa, watching movies together. But I was nowhere near ready to date again. Or was I? I'd been single for an entire year.

I jabbed the hot water spout.

"Sounds good, I'll have to check it out. Hang on, let me grab a lemon." I ducked to open the mini fridge, then popped back up.

His "usual" was hot water with lemon. It was a big, fat check in the minus column for Chief Noah Garcia. He didn't drink coffee. How was that even possible? To me, it was tantamount to blasphemy. How could he be boyfriend material if he couldn't snuggle on a Sunday morning while drinking a mug of robust, life-giving java?

Freak.

"Well, I'm a little out of sorts this morning," I blurted. Out of sorts? What was I? An eighty-year-old woman? An extra on *Downton Abbey*? I pressed on as I sliced a wedge of lemon. Now I was sweating, disarmed by the chief's spicy aftershave scent that blended perfectly with my café's roasted coffee aroma. "I've had to handle the morning rush alone. Fab's late, which is unlike him. And I can't reach him on his cell."

While I twisted the juicy lemon wedge into his cup of water, he leaned in.

"Uh, Lana? Fab didn't tell you?"

I scowled. "Didn't tell me what?"

"He's over at Island Brewnette this morning." Noah popped the rest of the cookie in his mouth.

"What? Why? That can't be possible." Island Brewnette was the only other café in Devil's Beach. It was newer, larger, and in my humble and unbiased opinion, nowhere near adorable as Perkatory.

"What's Fab doing there?" My voice was cross. "Oh. I know. He was probably having breakfast with Paige. His girlfriend's father owns the cafe. I guess he was so caught up with her that he forgot about his shift."

The chief ran his fingers through his short black hair and swallowed hard. "No. Fab's working."

"What do you mean he's working?" I scoffed. "He's supposed to be working here."

"I walked by on my way to the station at seven. Saw him behind the counter so I went in to investigate. He was in there telling everyone he'd quit Perkatory. That he's competing for Island Brewnette in the barista competition that's coming up. The one that was in the paper today."

I pressed my palms into the blonde wood counter. "That can't be right. Fab wouldn't do that to me. He's the one who talked me into entering. And he's been a dedicated employee. He's like family."

"Oh, jeez, Lana. I wish I was wrong. I'm sorry to be the bearer of bad news. I thought you knew. I didn't buy anything there.

Because I'm loyal to you." He grabbed his cup and a second cookie, then glanced at the clock above my head. "Listen, I have an eight-fifteen conference call with the Florida Police Chiefs Association. Gotta run. Chin up, cupcake. You'll find another barista in no time. Everyone will want to work here. It's the best place on the island, with the best boss. Have fun in Miami."

He shot me a sheepish, if not maddeningly gorgeous, smile. Then walked out. I was too incensed to dwell on the fact that for the first time, he'd called me *cupcake.*

I snatched my phone off the counter and speed-dialed my most reliable employee. He picked up on the first ring.

"Dad, I need help. Can you come down and start working a bit early? I'm in a jam."

"Dear, I'm headed to beach yoga. Today's New Moon Yin class. Yesterday you told me to be at the cafe at noon, so I've already planned my morning."

"Please? I'm alone. Fab isn't here. We're about to get the mid-morning rush." Usually that consisted of tourists getting up late, or tourists coming in from their first session on the beach, needing a break from the sun.

As if on cue, a family of four, all in matching orange T-shirts emblazoned with a ubiquitous cartoon mouse, wandered in. I slapped my hand on the counter, hard enough to startle Britt in pink shorts and bikini top. Her eyes met mine, then she returned to her phone. Had she been listening to me talk with Noah?

Had she overheard my conversation with the chief? With Dad? I didn't want it getting around town that my best barista had jumped ship, so I turned and hunched behind the espresso maker.

I heard my father take a long slurp of something. Probably his morning green smoothie. Last week I overheard him and Noah talking about whether to put kale or collard greens in a morning drink and almost barfed.

"Well, call Barbara. I'm sure she'll want some hours. Fab never takes a sick day, so I'm sure he's resting," Dad said.

Barbara, our part-time barista, was probably out gathering driftwood, shells, and other junk off the beach for her so-called beach collages. "Or perhaps Fab overslept. Did you call him?"

"Dad, Fab's not sick. He quit. He's working for Island Brewnette now. I need to have a word with him. And it won't be a nice word, either."

Dad sucked in a breath. "Oh LeLa," he said, using my childhood nickname, "I'll be right there."

*   *   *

Once Dad arrived, I tossed back my third shot of espresso for fortification. There was barely enough time to savor the notes of chocolate and caramel. I grabbed my purse. I was fully caffeinated and on a mission.

Dad glanced at me, tossing his head to the side so his short silver ponytail swished against his neck. He'd donned a black apron over his gray sweats and white T-shirt emblazoned with a red mandala, and stuffed his iPhone into the apron pocket.

"You sure you want to do this before you head to Miami? Maybe you should wait a day, after you balance your chakras. Or, I could try my new reiki skills to center you. Or I could have a talk with Fab at yoga. You know how we sometimes see each other at men's yoga class." He rubbed a grass-green stone attached to a strip of leather around his neck. "You know what being in Miami does to your energy. Hey, I can get you one of these. It's malachite. Absorbs negative energies."

I ignored his New Age prescription for bliss. He'd gone over-board with the woo ever since Mom died; somehow her casual interest in yoga while alive inspired him to be a combination of Dr. Oz, Eckhart Tolle, and Deepak Chopra after her passing. At first it was endearing because he'd been so comforted by all the trappings, but now? I blinked a few times as I remembered him smudging my kitchen with sage.

"So, I should hide? Ignore him? Pretend he didn't jump ship when we needed him the most?" My voice was a sharp hiss.

"Sometimes you need to live and let live. Maybe Fab had his reasons."

I huffed. "I just gave him a raise. He rents the fourth-floor apartment from you. What reasons could he have to go work for the competition? It's rude not to give notice, especially right before the barista championships. It hurts. We were a team. Or so I thought."

Dad shrugged. "People are strange, Lana. It's something you need to get used to if you're going to be a businessperson."

"It's Florida. Everyone's strange. They shouldn't be jerks on top of it."

"I know, I know. Drive safe, sweets. I've got everything under control. I'll try to find out what's really behind Fab's sudden departure."

I had my doubts about Dad's version of being in control, con-sidering when I took the café over, the place was teetering on the edge of collapse. It had been Mom's dream business, after all. At one time, he'd been the quintessential Florida real estate guy, always hustling and aiming to make a buck. He practically had a cellphone surgically attached to his ear for decades.

Now he handed out cell radiation blockers like candy, and his grief over Mom's death left him a little scatterbrained.

But I did have immense faith in his gossip abilities; being Zen didn't extend to learning all the dirt on people. As a lifelong realtor on the island, he knew more details about folks than most.

Dad extracted his cell phone, and I knew he was fiddling with the tunes because the volume coming from the café's speakers went up a notch. I leaned in and kissed his cheek, getting a noseful of an earthy scent. "Patchouli?" I grimaced.

"One of the ladies at yoga gave it to me," he replied. Next to Fab and Noah, Dad was probably the most desired man on Devil's Beach, which was an unsettling fact as his only child.

The strains of Fleetwood Mac's "Sara" came wafting through the air. A goofy grin had spread on Dad's face, and his eyes glistened with moisture. "Your mother loved this song."

"I know." I let out a soft sigh. I didn't have the time or the emotional bandwidth to reminisce or grieve. "Please don't be sad. I'll call you from Miami, okay?" I wrapped my arms around him and gave a tight squeeze.

"Not sad, dear. I just miss her. I know you do, too."

I released him and nodded. "I gotta run."

"Don't forget about my retreat tomorrow. I can't work at all," he called after me.

"Got it." Crap, I was already running late. This confrontation with Fab was going to be a short one.

I drove the three blocks to Island Brewnette instead of walking. Normally I loved strolling the island's historic downtown, taking in the Caribbean–Key West vibe. The island's Main Street was eight blocks of mostly historic, four-story brick buildings, housing dozens of businesses and boutiques. A handful of buildings were painted white, while others, like my family's, were untouched. Several of those brick buildings had turned to condo-lofts on the top floors and had shops at the ground level.

Those grand old structures were interspersed with graceful, old wooden buildings. Some were historic, original shops from the turn of the last century, while others were Victorian-style mansions that had since been turned into bed and breakfasts.

But today was not a time to soak in the town's beauty. I was on a mission and past the hour I'd hoped to leave for Miami.

Miraculously, a car was pulling out right in front of the coffee shop and I parallel parked like a champ. Killing the engine of my ten-year-old Honda, I peered into the large windows. Goodness. It was packed. Just as packed as Perkatory had been all morning.

A gaggle of customers, mostly women, tapped on laptops, twirling locks of hair while stealing furtive glances behind the counter. Cursing under my breath, I tore out of my car and slammed the door. My mood plummeted with every step, and by the time I yanked open the door to the café, I was good and angry.

In my mind, I had imagined customers gasping the moment I walked in. I had figured they'd drop their mason jars when they saw the rival coffee shop owner stalk into Island Brewnette. Over pour sugar. Slop creamer everywhere. That kind of thing.

But no. Instead, no one acknowledged me. The hipster music droned on —it was loud and grinding, an assault to the ear— and everyone continued to focus on their screens. My eyes swept around the minimalist, monochrome décor. I sniffed disapprovingly. Entirely too trendy for me. Where was the homey, cozy ambience? Coffee was a warm drink. This seemed more like a doctor's office. Or a South Beach club. One of the reasons I fled back to Devil's Beach was because it was nothing like where I used to live.

My gaze landed on Fab, who was holding court behind the counter. He'd been here for exactly one morning and already he worked the espresso machine like he owned the place. Goodness, that was a nice machine. It cost a cool thousand more than mine. I knew this because I'd wanted that particular brand, but had been more fiscally responsible when I helped Mom make her final selection.

I stopped in the middle of the café, fixated on my former employee. He slid a white mug to a redhead in a flimsy white beach cover-up and matching white bikini.

"Here you go, *cara*," he purred in that Italian accent. His English was flawless, but he often sprinkled in some Italian pet names for women. "A foam heart, just for you." The woman squealed and thrust her ample chest toward him.

I rolled my eyes. "Oh, come on," I muttered.

"Oh Em Gee! Thank you! Can I get a selfie? I promise to tag you!" The woman whirled around and extended her arm, phone in hand.

For a beat, Fab and I locked eyes, and I snorted. Arrogant jerk. He quickly glanced away. I hoped he looked derpy in that photo.

"Excuse me." I pushed my way past a couple of customers waiting in line. I ignored their grumbles. Out of the corner of my eye, I spotted Britt, the woman in pink who'd come into Perkatory hours ago. She was shooting daggers with her eyes at the woman in the white cover-up. Would Fab's departure cause me to bleed customers?

"What is going on here?" Maybe my voice was a touch too loud, probably because of the stupid music.

Fab grinned, crossing his muscular arms over his chest. "Change of plans, darling Lana. I was going to get with you later to explain."

I hated when he called me "darling Lana." It felt so pretentious.

That's when I lost it. Gesturing wildly, all my frustrations poured from my mouth. Being laid off from the paper in Miami.

26

Returning home to Devil's Beach, a place that harbored complicated memories. Running my mother's once-beloved coffee shop. My dismal love life. The fact that Fab's departure meant that we wouldn't have a chance of winning the Sunshine State Barista Championship. Everything.

"You are a traitor. Any reasonable person would have given two weeks' notice. And you could have told me you were doing this before we entered the barista competition, before I paid the five-hundred-dollar entry fee. We were doing this together. And now, you'll be competing on their team," I spat.

He shrugged. "It's beyond my control," he responded. "I wanted to be with my girlfriend."

"Don't pee down my back and tell me it's raining. You're being selfish. Why would you do this to me? I thought we got along well."

I glared at him, but he didn't respond. That only made me angrier. And sadder. Fab was one of the few people I regularly talked with. Even though most of our conversations revolved around Instagram, the beach, and his workout routines with his buddies. He was one of my few lifelines to the world after a difficult few years, and now it was severed.

His move to the competition left another little fracture in my already splintered heart.

"Your girlfriend wanted to keep an eye on you because you can't keep your pants zipped, and so here you are. Well, I hope you realize how you've screwed me over. I wish I'd never met you. Wish you never existed, really. You're a menace to women, you know that? You're a user."

Crap. This was nasty, especially for me. I needed to get a handle on my emotions, and yet I took everything out on him as the crowd in Island Brewnette looked on in horror. I took a deep breath and tried to count to ten.

"You're being so extreme in your response," he said in formal, Italian-tinged English. The kind that made women go gaga. "Darling Lana, let's talk tonight over Chianti. We're practically neighbors, after all."

"Don't remind me that we live so close. If it were up to me, you'd be evicted. How can you stay in our building now? Of course, I'm being extreme. You walked out at the worst possible time and went to the competition. You betrayed me. And I hope you fail at the barista competition."

Somehow, that was the worst part. Despite his flaws, I thought we were friends. I spat some choice phrases that may or may not have involved a few swear words that I'd learned in newsrooms. Then I stalked out and seethed all the way to Miami, hoping the city would take my mind off all my island troubles.

Chapter Three

S poiler alert: the city did not take my mind off my troubles. Not by a long shot.

For starters, because I was so late getting on the road, traffic snarled my journey, along with a nasty wreck on I-75 involving what appeared to be a tangle with Lamborghini and a motorcycle. I checked into my cheap motel room, threw on a little black dress and spackled on a layer of makeup. Rolling on deodorant in a bathroom straight out of a 1980s *Scarface* scene wasn't how I'd hoped to start the evening, but it fit my mood.

Grumbling to myself, I called an Uber, which took eons to drive downtown. The early evening ceremony was held at Icon, a downtown hotel where the Florida Society of Professional Journalists' annual award dinner was held every year. Somehow, despite a downturn in the news industry, the group managed to scrape together enough cash to hold the banquet on the top floor of the city's swankiest address.

Obviously, because it was Miami in late August, it was hot as heck. While riding the elevator up, I dabbed the sweat off my face with a tissue and peered in the mirrored door, trying not to think too hard about how this entire evening—celebrating the best of journalism while papers were cutting jobs every other month—was like rearranging deck chairs on the Titanic.

Futile.

Oh well. At least there was free booze.

I stepped out of the elevator and made my way down the corridor to the bar, where everyone would gather before entering the banquet hall. Free drinks made journalists as happy as clams at high tide.

The bar was packed with folks from papers all over Florida, and I recognized dozens of them. Panic seized my gut. Was I really welcome here? I was no longer a reporter, no longer a part of the tribe. I kept close to the inner wall, not wanting to get too near the floor-to-ceiling windows, with the expansive view of Miami. If I focused on the glittering skyline from this height, I'd get woozy and anxious.

More anxious than I already was.

I snatched a glass of champagne off the tray of a passing waiter. It was crisp and fizzy, but I could drink an entire bottle by myself back in my hotel room. There, I could inhale a box of guava pastries, too. A worthy alternative than all this . . . peopling.

"You made it!"

I turned to the familiar, rich male voice. "Erol!"

I wrapped my arms around his red smoking jacket, pulling him close. He was a features editor at my old paper, and my closest friend there. I immediately felt terrible for letting a few weeks go by without talking with him.

Erol was a gorgeous Haitian man, who was among Miami's most eligible bachelors. Women of all ages sought his company, but I was one of the few to know that he was nursing a broken heart after his girlfriend left him to take a job as a war correspondent in Iraq with a wire service.

We swept each other up in a hug and for a moment, I missed him desperately. Missed Miami. Yearned for everything about my old life. So much that I was a second or two away from weeping.

"You made it," he cried.

"Your hair looks amazing," I squealed, kissing him on the cheek.

"Yours does, too. So full and curly. Lana, you have some guts coming here," he said with an admiring grin while plucking two glasses of champagne off a wandering waiter's tray. He handed one to me, and I took a gulp.

"Hey, I'm up for an award." I shrugged. "I was invited just like everyone else. Even though the paper laid me off, they can't stop me from attending. Plus, I could win, and it would be sweet, sweet revenge."

"Hell yeah, it would be. And once a journalist, always a journalist. I think you're going to win. Screw the editors. Especially Ellis."

James Ellis was the managing editor of the paper. The guy who'd fired me and a dozen others six months ago. Oh, he'd been appropriately apologetic, even allowing his icy lizard eyes to glisten for a second. He'd blamed it all on corporate. On the new owners, a private equity group. On Craigslist, the Internet, Republicans, Democrats, life itself. Whatever.

"Is he here?" I tried to appear bored, as if news of my old boss's presence didn't faze me.

Erol rolled his eyes. "Yeah, somewhere. I saw him slithering around the appetizer table."

"Naturally. I'm over it. I'm in a way better situation now." I waved my hand dismissively.

"Of course you are. You're a business owner. Loved that write-up on Southern Living."

31

I shot him a coy smile. That had been my first and only triumph since leaving the paper, convincing the magazine to visit the café in the second week I was on the job. The two-hundred-word write-up in this month's edition was worth its weight in gold. "I've got lots up my sleeve. Perkatory's going to be the best-known coffee shop in all of Florida. In all of the South."

That sounded so breezily confident. I wish I believed it myself.

The lights in the bar area flickered, which meant the organizers wanted to herd us into the banquet hall to eat rubbery chicken and overly sweet chocolate cake. "Showtime," Erol said. "I already saved you a seat at our table. I want to be there when you win your award so we can rub it in Ellis's stupid corporate face."

"Or club him over the head with it."

Locking arms, we cackled and went inside. Of course he'd chosen a table in the center of the room, because Erol adored being surrounded by people. Wouldn't have been my choice, but being near him made me feel invincible.

At least I knew the people seated with us: three copy editors from the paper and a guy from a Miami lifestyle blog. We all hugged, and the editors launched into a diatribe about how awful things had gotten at the Tribune. Typical newspaper stuff. Stories were shorter, budgets were smaller, there was no staff to cover important news. Someone covered a court verdict by following a TV station's twitter feed because they didn't want to spend the money sending a reporter to Orlando. Mold had sprouted in a stairwell. The company sold one of the parking lots.

I nodded along sympathetically and drank a second glass of champagne. If there was one thing newspaper people were good at, it was complaining about work. No, I didn't miss this. Not really. My earlier yearning had been a fleeting emotion from the rush of all the glitz and familiar faces.

I listened to someone talk about how they bought their own notebooks and pens, only to have the losers in sports steal their stash. Yikes. As lonely as my life was in Devil's Beach, I was better off without this negativity.

"See? You're not missing anything here in Miami," Erol said, finishing his champagne. "But we're missing another drink."

"Amen to that," I murmured. Okay, this wasn't so bad. I could handle this. This was no longer my world. No biggie.

I was telling the lifestyle blogger about my café and inviting him to visit—hey, why not promote my business a little—when Erol emitted a low groan. He poked me in the ribs with his elbow. I turned toward him, and he pointed with his eyes toward the stage.

"What's up?" I asked.

"Look who it is," he said through gritted teeth.

My gaze went to the stage, where a tall, dark-haired man in a deep blue designer suit stood on the podium. He had exceptional posture and the carefully cultivated beauty of a TV news anchor. Not a hair was out of place, not a blemish on his spray-tanned skin.

I sucked in my breath. Well. Wasn't this awesome. It was my ex-husband, Miles Ross. He grinned and pointed at someone in the front row. I rolled my eyes. He'd become such a slick jerk, almost a caricature of a TV newsman. Maybe he was auditioning to be a game show host or something. He sure gave off the appearance of one.

I'd known him when he was just an impoverished local TV reporter, buying two-for-one suits at the discount mall and begging me to split a five-dollar footlong at Subway for dinner.

In the last year of our marriage, his newfound fame as a network correspondent had been one of many things that drove us apart. Well, that and the fact that he'd been sleeping with a woman who was barely old enough to drink. Yes, that had been the final straw.

"Good evening, folks, please have a seat," he said in that deep baritone that I once loved. Now it was mildly irritating, like that little runny spurt of ketchup that comes out when you first squeeze the bottle.

"In case you don't know me . . ." he guffawed and paused for dramatic effect. Obviously, everyone in Miami knew him because he'd have never gone to a red-carpet event that he didn't slavishly walk down. "I'm Miles Ross, the Miami correspondent for ACN, American Cable News. I'll be your emcee tonight, and helping to hand out awards to all of our talented Florida journalists."

"What?" I mouthed to Erol, whose face had twisted into a sour expression. I leaned in and whispered, "I don't recall him being on the invite."

"He wasn't." Erol hissed. "Jerk."

"You might be surprised to see me up here tonight," my ex boomed into the microphone. "But the usual emcee, the publisher from the Fort Lauderdale paper, had a sudden situation and was unable to attend."

Erol leaned into my ear and whispered, "That editor was canned yesterday."

I groaned softly and glared at my ex, who kept speaking.

"So, the Florida Society of Professional Journalists asked me to be the host tonight. I hope I'm a worthy substitute." Miles chuckled, probably hoping to sound humble.

I snorted softly under my breath. Had I known, I'd have stayed home on the island and watched the sunset or gone to dolphin meditation with my dad or . . . heck, scrubbed the tile in the café's bathrooms.

I swiveled in my seat; my cheeks hot. I caught the eye of one of the copy editors at the table, and she averted her gaze. Everyone probably wondered how I felt at seeing my handsome and rich ex-husband up there on stage. They all pitied me.

Poor Lana, who was dumped by her beefcake network correspondent husband. Poor Lana, who was fired from her high-profile crime beat at the *Tribune*, right as she'd written the best story of her career. Poor Lana, who had to leave Miami, tail between her legs, because she couldn't find another job.

I held my head a little higher as my ex droned on about the First Amendment. As if he cared about any of that. I was the one to show him how to request arrest records from the Miami Police Department, for God's sake. That's how we'd met. I was a cub reporter at the *Tribune*, filing a public records request at the police department. Miles was standing in the clerk's office with a cat-who-ate-the-canary grin. Like all women in his orbit, I was captivated.

He'd gotten my number—and the public records—by the time we made it to the parking lot.

"Before we start with the program, I'd also like to introduce someone special to me, and share some news of my own," he gestured to the middle of the room, and I drained my drink. This was the kind of thing he used to do, public declarations of his emotions. He'd proposed to me on New Year's Eve at the Shore Club, in front of several hundred people. I'd wanted the earth to swallow me whole.

"Right there," he said, pointing in my direction. I froze. What? Me? My stomach seized, much in the way it did when he'd asked me to marry him. I inched down in my chair, clutching my empty champagne glass. Was this being broadcast live on Twitter?

A spotlight flooded the table immediately beside us, and a perky, young woman with shiny black hair stood. Oh. Her. The local TV intern he'd slept with in the waning months of our marriage. I exhaled.

"That's my girlfriend, Yasmin Balenciaga. She was promoted to assistant producer at WSVN. I wanted to acknowledge how special she is to me. Where would I be without her?" Miles beamed, and she pressed her hands together in a prayer gesture.

"Still married," I muttered, as everyone clapped. Erol folded his arms in protest and scowled.

Well, good luck to Yasmin. Surely he'd dump her once she reached the ripe old age of twenty-nine. I inhaled a thin breath and waved down the waiter.

"I'll take a Scotch, but make it a double."

*   *   *

Three glasses of Scotch, one cockroach next to the bed in the hotel, and sixteen hours later, I pounded a sweet shot of Cuban coffee at a gas station at the edge of Alligator Alley and bought a colada—four ounces of the thick, high-octane blend in a Styrofoam cup—for the road.

Normally one was supposed to share a colada in thimble-sized plastic cups, but I was not in a sharing mood today.

Fab's departure meant my presence was required on Devil's Beach by six, because Perkatory opened at six thirty in the morning. Last week, Dad had told me that he couldn't do the early shift because of a prior commitment, and I'd assumed Fab could handle the first couple hours by himself. Now, of course, I was on my own. I didn't mind leaving Miami at the crack of dawn, mostly because it meant I could avoid the hellacious traffic.

Still, leaving in the middle of the night—when half of Miami was still out clubbing—was unpleasant, considering I was moderately hungover. As I drove across the state through the Everglades, a soft rain fell. Daylight broke, revealing a purple, bruise-colored sky, and I tried not to think about seeing my ex last night.

Tried to squelch the memory of the pity in his eyes when I'd gone on stage to claim second place in investigative reporting for the story that should have made my career. I'd lost to a reporter from a paper in Tampa, who had written an amazing series on the state's screwed up foster care system.

Still, second place stung. I'd put everything into that story on the serial killer, which had ended in a high-profile arrest. Now, I felt more like a loser than ever before.

Afterward, while posing for photos with the other winners and Miles, I'd been forced to shake his new girlfriend's hand and gawp at her smooth, young face. It burned an angry hole in my stomach, not because I wanted to get back together with Miles. It was from the regret that I'd spent years of my life with a disloyal man who cast me aside without a second thought.

I cranked the volume on the radio, drowning out my thoughts with Fleetwood Mac's *Rumors* album. Even though I was thirty years younger than the average Fleetwood Mac fan, I adored the band. I loved Stevie Nicks' songwriting talent, her vulnerability, and her style. She poured out her heart into her lyrics about Lindsey Buckingham's affairs and still managed to soar to stardom like the gorgeous, ethereal angel she was.

I shifted in my seat, trying to get comfortable for the long drive, tugging the hem of my white shirt that read, STEVIE NICKS IS MY FAIRY GODMOTHER.

As I sailed along, crooning and sipping the last drops of caramel-tinged foam from my Cuban coffee, I wondered if Dad had found out any gossipy details on Fab. For a few minutes, I pondered whether I should apologize to him for my outburst the previous day. I decided against it because he was the one who'd run out on me.

I dialed Dad's number, hoping to grab him before he went kayaking with dolphins or meditating in silence or whatever quirky thing he was doing. He didn't answer.

That launched me back into a dark mood, as dark as the sky. The clouds were even thicker on the Gulf Coast, and by the time I paid the toll and crossed the bridge to Devil's Beach, I knew we were in for a storm.

At least that would be great for the café—tourists loved to hang out at Perkatory during summer storms. The beachy, cozy décor meant people could sink into the overstuffed sofas and relax as the rain hit the windows.

It was almost Labor Day weekend, the island's busiest of the year. Maybe I'd see if Barbara could come in earlier to help.

I pulled into sleepy downtown Devil's Beach at five minutes to six, my mind churning at the idea of hiring and training a new barista. For a split second, I thought of driving to my house—it had been my childhood home, but now it was only me since Dad lived on the beach—and parking there. No, I was running too late. Best to go right to the shop and get ready for the crush of caffeine addicts.

I parked in the café's one spot in the alley. Today was unusually foggy, which sometimes happened when the humidity and rain descended on the island. I squinted to see in the gray, dawn light and killed the engine. What was that on the far side of the alley? It had the shape of a pile of clothes, but that didn't make sense. There were no clothing stores on this block.

Leaning forward in my seat, I studied the form. It was like something I'd only seen on the cop beat in Miami.

A body. No, that couldn't be. Or could it? There were a few homeless people on Devil's Beach, so maybe that was it. Could it be Dale, the older homeless guy who lived in the park downtown? Perhaps he'd suffered a heart attack. He'd told me about some health problems recently.

Oh, no. I hoped it wasn't him. Dale was a veteran who adored sunsets, the beach, and tallboys of cheap beer. He'd had a difficult life since Vietnam, and I had a soft spot for him. I often gave him unsold pastries and free coffee.

I hurried out of the car and slammed the door. With every step closer, my heartbeat grew faster. The person was curled almost in a fetal position, back facing me. Clad in khaki pants and a black T-shirt. Obviously a man, from the muscular body and short, dark hair, and way younger than Dale. Maybe it was a wayward tourist who'd passed out after partying at a local bar. I was used to drunks in the alley, but usually during the island's pirate fest in February.

I kept a wide berth as I circled to the man's front so I could get a better view. My hand flew to my throat, and I gasped in horror.

Even in death, Fabrizio "Fab" Bellucci couldn't wipe the smirk from his face.

Chapter Four

F ab was lying nearest to the brick building across the alley from my own, half under a scraggly palm tree that had sprouted between broken clumps of black asphalt. When it registered that his tanned limbs were splayed at physically impossible angles, I inhaled sharply. Despite his lifelessness, my mind went straight into denial mode, trying to find the positive.

"Fab?" I asked in a quavering voice while taking a step forward. Then, louder. "Fab?"

My voice bounced off the brick walls. A claustrophobic feeling settled in when there was no response. His expression was sardonic, seductive and smarmy every single day, so that's probably why I didn't want to accept he was dead.

I moved forward. "Fab, it's going to be okay. Hang tight. I'll call an ambulance." Still trying to apply logic to this scene while keeping as much distance as possible, I reached for my former employee with my free hand and gently brushed my fingers over his stubble-roughened jaw.

It was not the temperature that skin should have been. Not in this Florida heat. Wincing, I firmly pressed a spot at the base of his neck, checking for a pulse.

None.

I sprang back, a jolt of horror stabbing at my chest. He was really and truly dead.

A sob clawed inside my throat. Fab was the playboy of Devil's Beach. A local Instagram star. My best barista at Perkatory. Well, had been, until yesterday. He was also my dad's tenant on the fourth floor of our building. Dead, in the alley, a few short steps from my café's back door.

I should call someone. Police? An ambulance? Dad? Yes. All three. Now.

The morning's coffee in my stomach began to fizz. My last encounter with Fab had been so combative that a wave of guilt washed over me. I didn't hate Fab. Not really. Yesterday had been out of character, a vortex of stress and frustration because he'd left me high and dry.

"What happened to you?" I whispered.

How long had he been dead? An hour? Five? All night? Of all people, I knew what death looked like, and now that I studied him, it seemed like he'd been there a while.

It had been a year since I'd seen a corpse; the last one was in Miami. A homeless woman, on a cold, steel table at the morgue. A victim of that serial killer I'd helped put behind bars, the story that had gotten me a second-place award less than twelve hours ago. I shut my eyes. Last night's booze-soaked ceremony at the Icon Hotel in Miami seemed like a lifetime ago. My head throbbed with fear and the remnants of my hangover.

I whirled and ran to the back door of the cafe. The waistband of my jeans absorbed a trickle of sweat running down my back. It was crazy humid today, that blanket of moisture in the air that always settles in before a huge storm.

"Police. Call the chief. Noah," I muttered aloud, my trembling hands reaching for the keys in my purse. My arm was suspended in the air, about to twist the key in the lock, when a sickening realization came over me.

Was I in danger?

Lowering my hand, I turned, the early morning gray sky giving everything an eerie sheen. It all appeared normal. The back door to Beach Boss, the souvenir shop next door, was closed, as it always was. So was the back door to Dante's Inferno, the hot yoga studio that was the other tenant in the building. Our shared green dumpster sat against the brick wall, opposite of Fab's body.

My gaze landed back on him and I shuddered. *Police.* I needed to call the chief immediately. My stomach lurched again when I turned back to the door.

What had happened? What if Fab had interrupted a burglary in progress? He might have come downstairs in the middle of the night to throw away his trash and caught someone in the act. What if the person who'd attacked him was in my café right now? What if Fab had been trying to save me, even after I'd been so nasty yesterday?

Choking back tears, I took one last glance at Fab and hustled over to my Honda. I'd only seen him, what? Less than twenty-four hours ago.

When I'd confronted him at his new job at Island Brewnette and told him that I hoped he'd fail. That my father should have never hired him, should have never rented him an apartment above the cafe. That I wanted him out of the apartment in a month.

That I wished he didn't exist.

And now, he didn't.

My hands quaked as I dialed Noah. He'd given me his number last week. Had wanted me to have it "in case" I ever needed anything. I'd spent days wondering if this was a thinly veiled, slightly shy attempt at a date and had even considered contacting him.

I never thought I'd call him under *these* circumstances.

"Chief Garcia," he answered in a brisk tone.

"Hi. It's Lana. Lana Lewis, from Perkatory." My voice shook and I took a huge, honking sniffle.

"Lana, are you okay? What's wrong? You sound upset." His voice dripped with concern.

"I . . . I'm okay. But Fab's not."

* * *

The tourists who come to Devil's Beach say the island is a tropical paradise like no other. It's twelve miles long, three miles at its widest, a postcard-perfect spit of land in the Gulf of Mexico.

Visitors love the sugar-sand beaches, the majestic royal palms that line each side of Main Street and the quaint, historic downtown that's walkable and bustling with business. *The New York Times* raved about it being an example of "unspoiled Florida," and *Southern Living Magazine* called it "the New Gulf Hotspot." (That was when they ran the sidebar brief about Perkatory).

Today, downtown Devil's Beach was like an opening scene from *Law & Order*.

Yellow police tape stretched from my family's building across the alley to the brick building next door. All four of the island police department's cruisers were parked on the street outside the alley, and another half-dozen sheriff's vehicles from the mainland were scattered in spaces nearby. A county medical examiner's van stood at the ready, near the corner of Main and Beach streets.

By order of the Devil's Beach Police, I was not allowed to open Perkatory to the public. At least not until forensics combed through the place.

For the same reasons, I was prohibited from going to my second-floor office. I thought about heading home, but my curiosity got the better of me, plus I needed to explain to regulars and tourists why we weren't open.

So, I parked myself on a faded wooden bench outside the café as crime scene investigators, officers, and media descended on our block. It felt weird to not stand at the crime scene tape and take notes.

The rain had yet to arrive on the island, but thunder rumbled in the distance from the direction of the Gulf. The storm was coming soon, and from the looks of the dark cloud to the west, it was going to be nasty.

I dialed Dad's number and got his voicemail. Again.

"Hey, it's me. Call me right away. Something really awful happened. You're not going to believe this. 'Kay. Love you. Bye."

Two women who were probably in their fifties and both wearing tropical print caftans sauntered up. Each carried canvas beach totes and foldable chairs, and both looked like they'd already gotten too much sun for their fair complexions.

"You open today?" The one with a green floppy hat asked in a thick Southern accent.

"We want to meet that beefcake. The one on Instagram. We came all the way from Atlanta to get a shot of his coffee," said the other one. She seemed like she'd fit in on a reality TV show with her over-plumped lips. "What's his name. Fab? Fab with the abs."

They dissolved into giggles, and I cleared my throat. Little did they know that Fab with the abs was lying about thirty feet away, deader than a bag of rocks.

"Did, ah, do you know Fab?"

"No. We followed him on Instagram religiously and were here for a girls' weekend. Thought we'd get an eyeful of some man candy and a photo to make our husbands jealous."

I winced. "He's no longer with the café." Was that diplomatic enough? "And, er, we're closed for the morning. We're dealing with an issue here."

The women turned their attention to the hubbub in the alley.

"Ooh, that's too bad. What's going on there?" Green Hat stared toward the alley.

"I'm trying to figure that out myself." For all my years of being a reporter, I wasn't entirely sure how to break it to Fab's adoring fans that he was gone. I'd probably have to make a statement on Instagram. Ugh. I hated social media.

The women homed in on the crime scene van. "That's a vacation buzzkill right there. Let's find another place," Green Hat said to her friend. They both bid me a cheery goodbye, and I responded with a weak wave.

Several sweaty minutes passed, then Mike Heller, the publisher of the *Devil's Beach Beacon*, strolled up with a copy of the paper under his arm. Was it ten already? He usually came to the café about this time every morning to get his large cup of high-octane black coffee.

Time seemed to have stretched and slowed.

"Mornin'. How you holding up?" He glanced at me with a fatherly tenderness, probably because I'd known Mike since I was in high school and had written my first news articles as an intern at his paper. "You okay? Our reporter called in some early details and I thought I'd come check on you. You weren't robbed, were you?"

I gestured toward the alley. "No. Not robbed. I'm . . . I don't know how I am." I glanced at the photographer from the island's paper. He was about thirty feet away, his chest pressed against the police tape, trying to get a shot.

"Oh, come on!" the photographer cried, and Mike swiveled his head in the direction of the voice. "Officer, you're not gonna let me get a shot of the corpse?"

I winced. Had I been so crass and disrespectful when I was a journalist? I hoped not.

Mike turned to me, his expression impassive. He was an older guy, around sixty, with gray hair, deep golden-brown skin, and a trim body. He was one of a handful of folks on Devil's Beach who was extremely fit. Mike's specialty was ultramarathons, which made my muscles ache to even think about. How he managed to train while running a paper had mystified me for years.

"Guess I need to chat with our photographer about proper crime scene etiquette."

"Fab's dead," I said dully. "I can't believe it. I found him in the alley this morning."

Mike's brown eyes grew huge, and he sank to the bench next to me. "So, you were the one to find him? Aw, Lana. I'm sorry."

He extended an arm, and folded me into an awkward half-hug. I broke away and sniffled.

"I found him lying there." I waved my hand in the direction of the alley.

Mike took a deep breath. "Wow. That's a lot to process, Lana. Do you want to talk about it?"

His question hung in the air.

"Our reporter's around here somewhere." I couldn't even be offended at Mike's question; as a former journalist, I knew exactly what he was after. *Story first, emotions later.* After all, he was the one who'd taught me that, back when I was an intern.

"Yeah, I'll tell your reporter what I saw." I shot him a grateful smile. "It's weird. I'm feeling so many things this morning. And a little part of me thinks I should be reporting right now, except the best interview would be me. I've been sitting here zoning out, thinking about that. When I should've been calling you with the scoop."

Mike cracked a smile. "Lana, you're human. You just went through a trauma, from the sounds of it. You're not a robot."

I turned my head and wiped away a single, fat tear, then swiveled to look at Mike, who was being uncharacteristically tender. "I'm okay. Really."

"If only you could write this article. I know you'd do an amazing job, kiddo."

"Probably not in my condition. It was freaky, seeing him lying there, this morning."

Mike cleared his throat. "So strange. I wonder what happened. How old was he? Did he have family in the States, or were they all in Italy?"

"Twenty-eight. And I'm not sure." Since my father had hired him, I knew darned little about Fab other than his workout routine, and that he was an incorrigible womanizer.

"Terrible." Mike paused. "We need to tell Raina."

"Isn't she in Costa Rica teaching that ten-day yoga retreat with her new man?" I asked.

"Oh, that's right. She and Kai only left a couple days ago. I'll give her a call."

Raina was the lissome young owner of the yoga studio in my family's building, one of the other businesses on the ground floor. She specialized in hot yoga, something I stayed far from because it seemed ridiculous to stretch in a hot room when it was already the temperature of Hades outdoors. In fact, that was the name of her yoga studio: Dante's Inferno. Mike and Fab and the island's fit crowd—admittedly only a few qualified, since the rest of us liked to eat fried seafood and booze it up—flocked to her studio.

Raina was one of Fab's first conquests here on the island. According to the Devil's Beach rumor mill Raina had dumped Fab for some lithe bald dude named Kai, who was independently wealthy and spent his days drinking kombucha.

I'd tuned out the entire story because it was like a hipster *Desperate Housewives.*

"Mike, I appreciate that. There's so many people I need to call . . ." Who was going to tell Fab's girlfriend, Paige? My stomach clenched. Even though we weren't exactly friends, no one deserved that kind of news. "I've got to reach my father, but he's not picking up his phone." I stared at my cell, willing Dad to call.

"No worries. I'll take care of Raina; I've got her email. Hey, are you open and serving coffee? I mean, not to pressure you or anything."

"Sorry. Not yet. Can't. I'm waiting for the chief to give me the all clear."

Grunting under his breath, Mike rose. "Not long before Labor Day weekend. Wonder if this is going to turn away tourists."

"Thinking about a second-day story already?"

"You know it."

My faint hangover had migrated into my sinuses as a dull throb. The desire to talk about anything but Fab was palpable. "How was your barbecue last night, anyway?"

He shrugged. "The usual. Wish you had been there, but I understand you had a better invitation. How was the city?"

"Crazy. Like Miami always is."

"So are my barbecues. You'll have to come sometime. Now that you're home."

He'd invited me to his backyard cookouts a few times since I'd returned. I always had an excuse not to go. A little rebellious part of me resisted being woven back into the fabric of Devil's Beach so quickly.

I thought of my old life, in a sleek Miami condo. That hadn't felt right, either. "Home," I snorted, shaking my head.

He gestured in the direction of the idyllic, sugar-sand beach, which was only a block from where we sat. "Yeah, you can't beat Devil's Beach for serenity," he said, in an almost cheerful voice.

We both turned to stare at an officer directing traffic away from the alley. "Well, usually," I said dryly.

"Right. Good one. I'll be back, or send one of our reporters over. I need fortification for this. Gonna be a long day. You want this?" He offered me the paper.

"Sure." I gratefully accepted it, hoping for a diversion. Mike stalked off in the direction of Island Brewnette. Ugh. Between my outburst yesterday and today's events, my competition was poised to do a piping hot business.

I unfolded the *Devil's Beach Beacon* and my eyes zoomed in on the top headline.

Florida Man Finds Chicken Tender Shaped Like Manatee

I wasn't sure whether to laugh or cry and slumped against the cool brick of my family's building.

The nausea in my stomach had reached a crescendo and my entire body pulsed with jitters. Or maybe it was hunger. From my purse, I unearthed a stash of individually wrapped mints I'd scooped up from the swank Miami hotel lobby after the awards ceremony.

While sucking on the candy, I stared at the local media and police, a ragtag bunch of characters. After my eight years at the Miami Tribune, I considered the reporters here rookies. Competent rookies, since Mike hired eager young talent and groomed them well.

I could've been among them; I'd gone out to lunch with Mike when I was first laid off. But his budget could only afford $9.50 an hour, part time. It wouldn't even cover half of my student loans, so I'd politely said no. My chances of making way more at the coffee shop were greater, and Dad needed me.

I watched their reporter work the scene, feeling a mixture of amusement and jealousy. He had a clean-shaven baby face, and I guessed he was fresh out of journalism school. He was sweating and pacing, so probably this was his first homicide. Which made sense, because this was the biggest thing that had happened on Devil's Beach since . . .

"Lana?"

The rough baritone startled me, and I turned in my seat and sat up straighter. "Oh! Chief. Hello."

Chief Noah Garcia's voice was only one of many unsettlingly alluring things about him. He was incredibly intense, and today his eyes pierced mine. He seemed on edge.

Without asking, he sat on the bench next to me, which gave me a second to compose myself—and to marvel at how his crisp blue uniform fit his muscular body perfectly.

I moved my purse and scooted to the far end of the bench.

He slowly removed his police hat, revealing short, dark hair. Something about his masculine body and the way he always looked sharp was incredibly endearing. Even now, in the middle of a homicide investigation, I couldn't help but swoon a little as he adjusted his glasses.

"So," I said nervously.

"So." He ran a hand across his sharp jaw. "How are you?"

I pawed around my purse for another mint. "Gutted. You want one?"

"No, I'm good. And it's understandable that you're upset."

"I mean, I've seen a dead body before. As a crime reporter."

He tilted his head. "Yeah?"

"But this is different."

"I can imagine. Quite unusual, given the circumstances. We're going to have to formally interview you, but I'm glad you already gave such a detailed statement to the responding officer."

By "detailed statement," he meant ten minutes of non-stop verbal diarrhea. When the officer arrived minutes after I'd found Fab, I was nervous as heck and had unloaded everything I'd seen.

"Here's the good news. We found nothing suspicious in your office or coffee shop. No forced entry on the first or second floor, no obvious evidence of theft. The safe in the office is locked shut. We're going to need you to come inside with us and let us know if you notice anything that's out of place."

"Of course." I sighed, pressing a hand to my breastbone. "That's a relief, though. That no one's hiding in the storage room or the upstairs office bathroom. But, Chief, what happened to Fab?"

"Have you stopped calling me Noah because we're in the middle of an investigation?"

I opened my mouth and he smiled, showing that adorable dimple of his. Way to diffuse the tension in my body. If this was his signature investigative tactic to disarm people, it was working.

"Noah." I allowed myself to truly grin for the first time today.

His cheerful expression faded. "About your barista."

"Former barista. Fab and I had words yesterday at Island Brewnette."

He cleared his throat. "Yes. Former barista. I heard about what happened between the two of you."

I didn't like the pause he took after that, but I also knew enough from being a reporter that I shouldn't babble to fill a lull in the conversation. So, I stayed silent.

Noah trained his dark brown eyes on me. It was as if he was studying me, sizing me up, probing inside my brain. Normally when we stared at each other, I felt electric shocks of lust. Today, his gaze made me feel a touch uneasy. As if I'd done something wrong. Which was ridiculous, because I hadn't.

"Fab fell from the roof, it appears."

My jaw hung open as I imagined Fab plummeting down four stories to his death. He loved that rooftop. "What?"

"We found his flip-flops and a glass of half-finished wine on the roof. And his injuries seem consistent with a fall. But that's between me and you. Don't go telling your reporter friends at the paper yet. I'll handle the news releases. Can you recall if Fab was depressed?"

I scowled and straightened my shoulders. Suicide? Fab didn't seem the type to kill himself. He was many things, but depressed wasn't among them. "Of course, this is off the record. But I don't understand. He jumped? Or he fell?"

"Could be either. At this early stage, everything's on the table. We're going to do a full investigation."

"Naturally," I said, a little too forcefully. "He did like to drink wine on the roof, entertain friends. He'd told me that he'd put a table and chairs up there. But I can't imagine Fab committing suicide. He had a lot to live for." Women, latte art, flexing his muscles on the beach—he had a sunny, if not patronizing and arrogant, personality. Like the overgrown Peter Pan he was, Fab always acted like he'd won the lottery.

"No, he didn't seem the type, but you never know. Depressed people often hide it well," the chief said slowly. "That's why we want to get into his apartment so we can study his things. Do you have a key? We didn't want to break down the door if we didn't need to. Maybe he left a note. Or, maybe it was an accident."

I gave a little cry and jumped up, a jolt of awareness shooting through me. "Oh God."

Noah stood; his eyes wide. "What?"

"Stanley!"

"Who's Stanley?" Noah's hand hovered over the gun on his hip. My heart skipped a beat. His automatic instinct to protect made me adore him all the more.

"Stanley is Fab's puppy. He got him a month ago. He's probably upstairs on the fourth floor." I paused, a current of dread flowing through me. "At least, I hope he is."

Chapter Five

With rubbery legs, I followed Noah up the three creaky flights of stairs to Fab's apartment.

"Interesting place you've got here. How long has your family owned it?" Noah's voice bounced off the walls, which were covered in an antique, tropical-print wallpaper.

I paused. Usually most people on the island knew my family's colorful history on Devil's Beach—my great-grandfather had famously killed a man during a duel the year he arrived in 1899—but I guessed Noah didn't, being a newcomer and all. Then there were my family's ties to a problematic monkey colony. And the kumquat farm.

Best to gloss over my eccentric family legacy, especially today.

"My great-grandparents settled here around the turn of the century. They were among the first full-time residents. They built this as a hotel." We were passing the third floor. I hauled in a breath, trying not to pant like an animal. Noah, of course, wasn't even winded. "My mom opened the café about twelve years ago, when I went off to college, and she and my dad closed the hotel around the same time. When Mom died, Dad kept the café going. He has a plan to turn the third and fourth floor into condos. He rented to Fab about six months ago, saying he could stay until he started renovations. Fab liked the place because it had roof access and lots of light."

There I was, running off at the mouth again. I received no response from Noah, probably because we were at the top floor, hovering near Fab's door. My heart rate spiked, and not because I could smell Noah's spicy aftershave.

What were we going to find on the other side? Being an animal lover, my main concern was for little Stanley, a puppy so petite that he once snoozed in a shoebox under the counter downstairs.

"Do you want me to unlock it?" I wheezed while waving my set of master keys.

"No, let me. We don't know what's in there," Noah replied in a stern voice.

As if to punctuate his words, a sharp bark came from behind the door.

"Stanley," I cried. "Oh, thank God, he's okay. We're coming to get you, Stan."

"Step aside." Noah motioned for me to move away, and I obeyed, flattening my back to the wall. "And don't follow me in—I don't want you to contaminate the scene."

He briskly unlocked the top lock and turned the doorknob. A gold-and-white furball flew toward us.

"Oh, you poor little man," I said, kneeling and opening my arms. With those long, muscular legs of his, Noah carefully stepped inside and disappeared.

The puppy bounded into my embrace—I must admit, he loved me from the moment one of Fab's female admirers gave him as a gift a month ago—and I scooped him up. "Little pupper. All alone. Such a good boy. So brave."

As the tiny moppet licked my face in the hall, I inspected the dog, petting and kissing him. He seemed his usual, jolly self. Poor little thing didn't know his owner was dead. My heart squeezed thinking about what he might have seen, and how he'd been alone for hours.

Edging into the doorway, I caught an eyeful of Fab's living room. It appeared like it usually did—a messy bachelor pad. A pile of what appeared to be dog poop sat in the middle of the floor.

"Let's get you outside, Stanley, so you can do your business." His fur had the faint smell of baby powder. I smooched the top of the dog's soft head and furtively glanced inside the apartment.

Fab's place was a mishmash of former hotel rooms all interconnected. Over the decades, walls had been knocked down during my parents' half-baked ideas to turn it into offices, incubator space, and a meditation center. It was rundown, with giant, old floor-to-ceiling windows on one side. I shivered. Wouldn't be going near those windows. Just the thought of looking down at the alley made me woozy.

Stanley wiggled in my arms at the sight of Noah coming back in view.

"Well, there's no one else here." As if on cue, a ray of sunshine broke through the clouds, streamed through the glass, and lit up Noah's handsome profile with a rim of light. "Want to go upstairs to the roof with me, to see if you notice anything out of place?"

I shuddered. "I probably wouldn't know. I haven't been up there in years. It's not my favorite place. Hey, I think the puppy probably needs to do his business outside. Mind if I take him downstairs?"

The chief, who was standing with his hands on his hips, rotated his body and shook his head. "That's fine."

He stepped to a table by the door that was littered with junk. "You might need this. Looks like this is Stanley's leash."

I moved to the doorway as he pulled a red retractable leash off the messy table and extended it in my direction. A business card and pair of women's white lace panties fluttered to the floor. I rolled my eyes.

Noah scowled, then knelt. He studied the card. "Ace's Alligator Farm. Was Fab a gator hunter?"

I snorted and pointed at the panties. "Hardly. He liked the beach, but mostly because he looked great in selfies at sunset. And the only thing he hunted was his next conquest. As you can see by the evidence."

Noah slid a pen out of his breast pocket and lifted the panties with the pen's end. They appeared to be of the thong variety, a mere scrap of fabric.

I clipped the leash to the dog's collar. "Don't be surprised about what you find in here. Fab had an active social life. Which is a charitable way of saying, he got around."

Noah raised his gaze, fixing his dark amber eyes on me. "We'll be investigating into exactly where he's been, and with whom."

I tore down the stairs, a shiver crawling up my spine when I thought about Fab's final moments.

* * *

Stanley didn't move away from my side the rest of the morning. Not while police combed through Fab's apartment (I stayed in the doorway, my curiosity at that point equal to my fear of heights), not when reporters tried to interview me (I gave an exclusive interview to the *Devil's Beach Beacon* and said *no comment* to the TV reporters from the mainland) and not when Noah allowed me to reopen the café (I think he wanted to reward his officers after a long day with some of my coffee. Or maybe he wanted to eke out a few more minutes with me, but perhaps that was wishful thinking).

Around three that afternoon—I decided the day was a wash and wasn't going to reopen until the morning—I sank into a tall, wooden window seat with a cup of house blend, a day-old carrot cookie, and Stanley at my feet. He seemed to be in ecstasy as he gnawed on a donut-shaped dog bagel.

My black leather Moleskine notebook and a pen sat nearby, because I needed to make a list of everything I had to do tomorrow. I'd started bullet journaling—a detailed way to keep a calendar—only a couple of weeks ago. It was a way to wrestle organization into my out-of-control life.

For a few minutes, I fiddled with a music app on my phone, finally settling on a soothing seventies radio station to play on the shop speakers. My ex had always teased me about my love of yacht rock, saying I should listen to more electronic dance music. Which I hated. Yes, I was single here on Devil's Beach, but I could at least listen to whatever I wanted without feeling like I was the least hip person alive.

I watched as the county medical examiner's van rolled away with Fab inside. Almost immediately after, a yellow VW Beetle with a giant plastic cockroach on the roof inched past. The driver waved. It was Pete, of Pete's Pests, and I made a note in my journal to call Pete about a termite inspection.

Then I immediately felt terrible. I was sailing on with life, drinking coffee and scheduling appointments as if someone I knew hadn't been found dead at my back door less than twelve hours ago.

I dialed Dad for the fifth time today. He hadn't answered any of my messages. I rubbed my temples with my fingers. Was today the day he was supposed to go north for a real estate conference? Or was it a yoga retreat? A meditation thing? Why couldn't I recall? Blergh. Had seeing Fab's body given me PTSD? Was I dissociating from trauma? I was probably exhausted, judging how stiff and achy my bones felt, and I yawned.

I glanced down at the golden puppy, who yawned right back. For the first time, I realized the fur on his chest was lighter than the rest of his body, almost a cream color. "You sleepy, Stanley? What are we going to do with you, anyway?"

He met my stare with mournful, chocolate-brown eyes. He was adorable as heck. I racked my brain trying to recall which woman gave the dog to Fab. Was it Paige? No, probably not her. I had a vague memory that she was allergic to both dogs and cats. In high school she'd made a big deal about her allergy when a duo of state troopers gave a K-9 demonstration.

Maybe it had been the waitress at the Dirty Dolphin? I always got her confused with the woman who owned the all-organic clothing boutique the next block over because they had identical, pin-straight blonde hair. Fab's accent, his forearms, and his coffee skills had attracted so many women. It was going to be a delicate matter approaching all of them, asking if they wanted the puppy back. He rolled onto his side and stretched, showing me his downy, chubby belly.

"Aww. You're too cute to give away." Still, didn't I have an obligation to break the news of his death to some of his former lovers? As I was making a list of the many women I'd have to call, my cell rang.

"Café Perkatory," I said, mustering a chipper tone.

"Hi. Uh, is this where Fabrizio worked?" The man's thick New York accent was the vocal equivalent of burnt coffee.

"Um." I paused. Way to be articulate. "Fab's, ah. It was where he worked."

"Listen, let's not beat around the bush. I know about his death."

I snapped to attention. "Who is this?"

"This is his uncle Jimmy. His only living relative. Someone named Paige claimed to be his girlfriend called me a couple hours ago and told me what happened. Asked me if I'd be coming down to claim the body. I thought it was a prank but then saw online when I clicked on that local paper down there and sure enough, it was true. Damn shame."

"Uh-huh," I said, now in reporter mode. I wanted to know more. I'd never heard of an uncle Jimmy. I opened my notebook and clicked my pen, then turned to a few blank pages from the back.

"I'm from New York," he offered.

"So I gathered."

"Yeah, Fab and I weren't close. He lived with me a bit when he came from the old country. But I kicked him out because he wouldn't stop bringing girls home. I like my peace and quiet, yanno?"

"Sounds like Fab." I scrawled every word he said into the notebook. It was like second nature, writing during phone conversations. I'd done this for years as a journalist.

"You know him well? Then you know how he is with the ladies. Maybe he was like that with you."

"He most certainly wasn't like that with me. I'm his manager. Well, was. My name's Lana Lewis."

"Oh yeah, I think I saw something on Instagram. At your café. And he mentioned you in an email a few months ago, how you were taking over from your dad. I assumed you were one of Fab's latest girls."

"Absolutely not," I said sourly, still taking notes.

"Right. Anyway, I gotta business thing. Won't be able to come to claim him. So, I was wondering if you could arrange something.

Or maybe someone there will arrange it. Sounds like Paige might, but she seems a little flighty to handle it."

"It?" I grimaced.

"The funeral, the service, the wake."

I glanced down at Stanley, who wagged his tail every time we made eye contact. My heart cracked a little, both for Fab and his dog. "But what about his things? His body? Where do you want him buried? What about his puppy?"

Jimmy snorted. "Well his parents in Italy are dead, they passed when he was a teen. He's got no brothers and sisters. So you can't really send him back there. He was happiest in Florida. That's what he said, but probably because he bonked all the women he wanted. That's what happens to men with mommy issues, you know. Let him stay in Florida." Jimmy stretched out the word, so it sounded like *Flaaa-rih-duuuuh*. "He might as well be laid to rest there. Wish I could be there for the service. And as far as his things, give 'em away. I don't need 'em."

"Okay," I said slowly, wondering how anyone could be so callous in the face of the death of such a young man. "Hey, did Fab ever mention anything about an alligator farm?"

It was such an odd detail, that card. One that had stuck in my mind.

"Alligator farm?" Jimmy chuckled. "Do they really have those in Florida? And, no. Fab didn't. Did you say he had a dog? I didn't even know Fab liked animals. He was nothin' but an animal himself." He yawned with a roar. A real charmer, this Jimmy. But he gave great quotes, and I itched to use them in an article.

That wouldn't be happening anytime soon, though, because my days of journalism were over.

I muttered something in the affirmative and hung up. Somehow, I'd learned more about my former barista in a three-minute phone conversation than I had while working with him for two months. Maybe he had killed himself. It sounded like he'd had a troubled past.

Stanley pressed his fluffy little body against my leg. I leaned down and scratched his soft, golden ear. Both ears were the same color, and he had a white splotch on top of his head that extended to his liver-colored nose.

"Guess you're coming to live with me now, you little floof. At least for now."

The bells on the front door jangled.

"We're closed," I called out, swiveling in my chair as the door creaked open. A woman with black hair, sharp cheekbones and red lips poked her head in. I pressed my palm to my forehead. I'd forgotten that we had set a time to meet.

"Erica!"

Stanley bounded from my feet, and before I could stop him, aimed for her. Erica shut the door and knelt, grinning and cooing.

"I'm so sorry. I forgot that you were coming in, with everything that happened today. Stanley, don't harass. That's Fab's dog."

She straightened to standing. "No worries. I love animals. Yeah, I heard about Fab. Crazy that someone would murder him. Awfully sad."

I scowled. "Murder?"

She shrugged and walked toward me, almost with a swagger. It was then that I noticed she had on a black tank top, black shorts, and Doc Martens. Not boots, but shoes. Next to the soft, blue-and-white décor of my café, this woman stuck out like a goth in a Precious Moments shop.

"That's what people are saying around the island. It's all speculation."

"People are talking already?" Groaning, I slid off my seat and gestured to the counter. Why hadn't Dad called? By now he'd have the scoop on what the islanders were saying.

"Yeah. Over at the marina, where I keep my sailboat. That's where I heard the murder rumor. People said Fab was too full of himself to commit suicide. Dunno if any of that's true, though."

"I'd say that's pretty accurate." I paused as we stood near the cash register. "But I guess you never know. Would you like a cup of something?"

Her eyes widened and sparkled, a genuine expression that lit up her entire face. "I would. Black."

"Cool. Want to try our house blend?"

She gazed over my shoulder, up at the chalkboard menu. "Sure. But the Idido also sounds tasty. I had that when I traveled to Ethiopia a few years ago."

As I prepared the grounds, she leaned on the counter and a lazy smile unfurled on her face. "Hey, love your T-shirt."

I glanced down, having forgotten I was wearing my favorite Stevie Nicks shirt. It was a point in Erica's favor. Impressed, I made a special pour-over carafe, just for her.

Chapter Six

Erica was an excellent conversationalist, the kind of person who could talk about everything and nothing, without being too intrusive. She entertained me with stories of world travel, and I told her about my layoff in Miami and my ex.

"Sounds like a real tool," she sniffed. "Men."

"Can't live with them," I said.

"Can't kill them," she responded.

We stared at each other for a beat. "Too soon, probably," I said, a pang of guilt striking my stomach.

She nodded. "Probably."

That conversational gaffe aside, Erica made me realize that since I'd been back on Devil's Beach, I hadn't had much contact with other women my age on a personal level. I'd spent most of my time with Dad since coming home, and with Fab at the café. It was energizing to chat with Erica, like we'd been friends for years.

I took her on a tour of the café, showing her the stock room, the bathrooms with the vintage mirrored settees, and the bookcase wall that showed off some of Barbara's art and books by local authors. I pointed out the area near the sugar and creamer station. It was wallpapered with old album covers from the '70s and '80s.

"Whoever decorated this place did a great job," she said.

My chest swelled with pride. "Thanks. My mom went with the blue-and-white theme and I ran with it. When I came home after the layoff, Dad put me in charge. I freshened it up a bit. I think buying new stuff and going with my own vibe helped pull me out of a funk."

"Nothing wrong with a little retail therapy. Your mom must love what you've done to the café. Does she come in often?"

A thickness formed in my throat at the mention of Mom. I swallowed. "I wish she could see this. She's been gone three years."

Erica reached to squeeze my shoulder. "Sorry to bring it up."

"It's okay. This place was her passion."

"And you want to keep that going, understandably."

I tilted my head. "Never thought of it that way, but yeah. Once Dad suggested I take over the place, it made sense, you know? He didn't want to run the business, and I didn't have a job, so I stepped up."

"It's awesome you have that connection still with your mom."

I fidgeted with a napkin on the counter, rolling it into a skinny cylinder. "Mom spent her life in pursuit of excellent coffee. She worked as a green coffee buyer."

Erica's eyes widened. "Really? That is so cool."

"Yeah, for a good part of my childhood she specialized in Caribbean and Latin American beans. She traveled a lot. Sometimes I went with her, to places like Jamaica and Costa Rica. But she always wanted to open her own shop and she finally did."

"I love it. So, you grew up learning about coffee."

"I did. I even thought about following in her footsteps as a buyer. But I was bitten by the newspaper bug in high school." A cynical laugh erupted in my throat. "Good choice that was."

"I dunno. From what you said about your time in Miami, you did some pretty kickass work. Probably did more good for the world in those years at the paper than other people do in a lifetime. Do you miss it?"

I'd never considered it like that, but maybe she was right. I tossed the napkin in the garbage. "I do. A lot. But there's no going back, you know?"

"What about the local paper?"

I lifted my shoulders and sighed. "I interned there in high school. They don't have the budget for a full-time reporter. So, every month I'm out of journalism, the profession's further out of reach. I'm trying to make the best of what I have here. I mean, look around. This is pretty important, too, keeping the town hub alive. Mom did an amazing job of making this place into a coffee shop the whole island loves. I'm trying to keep that alive."

As I took in the pretty décor of my café—Mom's legacy—I almost believed myself, and sipped in a shaky breath. I didn't want to burst into tears thinking of Mom, so I changed the subject.

"How about you show me more of your coffee skills? Want to pull a few espressos? Make some specialty drinks? C'mon."

I waved her around the back of the counter and gestured to the La Marzocco. "It was the last thing Mom bought for the café."

Erica washed her hands, and I held out a clean towel. "It's really the best machine to work with. Now, how about I make a range of drinks?"

"Sounds good to me. Here's the fridge," I pointed to the stainless steel door below the counter, then to a rack beside the espresso machine, "And the syrups, the condiments, the glasses and the utensils. Let me know if you need anything else."

"Nope. This should be perfect."

She got to work, pulling shots and frothing milk. I leaned against the counter and watched her fluid movements. She set the first mug on the counter.

"That's a sweetened almond milk latte, with a shot of espresso."

It had no latte art, but was delicious. "We don't normally sell complicated drinks here because I wanted the menu to be coffee-focused and simple. But maybe we could do a drink of the day, because this is wonderful."

She reached into her bag and pulled out a plastic package of rosemary and a squirt bottle. "Mind if I use some of my own ingredients?"

"Be my guest."

Within minutes, the pungent aroma of rosemary mixed with the heavy, earthy coffee scent. She set down a mug. Two hearts were etched in foam on top, and a delicate sprig of deep green rosemary kissed the side of the design.

"Rosemary latte?" I raised the mug to my face and took a deep inhale. It was aromatic, with notes of herbs and something I couldn't quite place. "Interesting."

"Rosemary simple syrup. Honey. Caramel powder. Whole milk, and of course, espresso."

She watched as I sipped. "Whoa. *Whoa*. It's like," I took another sip to evaluate the party happening on my taste buds, "It's like the Mediterranean in a mug."

She pointed a finger in my direction. "You got it."

As I sucked down the rosemary latte, she made a few iced drinks with the syrups I had on hand—maple latte, toasted coconut, and finally, an iced mocha. I grabbed the mocha.

"These are deceptively simple yet difficult to master well. They can either be too cloying, or too bitter," I said.

"Tell me what you think." She rested her hand on her hip.

I took a slurp, and it was perfect. Satisfyingly creamy, with a wee bit of a bitter bite and a mouthful of chocolate. I sighed pleasurably. "Where'd you learn all this, anyway? Seattle?"

"Yeah, there, and I worked at a café in Boston for a bit. Then in various places around the world to support my travels. I'm thirty, and have been on my own since I was seventeen."

I figured there was a story there, and I'd eventually hear it.

"That explains your expertise." I sipped the mocha. "Listen, your drinks are exactly what I need. You're hired. But, are you sure you want to work here? Is it your style, your speed? We're busy, but probably not like Boston or Seattle." Holding the glass of iced mocha in both hands, I wandered around the counter and past the wooden tables. I stopped near a small, distressed wood bookcase that held various hardcover photo books about—what else—Florida living. Absentmindedly, I straightened one stack.

Erica grinned. "Why, because I'm dressed like this?" She motioned with her hand down her body.

"Yeah. I'd figure you'd want to work someplace more modern, I guess. Like Island Brewnette."

She shrugged. "I'd rather work with cool people."

"You don't mind a little Yacht Rock, do you? Between me and Dad, we play a lot of tunes from the '70s and '80s. I guess I'm kind of uncool." The strains of Daryl Hall and John Oats' "You Make My Dreams Come True" wafted through the air.

She took a sip of one of the plain, black espressos she'd just made. "You kidding? I love retro music. I get a good vibe here. Came in again yesterday afternoon to check it out again. Was going to drop off my resume. You weren't here. Older lady was. She was sweet. I need more of that in my life."

"Yeah, I was in Miami, getting drunk while trying to shoot fire with my eyes at my ex-husband. You must have met

Barbara; she's the afternoon barista a few days a week. She's also an artist."

"Right, she told me all about her work. And yeah, I feel you on the drinking part. I ended up going to a place called the Dirty Dolphin last night." Erica let out a little snort-laugh. "That might have been a mistake. Turned out to be one of those nights that lasted well into the wee morning hours."

"Oh, the Dolphin?" I chortled. "That place can get wild."

"No kidding," she muttered. "Anyway. I also stopped by Island Brewnette. Wanted to check out the competition. The guy behind the counter was unpleasant."

I scowled. "Fab? You saw him? When?"

"No, this guy wasn't young. I was there earlier today. Big man, gruff. Blonde-gray hair?"

"Oh, you met Mickey Dotson, the owner. Figures."

"Why, is he a jerk?"

I reached back in my memories to a school board meeting in my junior year when Mickey threatened to punch the cheerleading coach for proposing to cut his little girl from the team due to budget constraints. "He's a bit of a hot head, yeah. He also thinks he's a bigshot around the island."

I couldn't resist taking another gulp of the iced mocha Erica had made. "Anyway, you're hired. So glad you came in the other day."

She beamed. "Thanks."

"How long have you been here on island?" Somehow in our hours of conversation I hadn't gotten many personal details, only grand tales of foreign travel and adventures with men.

"Ah, only a few weeks. I'd been in the Keys and heard that this place was booming, so I thought I'd come check it out. Sailed on up by myself."

"It's fascinating the way you live life, going wherever the wind takes you."

She shrugged and sank into a seat at a table. "Sometimes it gets lonely. Have you traveled much since you left the paper?"

I laughed, and sat across from her. "No. I spent a month on the sofa, depressed. Other than my trips with Mom, I've never left Florida for any significant amount of time. Was born and raised here on Devil's Beach, then went to UF for school. Moved to Miami after that."

She tilted her head. "You never wanted to see what was outside of the Sunshine State?"

I shrugged, my stomach quivering from either all the coffee or the reminder that my life wasn't going as planned. I glanced out the window. It was raining now, coming down hard. A summer monsoon. Suddenly the day seemed about twenty years long.

"Thought about it, after I was laid off from the paper. A couple of online news sites in New York and D.C. wanted to hire me. But in the end, I couldn't pull the trigger."

"Why not?" She seemed like she was genuinely interested, as if I was a rare creature.

"Oh, I told myself it was because of my dad. I didn't want him to be alone here after Mom died. You'll meet him. He's a piece of work. But . . ."

"But what?"

"Even though life seems messy here, right now, starting over someplace new seems scarier. Florida's all I've ever known. It's the only place that's ever felt like home. And it will always accept me, you know? I can do anything, be anything, act any way I please. There's always going to be someone crazier or stranger. But everyone's welcome here."

"Everyone and no one, all at once," she murmured.

I blinked, wondering how things had gotten so philosophical so quickly. "Anyway, I'm glad to bring you on board. You make tasty drinks, and I'm sure you'll fit in here. We can talk about expanding the menu to include the rosemary latte, maybe next week even. The customers are laid back, as you'd expect of an island café."

"Nice. You need references? I brought a resume and list of people you can call." She walked over to her messenger bag, which was atop a table, then extracted two sheets of paper. "Call any one of those numbers on page two. They'll vouch for me."

I accepted the paper from her and studied it for a few seconds. I'd email folks later tonight, but since I was short-handed, I needed to rely on my gut and bring her on right away.

"Can you come in tomorrow? I'll be here, too, so you're not thrown to the hoards of tourists by yourself. Usually I'm here most of the time anyway, helping out. I try to work the rush hours, and then do paperwork and other stuff in between. I'm getting used to managing the place, really. Oh, and at night, I make a giant batch of cold brew."

"Sweet. Thanks. Can't wait," she grinned, and stood. Stanley reared on his back paws as if he wanted to climb her leg. She gave him a pat, then we said our goodbyes.

"Here, let me get you an umbrella." I moved toward the door, where I kept a basket of cheap umbrellas for customers.

"No need. I'm not gonna melt." She sauntered out, seemingly not caring about the pouring rain or thunder booming overhead. Erica was an odd one, quirky and tomboyish in a lithe, super-model kind of way. I sent a silent plea to the universe, hoping she'd be happy here and would jive with the customers, because I didn't need more problems.

As I twisted the lock on the door, a crack of lightning made everything go white. I inhaled sharply, and Stanley whimpered.

It was six at night, and a glance out the window revealed that the tourists who should have been packing the restaurants and bars downtown were painfully absent because of the storm that darkened the sky.

The streets were empty. Eerily so. The idea of staying in my apartment alone tonight made my stomach fold in on itself. Was Fab alone when he died? I shivered while dialing Dad, and stopped dead in my tracks when I got his voicemail. Again?

"Hey, I'm closing up and heading over with Stanley." I paused. Dad would probably assume Stanley was a new boyfriend. "That's Fab's dog. I think we're going to stay at your place tonight because of everything that has happened."

I hung up and frowned. It wasn't like Dad to not answer his phone this long. I hoisted Stanley into my arms, hoping we wouldn't get too drenched while dashing to my Honda out front.

"We'll buy you a raincoat tomorrow, little dude," I said, stepping into the rain. Thunder and lightning made the air crackle with electricity, and I yelled as I stepped in a puddle on the way to the car. My sneakers were soaked.

Chapter Seven

By the time I got to Dad's beach house on the other end of the island, the rain had vanished. That was Florida: stormy in the rearview mirror and sunny out the windshield.

My concern wasn't the weather, though. Maybe I was exhausted, or still spooked by the sight of Fab's dead body, or perhaps it was my usual, overprotective feelings about my father. But the fact that he hadn't called back was unsettling. We pulled into the driveway of the beach bungalow and my stomach clenched at the sight of his car (a Prius, of course). So, he *was* home after all. Which meant he'd been ignoring my calls. Or worse.

Grabbing Stanley and my purse, I stepped over puddles as I made my way up the walk. Dad lived in the same place he and Mom had built in the years before her death—a two-bedroom beach cottage with vast views of white sugar sand and Gulf waters. Unlike the McMansions that surrounded it, the low-slung bungalow with bright yellow shutters was a tropical wonderland, with giant foliage and flowers that attracted wild parakeets.

Tonight, probably because of the rain, it was silent. Steamy. A tad eerie. As usual, I didn't knock. Even though I was born and raised in my own house closer to downtown and had never lived in this place, I still thought of it as home, because my parents lived here. Funny how that worked, even at the age of thirty.

"Dad?" I called out. Strange. All the lights were on.

"Dad?"

Stanley let out a muffled woof in response. I called for my father again, and got no answer. Stanley wriggled. I gripped him tighter and froze. Why was it so silent? Usually Dad had some chant music or something going. Even the usual *Nag Champa* incense odor wasn't thick in the air.

I did a quick survey of the kitchen. Nothing amiss there, unless you count his fermented tea experiments that looked like science projects gone bad. Dad's cell phone sat on the counter. Odd. He usually kept it in a little holster on his waistband.

While holding an increasingly slippery Stanley, I poked my head in the sunroom off the kitchen. Nothing.

The rasp of an inhale filled the air. Then a slow, rattling exhale. Oh God, what if Dad had a heart attack and hadn't been able to call for help? I gulped a breath through my mouth.

It sounded like a cross between a wheeze and an ocean wave. Was there an asthmatic serial killer in the house? What the heck? I whirled around, ready to barrel into the living room.

I yelped when I spotted my father, dressed in white.

"Goodness, you scared me," I cried.

Stanley fought my embrace, so I released him. The dog launched himself at my father, who knelt, grinning.

"What the heck, Dad? First you don't answer your phone, then you creep up on me while breathing like a monster and dressed like a ghost." I eyed him, noting that Stanley had left small black paw prints on Dad's flowy linen pants. "And why are you wearing all white?"

Dad stood, reached in his pocket, and took out a small notebook and pen. He scribbled madly, tore off a page, and handed it to me.

I'm sorry, dear. I've been on a silent retreat today. Don't you remember? I told you yesterday. Purification. I was doing deep Ujjayi breathing.

Oh, crap. He had mentioned the silent retreat. I rolled my eyes and snorted. "Dad. You didn't get any of my messages? I didn't think that extended to the phone and emergencies!"

He shook his head.

"What? None of them? I was worried about you. Come on. How long is this going on for?"

Dad scribbled another page, and ripped it off. I snatched it out of his hand.

Until midnight, he'd scrawled.

"Are you serious? I need to talk. Don't you know what happened today?"

A shake of his head sent my anger spiking.

"Big, terrible things happened today. I can't believe you. I came here so I could work through my emotions and all that jazz you claim is good for me." I moved into the kitchen, where I grabbed a bowl out of the cupboard. I filled it with water for Stanley, then placed it on the floor. He lapped it up gratefully, leaving his golden moustache soaking wet.

Dad cleared his throat and I shot him a glare. "Okay, I'm going to tell you the entire story, start to finish. You can listen during silent retreat, right?"

Dad nodded.

"Great. So, you don't know what happened?"

Dad slid into a chair pulled up to the kitchen island and shook his head, then started playing with Stanley. You'd think he'd ask why I brought a strange dog home, but no. Not during silent retreat. I opened the fridge, searching for chilled white wine. Finding only green juice, I shut the door.

"Don't you have any booze?"

Dad pointed to a rack above the fridge.

I pulled out a bottle of red. "Not my usual, but whatever. Desperate times seek desperate measures."

I fished around for a corkscrew. "I don't know how to tell you this, because I know you liked him. You rented him an apartment. You hired him."

I uncorked the wine and poured a giant glass, then took a long guzzle. The wine slid down my throat, heavy and warm. "Truthfully, I could drink from this bottle after everything that happened today."

Dad's eyes went wide and he lifted his hands.

"What happened?" I prompted, hoping he would respond.

He nodded vigorously.

"Fab. Fabrizio Bellucci, our former employee. He was found dead. In the back alley of Perkatory."

"What?" Dad yelled, gripping the counter.

"So much for your silent retreat."

He pressed a big hand to his chest, his blue eyes filled with sadness. "Fab? He was so full of life. Such enthusiasm for so many things."

"Well, really only one. Women. But now isn't the time to quibble. Or speak ill of the dead. Yes. I found him dead."

"Oh, precious. Want a hug?"

I waved him off and took another slug of wine. "No. I'm past the hug stage and onto the binge drinking phase."

"Substance abuse won't drown out reality," he intoned.

"Says the man who smokes weed like he's in a *Cheech and Chong* movie."

"I'm only trying to avoid glaucoma."

"Right. Anyway. So, the chief—"

"Noah?"

"Yes. Chief Noah. He thinks Fab fell off the roof. Maybe committed suicide. But that doesn't make sense. Why would he jump?"

Dad stroked his beard thoughtfully. "No. It doesn't. He never struck me as the type. Unless he fell accidentally."

"I guess. But who is the suicide type, really? People do strange things. I mean, he'd just gone to work for Island Brewnette, and I assume he'd gotten a raise there. He had a girlfriend. Or three. What was he depressed about? And how would he lose his balance? It doesn't make a lick of sense."

Dad folded his arms. "What if it was murder?"

"That's what I was thinking." I pointed at Dad excitedly. "Maybe it's my crime reporter background, but something's off here."

Dad smirked. "Well, he did have several lovers. Maybe he made some enemies along the way. I'd heard at the Chamber meeting that he'd been involved with the Clarkes. It started when he was visiting Mrs. Clarke on Tuesdays when her husband was on the mainland for dialysis."

"Joanie Clarke?" I pretended to clutch my pearls. "Isn't she old?"

"Old-er," Dad said. "My age. But still a good-looking woman. I'd heard she bought Fab that scooter of his."

"Really?" I pondered this as I sipped. Mrs. Clarke was a hot and rich sixty-year-old, especially with her Maserati convertible. Maybe Fab was more than a barista. Maybe *gigolo* was a better title.

Dad wagged his finger at me. "You know, Mr. Clarke's no saint in that marriage, either. And rumor has it he liked to watch Joanie and Fab, well, you know."

"What?" I grimaced. "You're kidding? So, I guess they wouldn't want him dead. Or would they?"

Dad shrugged. "Dunno. But I'd be careful if I were you. It's not like you were exactly on great terms with him when he passed into the next dimension."

I scowled. "Me? Why? I didn't kill him. I was in Miami."

"Of course you were. But that dustup you had with him at Island Brewnette yesterday complicates things. That was all over town. You were pretty upset, dear. I hope Noah doesn't think you wanted Fab dead."

I wish you never existed. I swallowed hard. "I didn't kill him."

"Of course you didn't. You wouldn't hurt a fly. But you know how rumors spread around the island."

I finished the rest of my wine in one gulp, then went to the fridge to rummage around. Did Stanley need more food? He'd eaten the dog bagel and a can of kibble earlier. Was he as stressed as I was from the day's events? I found a tub of cottage cheese that I'd brought over a few days ago, and placed a dollop in a dish, then wolfed down a spoonful myself.

Stanley lapped it up eagerly.

"You're a cog in that well-oiled rumor machine, Dad. Maybe you can get on the horn and find out what people are saying." I pointed to his cell on the counter.

Dad reached for his phone and pressed the button on the side. "Let's see if I have any messages. Oh!"

"What?" I leaned in.

"Wow. Dozens of messages. It's going to take me some time to get through these. Where are my glasses?" He glanced around, and we both searched the counter. Nothing. Dad had several pairs stashed in various places because he constantly lost his specs.

"Maybe in the study."

"No." I pointed at his face. "They're on your head."

He giggled and lowered them to his nose. Stanley started running in a tight circle.

"Oh, and who's this?" Dad asked, reaching down to pet the dog. "He looks familiar."

"That's Fab's dog. I need to find out which woman gave him to Fab. I can't remember, can you? Maybe she wants him back."

Dad screwed up his face. "Can't remember. I think it was a tourist. She wanted him to remember her. Or something."

"I'm thinking of keeping him."

His eyes widened. "You? You can't even keep a plant alive."

I snorted, but a pang of shame went through me. "Whatever."

He paused and we both stared at Stanley, who was still running in a circle, near the door. "That dog seems like it needs to do its business."

Yeah, the last thing we needed tonight was puppy puddles amidst all this chaos. I peered out the window. The sun had recently set, leaving behind silvery blue clouds. "There's still a little light left. I'll take him down to the beach for a quick walk. Oh, and by the way. I hired someone to take Fab's place at the café today."

"I knew you'd be a great businesswoman. You're on top of things, LeLa, even when the chips are down. By the time you get back, I'll have found the scoop on the Fab story. You scoop the poop."

I grinned and took Stanley's leash out of my purse.

"I'm telling you, we need to do a book," Dad called out as I opened the door. That was Dad's thing—he'd been reading true crime novels and was convinced we should do one together. He wanted to somehow tie crime to Buddhist suffering, and to be honest, I didn't quite see how that would be a popular niche. I waved and pretended not to hear him.

Stanley and I walked out the back door and within fifty paces, were on the beach. The sand was still damp from the earlier rain, but I was grateful for the silence. There was no one out here, probably because of the rain—although this was one of the least popular beaches on the island. Why, I wasn't sure, since it was the most beautiful in my opinion. I inhaled salt air deep in my lungs, then exhaled. I repeated this several times. Maybe Dad was onto something with this yogic breathing.

"This is what we needed, right Stanley?"

The Tzu was crouched, peeing on a clump of seaweed. He shook himself and we were off. We worked up to a brisk pace, which surprised me because of his little puppy legs. He sure was energetic, dodging waves and bounding over pieces of driftwood.

Ten minutes of this and my shoulders came unglued from my ears. I *would* keep Stanley, and I'd be the most amazing dog owner on the island. It would be nice to have a fluffy little companion. Someone to love. Maybe get him one of those colorful bandannas for our jaunts around town. As we walked, I imagined us having all sorts of adventures together. Going to the island's dog park, cuddling on the sofa while watching Hallmark movies together, and romping on the beach.

Yes, I'd be an incredible dog mom.

I let a little slack on the retractable leash, allowing Stanley to run ahead. He was so adorable with his little tan paws. Well, they were closer to brown from the sand now. Maybe I'd give him a bath when we returned to Dad's.

Anything to avoid going to sleep. Anything to forget about what I'd seen today.

About ten yards ahead of me, Stanley stopped at something sitting on the beach. He sniffed, then started digging at the wet sand next to the round thing. What was that? I squinted. It was grayish white, about the size of a softball. Probably a rock. I pow-ered toward him, allowing the leash to retract.

I scowled as Stanley growled and pawed at the sand. Was he about to poop? I didn't bring a bag. If I was going to own a dog, I needed to be better prepared. "What is it, Stan?"

He made a loud snuffle sound and I crouched down.

"Gah," I reared back, gagging at the sight. And the smell, like dead, rotten fish.

It was a giant eyeball.

Chapter Eight

Feeling equally foolish and queasy, I dialed Noah's number for the second time today. Since I grew up on the beach, I was used to weird stuff washing ashore. Still, I felt it was my civic duty to tell someone about a giant eyeball.

The call went to dispatch and I groaned silently. This didn't need to turn into a big deal. All I wanted was to let Noah know. At the very least, I figured he'd get a kick out of it.

"What is your emergency?" The woman's pack-a-day tone sounded familiar. It was probably Bernadette, the department's longtime police dispatcher.

"Hey. This is Lana Lewis, Peter Lewis' daughter. I'm on North Beach. Only a couple hundred feet from the jetty. And there's a giant eyeball on the sand."

A pause. "A giant eyeball?"

"Yes. It's about the size of a softball. It's blue. I mean, I'm sure it's some sea creature. Or was from some sea creature. But it's unusual. I was born here and have never seen anything like this. I mean, I've seen a lot of other stuff. Dead jellyfish, wrecked boats, one time a barrel of hashish. But nothing like this."

"Okay. Giant eyeball, North Beach. Lana Lewis, did you say?"

"That's me. Owner of Perkatory. I actually was trying to reach the chief."

"Didn't you call the homicide in to him earlier?"

I held a squirming Stanley close to my body. He'd wanted to tear into the eyeball, so I'd been forced to pick him up. Who knew that Shih Tzus had such murder in their hearts?

"I did. Yes. Goodness. What a day."

"You're not kidding, sister. I'm working split shifts. Listen, an officer will be there soon, okay? And I'll let the chief know. He forwarded his phones for a half hour. Just hang tight with the eyeball. Or whatever it is. You sure it's an eyeball?"

I assured her that yes, it was an eyeball, and that I would hang tight. Stanley and I wandered a few paces away to where a child's lumpy, half-destroyed sandcastle still stood like a sentinel on the beach. I let the dog down and watched as he sniffed the mound.

It didn't take long for police, including Chief Noah, to arrive.

"We need to stop meeting under these circumstances," I joked. By now, Stanley and I had parked ourselves on the sand. He was sprawled on his side, sleeping. He was a trooper, that little dog. Not even a giant eyeball would deter him from a beachside nap. A soft, warm breeze rustled his longish puppy fur.

Noah rested his hands on his hips as he watched a crime scene tech snap photos of the giant blue orb. At first, I thought my lame joke had fallen flat, then he grinned.

"Well, that's something," he said, staring down at the eye. Which stared back at us. It was an unsettling cornflower blue, almost glowing in the semi-darkness. Disturbingly the tide was coming in, and I'd had a tense few moments while waiting, wondering whether I'd have had to move it from the surf line.

I'd briefly pondered kicking—well, nudging—the eye further up the beach with my foot so there was no danger of it getting wet, but fortunately, the officer, Noah and the CSI tech had arrived.

Noah sank to the ground, sitting next to me.

"I didn't want this to turn into a federal case. I'd really just intended to call you."

"You knew I'd get a kick out of an eyeball?" He gave me a little smile, as if we shared a secret. My skin tingled.

"Maybe." I unsuccessfully fought back a grin. "What do you think it is?"

"Hard to say. Giant octopus? Whale?" He ran his fingers through his short hair. Tonight he wasn't wearing his glasses, I stealthily studied his eyes, trying to determine if he also wore contacts. "Definitely not human."

"Obviously. It almost doesn't seem real. Except for the smell. That's how I knew it wasn't a movie prop or something. Gah. I can smell it from here. Well, that and the fact that no movies have been filmed here. But I guess it could have traveled with the currents and washed up. Or something."

Good lord, Lana. Way to babble like a dolt. Noah and I watched as the tech donned gloves and gently scooped the eye into a plastic bag. I turned away.

It was almost fully dark now—save for the crime scene tech's flashlight—and a full moon peeked through eerie gray clouds.

"Sorry to call you out for this. I'm sure you were busy, especially after the events of this morning."

He shook his head. "I'd gotten home and was in the gym at my condo. Trying to decompress. There's no downtime as chief. This is relaxing out here, though. The beach. The moonlight. Should have come here for a run. Seriously, I'm glad you called."

"You run on this beach?" Hmm. Maybe I should reconsider Dad's invitation to those morning beachside Tai Chi sessions.

"Sometimes. My condo's about a mile away. I usually run in the morning, when it's even more peaceful."

"Surf. Sand. A giant eyeball. What more could you ask for?" I cracked, trying to distract myself from his biceps. He wore gray sweatpants and a sleeveless black T-shirt. Was that sweat on his skin?

Noah groaned. "You're something else, you know that, Lana? In the morning you discover the first suspicious dead body on the island in years, then at night you stumble on a giant eyeball."

"That's how eye roll," I deadpanned.

I loved the sound of his laugh. Still, this was dangerously close to flirtation, being here in the dark with the island's police chief. A handsome, older police chief, exactly the kind of guy I was trying to avoid.

"Well, thanks for coming out. It was a little freaky, seeing this. Or being seen." I stood, and Stanley snapped to his little fluffy feet.

Noah also rose. "Where's your car? In the public lot? I'll walk you."

"No, it's okay. I'm parked at my dad's, he lives down the beach, not too far." Holding Stanley's leash tight, I gestured with my free hand.

"Oh. I'll walk you. I won't let you go alone. One second." He waved goodbye to the crime scene techs, then walked over to a detective. They spoke briefly, then Noah jogged back to me.

Our feet crunched against the sand as we walked. Awkwardness hung in the air. It seemed rather familiar to be strolling on a beach under the moonlight. His rich baritone broke the silence, sending pleasurable tingles down the back of my neck.

"Your folks always have a place out here?"

"No. I grew up closer to the café. Downtown Devil's Beach, in a bungalow on Hibiscus Street. The one I'm living in. I'd already moved away and was in Miami when Mom and Dad built this one here. Dad had picked out the empty lot years ago, and no sooner did they have it built and decorated that Mom had her stroke and died."

"That's a real shame. Sorry to ask."

"Thanks. You wouldn't know. You're so new here. Now it's just me and Dad. I wanted to stay with him tonight because of everything that happened today at the café."

"Of course. Hey, now seems like a good time to ask: how did you get into journalism, anyway?"

"It's a little twisted."

"Oh, really?" His voice deepened.

"When I was fourteen, a friend disappeared."

"Really?"

"Yeah. Her name was Gisela Sommer. She was my best friend, my first real friend in high school. It was right at the end of freshman year. We both went to a party at some senior's house downtown, then left. I walked home—to the house I live in now, that's where I grew up—and she walked in the opposite direction to her house. She was never seen again."

He blew out a sharp breath. "Lana, that's disturbing. I didn't know."

My stomach clenched. "You should find the case files. Some people thought there was a serial killer on the island. Others blamed her dad, who left a few weeks later for Germany. Some thought it was a custody kidnapping. But that was never proved, and she never contacted me. I think she would have, somehow, had she gone to live in Germany. It was so awful and strange."

"I probably will. Man, today must have brought back all those memories for you, no?"

"No." I paused, then realized how my stomach had felt like a brick all day, similar to that awful week she'd gone missing. "Her memory's always with me. Even though she'd only transferred into the school that year, we were really close. She was the first true friend I'd had. The first one who I talked about adult stuff with, you know?"

"Oh. Wow. You must have been terrified, being that young."

I could tell Noah was trying to piece together my slightly disjointed story. "I was. My parents wanted to channel my fear into something productive, so Dad helped me get an internship at the *Devil's Beach Beacon*. The local paper. I wrote a weekly column from a teenager's perspective. That summer I wrote about Gisela."

I fell silent, my entire body tensing up. I hadn't thought about her, or talked about her, for years.

"I see. So that's how you got into journalism?"

"Pretty much. Gisela's disappearance made me want to write about crime and dig for the truth. To tell the stories of victims. That's why the *Miami Tribune* job had been so perfect. I could shed light on cold cases, write about unsolved murders, hold police accountable. So, when you ask if today brought back memories?" I paused, trying to answer my own question. "Not consciously. This is an entirely different situation."

Noah side-eyed me. "Really? Is it? Isn't trauma still trauma?"

I shrugged, but his question unsettled me. "Perhaps. I feel like I worked through a lot of the feelings I didn't even know I had about Gisela while covering crime in Miami."

Noah nodded but didn't say a word. The awkwardness was back and now my mind was on Gisela. In situations like this where I felt uncomfortable, I defaulted to my old journalist self: fill the air with lots of questions. Or crack jokes.

"Since you asked me a question, I'll ask you one. Why'd you come to Devil's Beach? I'd read in the paper that you came from the Tampa Police Department. That's a pretty big force to leave, especially to take a job on a sleepy island where there's no crime. Or virtually no crime."

"I was searching for something a little more low-key. I'd gone through a few rough years heading the internal affairs department in Tampa."

"Oh. Wow. That must have been something." The words came out in a serious, inquisitive tone. I'd learned enough about police departments to know that IA cops were often viewed with deep skepticism—at best—by their fellow officers.

"Yeah. It was quite an experience. My philosophy is, and always has been, that law and order is about treating people fairly and equally. That view wasn't shared by some of my former collagues." He was silent for a moment, and I became all the more curious about him. "Then some personal stuff happened and I decided to make a change. It was either Devil's Beach or out of state, and I didn't want to be that far from my family. I wanted to land at a progressive department where I could make a difference in the community. Partner with social workers and addiction counselors instead of putting people in jail. That sort of stuff."

My heart swelled as we approached my dad's house. Noah was an even better human than I thought. "I can understand that part, about whether to stay or go. I had a job offer in D.C., but I couldn't leave Florida, you know?"

"I do know. I love this state, despite its shortcomings."

"Shortcomings?" I asked.

He shrugged. "You know. Rampant crime, destruction of the Everglades, unchecked development. Oh, and giant eyeballs."

A laugh erupted from my mouth. The more I got to know Noah, the more I liked him. Too bad he was ten years older than me, and I'd sworn off dating older men—well, all men, really—after my marriage imploded in Miami. Noah was in his early forties, the same age as my ex. As far as I was concerned, men like Noah weren't boyfriend material, no matter how foxy.

Still, it was exciting to flirt. Even under these weird circumstances.

We stopped and faced each other. A pang of awareness went through me. I must have been exhausted, because for some reason, it almost felt like the end of a short, yet emotionally intense date. Which was crazy, considering I'd called him here because of a giant eyeball. Or maybe not so crazy, since I hadn't been in the presence of a man after dark in months.

"Thanks again for walking me. My dad's house is right there." I gestured to the giant stone Buddha statue near a palm tree that sat at the short wooden boardwalk leading to the bungalow.

"Anytime, Lana." His tone was low and growly, awakening parts of my body that I'd thought were long dead. Pure danger, this man.

I chewed on my cheek and to avoid a weirdly intense staring contest here in the dark, my gaze landed on his forehead. It was lightly perspiring. A part of me didn't want this moment to end. "Hey, it's warm. Did you want to come in for a glass of water?"

"Sure, I'd like that."

We plowed our way up the heavier, thicker sand. At one point, Stanley refused to walk any further and flopped onto his belly. Noah scooped him up. Seeing his big, masculine hands cradle the puppy tugged at my heartstrings, and then I stopped.

"Uh, I should tell you something," I said.

He came to a halt and turned. "What?"

"My dad. He smokes weed. Pot. Er, marijuana." Duh. I was a dolt. Noah was a cop with nearly twenty years' experience. It wasn't as if he was unfamiliar with the terms weed or pot. "He has a medical marijuana license. I didn't want you to be surprised, or arrest him or anything."

"Lana, I know. He told me all about it. His eye pressures and glaucoma. He showed me his license a while back."

"He did?" I started walking again. "How well do you know my dad, anyway?"

"He's told me a bit about himself. Not too much about his wife, your mom. He gets too emotional. He's not ready to talk about that. At least not to me."

"Wow. I didn't realize you two were so close," I quipped.

"We got to talking when he sold me the condo. Said he's working through the feelings about your mom's death with his yoga and meditation. But he talked about you a lot." Noah grinned, and we started back up the beach.

I decided not to unpack that last statement, partially because we were at Dad's back door and because I wasn't sure I wanted to know what my dad had told Noah about me. Not only was Dad like me—he often babbled—but his weed-addled mind meant that he occasionally overshared. Noah probably knew all about my birth and divorce, and every detail in between.

"Dad," I hollered as I opened the door. "I'm here with the chief. The Police Chief. Please tell us you're wearing pants."

Noah chuckled.

"C'mon into the kitchen, Chief."

"Noah," he corrected sternly.

We walked through the sunroom, followed by Stanley, and found my father in the kitchen. A faint odor of marijuana laced the air.

I kissed his cheek. "Hey there, look who I found on the beach."

"Chief," Dad said warmly, shaking his hand. As if it was the most normal thing in the world for his daughter to go on a walk and return with the island's police chief.

"Sir, nice to see you."

Dad stared at me and squinted. "I didn't realize you were going to be so long. Guess I lost track of time. I've been watching Dr. Who and thought I'd grab myself some munchies." He held up a bag of blue corn tortilla chips.

"I was taking Stanley to do his business, remember? Then I called Noah because we found a giant eyeball on the beach. It was wild." I poured Noah a glass of water from the fridge spout on the door.

Dad froze, chip in hand. I could tell he was trying to figure out whether I was joking or if he was incredibly high. He let out a giggle.

"Yes, it was a blue eyeball, from some sea creature, probably," Noah shrugged.

"Probably?" I muttered while filling a water bowl for Stanley. "What else could it be from? An alien?"

"Trippy," Dad whispered.

"Yep, it's been a banner day on Devil's Beach." I leaned on the black granite counter. Noah's Adam's apple bobbed as he gulped down the water. His eye went to a framed Fleetwood Mac record album on the wall, and he walked over to study it.

"Check this out," he said.

"*Rumors* was Mom's favorite album. To surprise her for their anniversary one year, Dad tracked down a friend of a friend who knew everyone in the band and got them to sign it."

Noah turned to Dad and I. "Impressive," he said.

"Yeah, that's where Lana was conceived, in fact. At a Fleetwood Mac show. November 7. University of South Florida Sun Dome."

"Dad," I cried, while Noah nearly choked on his water. "You didn't conceive me at the show."

"Well, no. But after. We'd been dating about a year." Dad turned to Noah and I winced, wondering what deeply personal family detail he was about to reveal. "I'd just started selling real estate on the island, and Sara had come here to work for the summer as a waitress and never left. I surprised her with two tickets to the concert and we got a hotel room. That's where we—."

"Okay. How about a glass of wine?" I grabbed the bottle I'd been drinking earlier.

A mournful-looking Dad shook his head. "Noah?" I held up the bottle.

"No, I'm good."

"You don't drink coffee or alcohol?" I asked, pouring myself a glass.

"I do drink alcohol. But I'm hoping to get back to my workout tonight."

I grunted, wondering what it would be like to have that kind of dedication to a personal fitness routine. Since I'd likely never know, I savored my sip of Pinot as silence descended on the kitchen.

"Oh, while you're here," Dad had snapped out of his reverie. "Any word on Fabrizio? I was stunned by the news, Noah. Just shocked."

"We all were. And no, not really. We're still leaning toward suicide, but we've got to talk with his girlfriend, Paige . . ." he drummed his fingers on the counter.

I screwed up my face. "Paige Dotson. I went to high school with her."

Noah raised an eyebrow. "From your expression, I can tell the two of you have a history."

I shrugged. "She was a cheerleader; I was a band geek. We weren't friends. That's about all there is to say."

"Wait . . . a . . . minute," Dad chimed in, his voice slow and drawn out. I could tell he was super high because he was about ten steps behind in the conversation. "Why would Fab kill himself? Something's not adding up."

"Did you find a suicide note in his apartment?" I asked Noah. Noah shook his head.

"Any other evidence that points to suicide? Did anyone say he was depressed?"

Noah shot me a devastatingly sexy grin. "Are you back on the crime beat?"

I smirked. If only I could write this as a news article. The desire to tell stories was a gnawing, living thing, and would probably never go away. "Maybe," I teased.

Wait. What if I *could* write an article? Would I uncover enough information to find out why Fab killed himself? Or *if* he killed himself. Hmm. I mulled this over while Dad mentioned Fab's enthusiasm for Instagram.

Noah sighed. "So far, no one we've talked with said he was depressed. But we weren't able to reach Paige."

"Did you talk with his uncle Jimmy in New York?" I asked. Noah's grin faded. "I wasn't aware he had an uncle Jimmy."

"Yeah, he called the café today. Said I should handle funeral arrangements." Another reason I should write the article. After all, I had taken notes when I spoke with Jimmy. Quotes and all.

Noah nodded thoughtfully. "Can you give me the number?"

I shrugged as I reached for my phone, sliding it to him. "Sure. It's the 212 number."

Dad munched on a chip. "Did you talk with the Clarkes?"

"Dad, you have crumbs in your beard."

"Ooh, sorry." He brushed them off over the sink.

Noah finished his water. "I heard the rumors about the Clarkes. Their housekeeper told me they're on a fifteen-day cruise. They left five days ago."

"Pfft," I said, resting my hand on my hip. "People can hire others to do their dirty work."

"Are you saying the Clarkes killed Fab?" Noah raised an eyebrow.

"Anything's possible, right?" I could tell he wasn't on board with my theory that Noah didn't commit suicide.

"No offense, but I'd like to study the more obvious suspects, the ones who were on island, first."

I ignored Noah's snark and sipped my wine.

"Who did Fab have problems with?" Dad stroked his beard. In his mind, he was probably Sherlock Holmes, poised to make a break in the case.

Noah took a deep breath. "There's only one person who's had issues with him recently, and that's Lana."

"I was in Miami," I yelped.

"I know." Noah said. He stared at me for a beat and gave a slight shake of his head. "Lana, Mr. Lewis, thanks for the water. And make sure you come by tomorrow so you can give your formal statement." Noah's voice was all business now, and a chill went through my body. Surely, he didn't think I had anything to do with Fab's death? More reason than ever to pitch an article to the local paper: to prove my innocence to Noah, once and for all.

That night, in Dad's guest bedroom, I tossed and turned. My mind raced from the events of the day. Fab's body. The eyeball.

Fab's uncle's gruff New York accent. Little Stanley, who had flopped down next to me in bed and was softly snoring.

Once I drifted to sleep, I was restless even then. My missing high school friend Gisela flitted in and out of my dreams, and Noah made an appearance. By the time I awoke at six, it felt like I hadn't gotten a minute of rest.

Chapter Nine

Saturday mornings were usually busy at Perkatory, with tourists and locals stopping by to get their fix of high-octane coffee. Usually the dozen tables inside and the five spots on the sidewalk were jam-packed.

Today, not so much. Which was weird for a late summer weekend.

I glanced around the half-empty café, then turned to Erica. She'd brought in a basket of dog goodies for Stanley. Was she trying to send a message about my new puppy by including a bottle of oatmeal-flavored shampoo? He did smell a little clam-like this morning, but I chalked that up to our stroll on the beach last night.

At the moment, he was back at my Dad's house, probably snoozing on the lanai. Lucky dog.

Still. I was grateful Erica was here, and happy that she'd caught on so quickly to the quirks of our espresso machine. She was slamming out shots like a pro, and decorating lattes with Instagrammable foam hearts, to the delight of the trickle of tourists.

But where were the regulars? I drummed my fingers on the counter.

"Well, at least I can teach you the cash register properly and not have to deal with all the stress of serving a morning rush," I said.

"Why do you think it's so slow?" she asked.

I shrugged. "Maybe because Fab's not here? He had a cult-like following."

She scowled. "No. You think? People still need coffee."

I rolled my shoulders, trying to appear casual. "Dunno. It's weird more islanders haven't come in. Apparently, it's all over town that I yelled at Fab the day before he died. I seem like a big bad witch because of it. Or that's what my dad suggested."

Erica gave me a funny, quizzical look.

"My dad's kind of the island gossip. Imagine a busybody, with a ponytail and a crystal necklace."

"Gotcha," she said.

"Speaking of Dad, he's supposed to be here any minute. I need to go to the police station to give a formal statement about Fab. You think you can handle being by yourself for a little while?" It was risky, leaving a new employee here by herself. She was incredibly competent, though, and it's not like there was more than fifty bucks in cash at the register. What was the worst she could do? I figured the three regulars sitting at a corner table—the only ones who'd come in this morning, a trio of elderly women who'd known my mother and visited the shop every Saturday—would let me know if Erica started wheeling out major appliances.

Erica waved her hand in the air. "I've got this."

"Cool. You're a lifesaver. Thanks. My dad's name is Peter. Peter Lewis. You can't miss him. Tall, ponytail, goatee. He might try to balance your chakras. I'll only be an hour or so. Hopefully less. That is, if I'm not arrested."

Erica's eyes went wide.

"Joking," I said, making my way out the door.

I walked the few blocks to the police station, passing my three favorite stores: Whim So Doodle (a cute craft store), Culture Waves (island-themed knickknacks and housewares) and Beach Books. The latter had been here since I was a girl, and had it been open, I'd have been tempted to wander the stacks, searching for a new read. But I needed to get this interview out of the way. The thought of answering questions—not asking them—made me a tad nervous.

As I strode down the sidewalk, I figured that from here on in, I'd stop with the arrest jokes. Especially if it was true that people around town thought I had bullied Fab prior to his death. As a painful reminder, I spied Island Brewnette while walking. I'd intentionally kept a wide berth and stayed on the opposite side of the street, and still, I could tell that it was packed.

That made me walk quicker in defiance. I tried to focus on the bursting orange-and-blue Bird of Paradise flowers planted by the city in between the sidewalk and street, one of the only flowers that blooms in the dead of summer here.

The receptionist at the cop shop buzzed me in, then told me to go straight to Chief Garcia's office. I padded down the short hallway, my Converse sneakers making soft pat-pat noises on the gleaming white linoleum floor.

I came to the last door on the left, and paused before rapping my knuckles against the wood frame.

"Knock knock," I said.

The Chief raised his head. "Lana," he said, and his eyes brightened.

Gah. Why did he have to be wearing a dark blue polo shirt that stretched across his tan biceps like that? Didn't he have any-thing baggy and less enticing?

"Chief," I said, as he motioned for me to sit in a chair on the opposite side of his desk. I notice he didn't tell me to call him Noah, and I straightened my spine. This was a professional visit. I crossed one jean-clad leg over the other.

He took out a notebook and uncapped a pen. His desk was predictably clean.

"Let's get right to it. I know you're busy with the café, it being the end of summer and all."

I smiled, tight-lipped, thinking of the four customers back at Perkatory—and the twenty-four I'd seen at Island Brewnette on my way here.

"You're doing the interview?"

"Yes. This isn't Miami or Tampa. We're a small force, and I help out with the investigations when I can."

"Okay then." I hadn't anticipated this.

"Tell me about your relationship with Fab, please."

I inhaled. "My dad had hired him before I returned to the island. He'd brought him on as the morning barista and rented the apartment on the fourth floor of the building. But you know that part."

Noah nodded.

"And . . . nothing. When I was laid off, Dad figured I could run the café. Dad wanted to semi-retire and work on selling a few condos here and there. He never much enjoyed running the place, but he does still like working there from time to time. Mostly to socialize."

"I've noticed. Back to you and Fab."

"Yes. Well, we had a decent relationship, I guess. When I first arrived, he tried to, ah . . ." I paused.

Noah tilted his head. "Tried to what?"

"He tried to seduce me. Because that's how he was with every woman. Young, old, it didn't matter. Anyone with two X chromosomes was fair game to Fab."

"And you didn't succumb to his charms? Why not? He was a handsome guy."

I squinted. "Isn't that a little personal? And no, I wasn't charmed by him. For your information, Fab wasn't my type."

Noah nodded slowly. "Would you say you were friends with him? Did you socialize together?"

I shook my head. "Friends? I guess. I felt like we had a good relationship. Were we friendly, in a boss-employee way? Sure. He was an extremely loyal employee and loved being the public face of the coffee shop. At least he did until that last day."

"Mmm-hmm." Noah scribbled some notes on his pad.

"We once ran into each other at the Dirty Dolphin and had a beer together. But he was with three women, and I was with my dad, so it was more of a group thing. Honestly, I didn't know much about him until he died. Fab was like the court jester of the café. He kept everyone entertained with his amazing latte-making skills and his relationship drama. When I first started at the café, I was so overwhelmed, between running a business and . . ." My voice trailed off, thinking about those nights when I'd go home exhausted, and cry. Sob over how much I grieved for my old profession.

"And?" Noah prompted.

I shook my head. "I was in a bad place back then because I missed my old job in Miami and wasn't sure I wanted to be here on Devil's Beach. It's hard spending your whole life wanting to be a certain thing, then achieving your goal, only to have it ripped out from under you. I miss being a reporter."

"Okay." He paused, and an expression of sympathy crossed his face. "What do you know about Fab's relationship drama?"

What did I know that wasn't pure speculation and scurrilous rumor? "He was dating Paige. That I knew for sure. I think they were on the outs this month, though. And there was the scuttlebutt that he had a fling with Mrs. Clarke. Or Mr. and Mrs. Clarke."

Noah tilted his head. "Huh?"

"You should ask my dad. He said that Mr. Clarke used to watch Fab and his wife. Doing, well, you know. And Mrs. Clarke bought him a Vespa scooter."

Was that a flush of embarrassment creeping on top of his cheeks? Noah's gaze went to his notebook and I plowed on. "Oh, and there was the woman who gave Stanley to Fab. I can't recall who that was—it might have been a tourist who's long gone, or this other woman he'd met at the Dirty Dolphin, the clothing store owner. Honestly, I didn't pay much attention. It was literally a parade of women. I tuned it out."

"Why not? You were a reporter. I'd think you'd pay a lot of attention to everything?"

I curled my lip. "Are you always this judgmental in your line of questioning? I thought cops were more dispassionate."

"I'm trying to make sure all the puzzle pieces fit."

I leaned forward. "I pay attention when it matters. I didn't think Fab's social life was any of my business. He did his job well, promoted the café on Instagram, and showed up on time every day. Well, at least until that last day."

"Did you want to retaliate against him for quitting without giving notice?"

I reared back, shocked. "Retaliate? Are you trying to say I'm a suspect in his death?"

Noah shook his head. "No. Not exactly. We don't know how he died. I'm waiting for preliminary results from the medical examiner. Tell me about where you were the night Fab died."

"You know. I told you already. I was in Miami for that award ceremony."

"And where did you stay?"

I rolled my eyes. "At the Motel 8 near the airport. Bad choice. Terrible coffee, cockroach near nightstand."

"Bummer."

We locked eyes and I tried to summon a measure of defiance. Why did it feel like he was questioning me as a suspect?

"How late did you stay at the award ceremony?"

"Let's see. About midnight. I took an Uber to my hotel because I'd been drinking."

"How much did you have to drink?"

"One glass of champagne and three glasses of Scotch."

His eyebrows notched up by a millimeter. "Were you drunk?"

"Too drunk to drive, that's for sure."

"And what time did you leave Miami?"

I twisted my mouth. He was being thorough. "About three thirty in the morning. I had to be back on Devil's Beach by six to open the store. Because Fab had quit and my dad had a prior commitment."

"Did anyone see you leave? The desk clerk? Did you check out?"

"No. I was too worried about being the victim of a robbery at the front desk. So, I scrammed to my car, which was parked right out front. But I did stop for some Cuban coffee at a gas station."

"I see."

"But they probably have surveillance video. And there's a toll on Alligator Alley, and probably some traffic cams on the bridge to Devil's Beach, if you're that concerned I somehow slipped back onto the island unnoticed and killed Fab. Oh, and here."

I reached for my phone and swiped to the car share app, then held the cell to Noah. "My receipt for the ride back to the hotel that night in Miami."

Taking the phone, he paused to examine the screen. "Send that to me, please."

He returned my phone and clicked a pen, then wrote on a card. Our fingers touched when he handed it to me, and I fought back a grin.

Noah's expression was like a stone: flat and hard. He sure was a by-the-book cop when he wanted to be. No cookie or Netflix jokes today. "Thank you for your information, Ms. Lewis. I appreciate it."

"Ooh, now we're all formal, Chief Garcia?"

The corners of his mouth quirked up. "A couple more question. Do you know anyone who wanted Fab dead?"

I shook my head. "I've been asking myself that question for twenty-four hours. And hey, I thought it was a suicide. That's what you said."

"Everything's still on the table. Did you see Fab talk with anyone during your last week together? Rather, who did Fab talk with?"

I rubbed my temples with my index fingers. "Lots of customers. We were super busy, and he always treated people as if he knew them, even if he didn't. I think the mayor came in. And Mike, the editor of the paper. He always comes in. You came in, too."

"Anyone stand out?"

"He greeted a guy by name. A tall guy, looked like a surfer. Len? Lex? He was with a pretty woman. She was older. Fab kissed her cheek and seemed to know them well. I vaguely recall Fab talking about going out on a boat with Lex."

Noah scowled while making a note. "Nobody else that you recall? Was he angry with anyone? Annoyed? Anyone angry with him?"

I squinted. "My new barista came in. Her name's Erica Penmark. They met that last day and Fab seemed annoyed when I said I'd hire her."

"Why's that?"

"Dunno. Maybe because he was threatened that I was about to hire a woman who was better than him?"

Noah nodded slowly. "That's all I need from you today."

"Am I free to go?"

He gave a curt nod and stood up, which was my cue to leave. I walked out, confident I was no longer a suspect in the investigation. As I strolled through downtown, I replayed my conversation with Noah.

Instead of heading immediately back to the café, I took a turn and wandered two blocks down to the beach. I plopped down on one of the benches overlooking the Gulf. An invisible cloud of suntan lotion wafted in my direction, and I closed my eyes and inhaled the sun and coconut-scented air.

Why had Fab been so annoyed by Erica? Had there been something more between them, a relationship I was unaware of? She seemed to be unimpressed by Fab, but I wouldn't put it past him to try to get her in the sack.

I opened my eyes and reached into my purse, where I still had her resume and references. I pulled out the papers and my cell, and began to call. The two people I reached—managers of independently owned coffee shops in Boston and Chicago—both gushed about her.

"Best barista I've ever had," one said.

"A bit quirky but super sharp," said another.

A bit quirky. Now that I think about it, the events of the past few days were unusual. Erica showed up; Fab quit abruptly; Fab ended up dead. Where had she been the night he died? Oh, right. The Dirty Dolphin.

I searched for the bar's number from my smartphone, then dialed.

A gruff male voice answered. "Thanks for calling the Dirty Dolphin, where every hour is happy. And dirty."

"Bill, is that you?" I'd gone to school with Bill Alvarado. Not like we were friends—he was a couple years ahead of me and on the football team. Hung out with Paige and her clique. I rolled my eyes, realizing that I hadn't thought about high school cliques in over a decade, not until I returned home.

"Yeah. Who's this?"

"Hey. It's Lana Lewis from Perkatory. How are you?" I steeled myself for him to say something snarky about my high school geek days.

"Hey, Lana. I'm pretty good. Tired. The real question is, how are you? I read about your barista in the paper. I'm real sorry. It's a shame." His tone was warm and genuine.

I relaxed. "Yes. It's terrible, isn't it?"

"Yeah, I heard you and him had a real blowout right before he died."

"Well, I wouldn't call it that, exactly. He quit abruptly and left me in the lurch. I blew up a little, which was uncool."

"He quit without giving notice? Well, that sucks. I hate when waitstaff does that. He obviously had some troubles. What's up?" The sounds of a bustling bar almost drowned out his voice.

"I was wondering." I paused for dramatic effect. "On Thursday night, did you happen to see a woman with black hair at your bar? Dark blue streaks, sharp cheekbones, pretty in an unusual way?"

"Oh, you talkin' about Erica?"

"I am, yes." I sat up straighter. Bill knew Erica?

He laughed. "Man, that chick is crazy. She stayed until closing, doing shots. Then a bunch of us went out on my boat." His voice dropped. "She and I went swimming in the Gulf. We must have been out until, gawd, five in the morning, all of us. I was so freakin' hungover. Still feeling the effects today. You know how that goes. We just can't drink like we used to."

"Mmm-hmm."

Hunh. She'd also mentioned a hangover. His version of the story seemed to match hers. So, Erica couldn't have been with Fab the night he died. I exhaled and listened to Bill talk. He had an excited tone to his voice, and I wondered if he and Erica had done more than swim.

"Wait, no. It was later than five because we watched the sun come up together. Real fun, that Erica. Why? You going to hire her? She mentioned something about maybe working for you . . ."

I stood up and started to walk back to the café. "I've already brought her on board, so come on by and say hello some morning."

Bill promised he would, and we hung up. I spent the rest of the way back to the café thinking about Fab. A single, burning question lingered.

How did he *really* die?

* * *

At eight that night, hours after I'd discovered Erica and Dad playing air guitar to the Grateful Dead in the café, I closed up shop. I walked the short distance home to my family's bungalow. Well, my bungalow.

When I moved back to Devil's Beach, I'd considered living with Dad. Certainly, his home was more spacious and nicer, it being on the waterfront and all. Mom had amazing taste, and had decorated the entire place in British Colonial beach chic. But Dad had insisted that I stay on my own, which made me wonder if he had a girlfriend. (He didn't, as least as far as I could tell). He'd said I needed to "sit with my grief" regarding my ex and my job.

So, I'd had the option of either paying to rent a place, staying in one of the apartments above the café, or living in my childhood home. Since I'd been living on a reporter's salary for the past ten years and hadn't saved much, thanks to my ex's love for the finer things in life, I thought it wise to choose one of the latter two options. The apartment above the café was a bit run-down, and, frankly, Fab had made me uncomfortable enough with his never-ending seduction schtick that I didn't want to be under the same roof alone with him.

Also, something about the family bungalow felt safe. Stifling at times, but homey and snug. It was two blocks off the main drag, in a neighborhood filled with colorful, old wooden homes.

Ours was pink on the outside. Inside, it was filled with art and knickknacks from my mom's travels as a coffee buyer, with paintings from almost every Caribbean island on the walls. I'd also been slowly trying to make it my own, and had taken on a few reupholstering projects with varying degrees of success.

Now, though, I had someone else to think about: a puppy. Stanley seemed to fit right into the three-bedroom, one-bath home, and when I arrived home from work, he was snoozing on a makeshift bed I'd made for him in the kitchen.

Earlier, I'd instructed Dad to bring him to the house and barricade him in the kitchen because of the tile floor. When I saw he hadn't had an accident, I praised him mightily, then led him to the backyard where he did his business. We romped for a solid twenty minutes, chasing each other and playing with a tennis ball. The best twenty minutes of my day. The week, actually. Possibly even the year.

Then I scooped him up and brought him back inside.

I'd searched online for a homemade dog food recipe, and got to work on it straight away. I had all the ingredients—eggs, hamburger, oatmeal, brown rice, sweet potatoes—and for the next hour, I simmered and sautéed until I had something that resembled a fine pâté.

While I cooked, I reminisced about Fab. Although we'd technically been semi-neighbors for a few months—I could see the top of the café building and his apartment windows from my street, I was that close to downtown—we rarely saw each other outside of work. I had a separate stairway entrance to the second-floor office; he used a back staircase.

Had Fab been on the roof long the night he died? I knew he went there to drink wine and entertain. He'd invited me up several times, and I always said no, not wanting to reveal my fear of heights. Or be the target of his interest. He made a pass at me that first week I was in charge, his voice as smooth as a generic cup of Dunkin' Donuts coffee.

"Lana, with that curly dark hair of yours and those beautiful espresso-colored eyes, you're so pretty I forgot what I was going to say," he'd murmured when we were both in the stockroom. "I think we should have dinner tonight at my place and get to know each other better."

I'd curled my lip. "Does that work with most women?" I'd snorted.

"Actually, yes." He grinned sheepishly.

"Save it for someone else." The ink on my divorce papers had been dry a year, and yet I was repelled by men who thought they were God's gift to womankind.

I never imagined that he'd kill himself, though. Or that an argument with me would push him over the edge. Just another reason that suicide didn't seem right. While pondering this, I scooped a teaspoonful of Stanley's pâté onto a paper plate. He wolfed it down and looked up with his chocolate-colored, button-like eyes.

"Ah, you liked that, didn't you?" I scooped about a quarter cup onto the plate and he tucked in.

I made a mental note to buy him cute dog bowls from that new pet store down the street, but paused before indulging him with another spoonful. Surely Fab had dog bowls. I could run over to the café and up the stairs to Fab's and grab them. Maybe he had other dog-related things. Leashes, little jackets, vaccine records.

Oh, who was I kidding? Once a reporter, always a reporter. I was being nosy and wanted to poke around. It wasn't a crime, was it? After all, I was the owner of the building. Well, sort of. The daughter of the owner. What if I happened upon something the police had overlooked? And Fab's own uncle *had* said I could do whatever I liked with his things.

Leaving Stanley with one last spoonful of homemade dog chow, I slipped my phone and the building's master key in a canvas satchel, printed with a peace sign (a gift from Dad), and slung the strap across my body.

I walked briskly down the live-oak-tree-lined streets, and it didn't take long to arrive at the café's back door, the one that led down a corridor and to the stairs. Unlike the other day when Noah and I tore upstairs, I took my time. When I opened the hallway door to the fourth floor, I heard the jangle of keys.

The noise didn't come from my key ring. I froze. Then poked my head into the hall. Because it was formerly a hotel, the stairs were at the far end of a long corridor, and it was illuminated by a wan yellow light, like something out of a flophouse, or a horror movie. My heart pounded insistently against my ribs, and common sense urged me to run back down the stairs.

But I pressed on, curiosity overcoming all logic. Fab's apartment was all the way on the other end of the narrow corridor.

And there was a woman at his door.

Chapter Ten

E^{*ek.*} I froze, wondering what to do. Then I came to my senses and remembered that I was the owner here. Sort of. I barreled down the hall.

"Hey," I called out in a sharp voice.

The closer I got, I realized who it was: Paige Dotson, Fab's on-again, off-again girlfriend. The person who'd teased me mercilessly in high school for being a geek. A flashback came to mind, of walking into Beach High's girls' bathroom in the sophomore year and finding her scrawling my name in Sharpie on the bathroom wall along with the word *nerd* and another, less pleasant, adjective.

She greeted me with a sneer and a flick of her blonde hair, perfectly tousled with beachy waves. She was clad in a gray sweatshirt and black yoga pants, and I recall once how Fab said that yoga pants were God's gift to men. I'd silently gagged at his declaration.

"What are you doing here?" she asked in a snotty tone.

Since coming back to Devil's Beach, I hadn't had much contact with Paige, save for some pitying stares when she'd come into the café and harangue Fab. Which wasn't often. Clearly, she was still the same nasty person she'd been as a teenager.

I stopped about three feet from her. "I live here and my family owns this building. The real question is: what are *you* doing here?"

She sniffled. Her eyes practically glowed they were so red, and her nose was also an angry shade of pink. I willed my shoulder muscles to relax. There was no need to get in a fight with someone who was obviously upset. I genuinely felt bad for her.

A black duffel bag was slung over her shoulder and she waved a key in her left hand. "I'm here to pick up some things. Fab had given me a key, and I was about to go in and collect my belongings."

I wondered if the panties I'd seen with Noah were hers. "Okay. You could've called to tell me you were coming. And did you inform the police you were going to take stuff out of his apartment?"

"Why would I tell you or anyone? They're my things, and I don't see any crime scene tape on the door." She scratched the side of her scalp with the key.

"I dunno, you could be stealing, er, moving evidence."

She narrowed her eyes. "You could be doing the same. In fact, I'd say you have a bigger reason to steal evidence than I do. You already have his dog."

"What? Why on earth would you say that?" I blinked. "Someone had to care for Stanley. Did you want to?"

Please say no. Please say no. Please say no.

"Pfft. I hate dogs. I didn't want Fab to keep that little rat in the first place."

Relieved, I pushed out a sigh.

"You're the one who should be questioned for his death."

A surge of indignancy went through me. "Excuse me? Why is that?"

"You pushed him over the edge. Hurt his feelings. Isn't there some kind of bullying law?"

"Bullying law?" I crossed my arms over my chest and snorted. "Too bad it wasn't on the books when we were in high school. And no. I didn't bully him. I explained why I was so upset. Sure, maybe I could've used some different words and phrases, but I felt betrayed. Fab had convinced me to enter the barista contest. We had been spending hours together on our coffee presentation."

"You metaphorically pushed him over the edge." She glared at me with cold, blue eyes. "You were so harsh to him that day in the café. You don't know the stress he was under."

I leaned against the wall. "Not to speak ill of the dead or anything, but we're all under stress. Him leaving without giving notice caused me a lot of stress. I figured a guy in his mid-twenties could handle a mild reprimand."

"Whatever. I'm sure you were just jealous."

I squinted. She wasn't making sense. "Jealous? Of what?"

"I know he was with a lot of other women, and probably you, too. That's why you spent so much time together."

I grimaced. "No. He was teaching me to make latte art."

"Whatever. He loved me. Me. That's why he came to work for my dad, and that's why you were so unhinged." She slapped her chest with her palm.

Goodness. The only unhinged person was her. But maybe now wasn't the time or place to point that out. What if she attacked me? She was still in great shape, muscular and fit. I, on the other hand, had spent the last eight years eating dinners out of the *Miami Tribune* vending machine.

"I never hooked up with him. Wouldn't have been with him had he been the last man on earth." Oof. I should probably be a little kinder, under the circumstances. I took a deep breath and steeled myself. Then I allowed a little smile to lift the corners of my mouth.

"Let's start this again. I'm sorry for your loss, Paige. Truly. And I'm sorry for the attitude when I first saw you. I was a little startled, honestly. I didn't recognize you, or expect anyone to be here. I came by to get Stanley's vaccination records."

While hitching the duffel bag higher on her shoulder, she narrowed her eyes. "Stupid dog," she muttered.

Yeah, she was going to be a tough one to win over. Her crack about Stanley didn't sit well, either.

"Paige, I know you loved Fab. And he cared for you so much. He talked about you all the time." Okay, that was a lie. Fab didn't mention her at all, and instead talked about himself. "Want to come downstairs for a coffee? Talk it out? Then we can go inside his apartment together?"

"With you? No. Fake-ass geek. I'll come back with an officer to get my things. And I'll make sure to tell the police you were snooping around, too."

Crap. Now I wouldn't be able to go in because my fingerprints would be all over the place. Or could I? My face crumpled into a scowl.

"I'll never forgive you for what you did to him. How you made his life a living hell." She brushed past me, letting out a huff. "Maybe you did actually push him over the edge of that roof. The way you acted that day at Island Brewnette, you're crazy enough to do anything."

She shuffled down the hall in her flip-flops.

"Well, where were you the night he died?" I yelled.

She didn't answer and slammed the door at the end of the hall. I slumped against the wall, and once I was alone, was too creeped out by the silence and the weak yellow hall light. I didn't feel like going through a dead man's belongings, so I left.

* * *

The next morning, as Erica made friends with some of the customers—she even got a few shout-outs on Insta for her palm tree latte art—I called Noah around eleven, figuring he'd want to know about my conversation with Paige.

"Are you coming in this morning? Or are you avoiding us like half the island?" I half-joked. Business was still down, which had me worried. Tourists were streaming in, but the island's regulars appeared to be staying away. I needed to let Noah know about Paige. Figured I'd get to him before she did.

Noah chuckled. "No, I had an early meeting. Was planning on coming in soon for my usual. What's today's snack?"

"Your favorite."

"Three ingredient Nutella brownies?"

"Mmhmm." I smiled, smug.

"I'll be right there." He hung up.

Maybe I'd been moved off the suspect list.

Ten minutes later, Noah strolled in. His dark blue polo shirt stretched across his muscular chest, and his jeans fit him nicely, too. Why wasn't he in uniform? Oh. Duh—it was Sunday. I was losing track of time. Grinning, I slid a brownie onto a plate and went to prepare his lemon water.

"Have a seat. I'll bring it to you," I called out.

"Who's that?" Erica hissed, and a frisson of jealousy went through me.

"Noah Garcia. The police chief."

"Why is he staring at you like you're a bigger snack than that Nutella brownie?"

I shrugged. "Either he's planning to arrest me or he's madly in love with me."

She burst out laughing. "I suspect it's probably the latter."

I shot her a warning glare, and she clapped her fingers over her mouth. "I'll explain later."

I made a big production of setting his water and brownie in front of him and scurried to get a napkin. Today I'd dressed up. Well, dressed up for me. I usually wore jeans and a Perkatory T-shirt to work. Today I was in a cute olive shirtdress and white sneakers. As I walked back with the stack of napkins, I spotted Noah's eyes flicker for a nanosecond to my bare legs.

A surge of triumph went through me and I slid into the seat opposite of him.

"So," I said.

He bit into the brownie and the corner of his mouth lifted. He was so heckin' adorable. Focus, Lana, focus.

He wiped his mouth. "I have news."

My eyes widened and I leaned in. "Oh, really?"

"The eye that you found on the beach? It was a swordfish."

My body slumped against the chair. "Oh."

He took another bite of brownie. His eyes were smizing. Like honest-to-goodness Tyra Banks' *America's Next Top Model* smizing. It was both maddening and hot.

"Interesting thing, that eye. My theory is there's a poacher or a wildlife smuggler—"

"I don't care about the wildlife," I cried. "How's the death investigation going? Get to the good stuff."

He chuckled. "Oh, you want *that* news."

"Stop teasing me." My nostrils twitched.

"You're cute when—"

I held up a finger. "Don't say it."

He licked his lips and I nearly spontaneously combusted, so I grabbed a menu and fanned my face. "Noah, please."

"Okay. Here's what I can tell you. Autopsy results came back. That's why I couldn't come in this morning. Had an early breakfast with the medical examiner on the mainland."

"Impressive. On a Sunday, no less." I leaned in and stopped fanning myself.

He chewed another bite. "The ME and I went to college together. We're old friends." He pointed at the brownie. "These are incredible."

I inhaled, impatient. "Aren't you going to tell me what the autopsy report said?"

He polished off the rest of the brownie in one bite and shrugged.

"It's public record, you know," I said through a clenched jaw. "I'm not above filing a freedom of information request for the report."

He took a sip of his water. This guy was entirely too cool and collected.

"I'll bring you another brownie if you tell me."

Lord, even his smirk was adorable. "I think that's blackmail. I could arrest you for that."

"And I have some info that might be of interest."

His dark eyebrows furrowed. "Have you been snooping around?"

"No," I yelped. "I ran into Paige Dotson, that's all. Have you talked with her?"

"Not yet. She hasn't returned my calls."

My eyes widened. "Oh, really? That's suspicious, no?"

"What did Paige say to you?"

I shrugged, trying to play it as cool as Noah. "She was trying to get into Fab's apartment last night. Claimed she had a key."

"What were you doing in Fab's apartment?"

I straightened my spine indignantly. "My family and I own the building. I was cleaning the hallway and stairs."

"Sure you were," he muttered.

"I confronted her. We had a nice chat. She talked about how he was with other women, but claimed she didn't care. And she was prepared to take her things from the apartment. I suggested she speak with you first. See? I'm on your side."

I paused and we stared at each other. The temperature in Perkatory rose about ten degrees. "I'll get you that other brownie and you can tell me about the autopsy report."

He fiddled with the collar of his polo shirt, as if he could feel the warmth, too.

I fetched the brownie, my skin on fire because I knew he was staring at me. I set the brownie in front of him and folded my hands primly on the table. "Spill."

"I can't make a final determination on the case based on the autopsy alone, but signs are pointing to suicide, or an accidental fall. We know that he wasn't killed prior to making contact with the pavement."

I winced. "So why can't you call it a suicide or an accident?"

"Mostly because the toxicology report's going to take another week. Maybe two. I put a rush order on it."

"Doesn't it usually take longer?"

"It's a slow month at the medical examiner's. Unlike Tampa and Miami, there's not a lot of death in this county. I could almost make a determination now, but I want to be sure I'm not missing anything. Don't want to overlook important clues." He studied me.

"You don't think I killed him, do you? Paige all but accused me, and I thought that was completely inappropriate," I hissed.

"My gut tells me you didn't, but I don't base my police work on my gut. That's why I've gotten a warrant for the surveillance camera from the motel where you stayed that night."

I rolled my eyes. He thought I was a suspect! "You really think I'm a killer?"

"It's called thorough police work, Lana."

I snorted. "Glad you're being so diligent with my details. What about everyone else on this island? He had plenty of complicated relationships. Paige, because he screwed around on her? Mr. Clarke, because Fab screwed his wife? And God knows who else."

"Patience, Lana. Police work is about patience, not emotion."

I glared at him.

"Here's a detail you'll like: Fab had something interesting in his pocket when he died."

"What?"

"A key ring with a dried alligator foot attached."

I wrinkled my nose. "Ew. Any significance?" Hadn't there been an alligator farm business card in Fab's house?

He shrugged. "I know what you're thinking. The business card. I'm not sure it means anything. It looks like one of those trinkets you buy at that gas station in the Everglades. Or a roadside tourist trap off the interstate. Tons of people have them."

We stared at each other for a couple of beats in silence.

"Okay, gotta run, Lana. Thanks for the brownies. They were delicious."

We both stood, and I wondered why he was in such a hurry. My heart sank when I realized that it was entirely possible that he had a date.

"I'll keep you posted if I find anything else out," I said.

Noah took me by the elbow, which sent little sparks through my body. He was close enough that I could smell his Irish Spring soap. Swoon city.

"Lana, I know your reporter's antennae are quivering over this. But I'd like to caution you. Do not do your own investigation. Please."

I smiled prettily, but didn't say anything. He smirked and shook his head, probably because we both knew I wasn't going to follow his orders.

Chapter Eleven

"What's the story with the wild monkeys on the island?" Erica asked, rinsing off a glass. "I read that article in the paper today."

I glanced up from the *Devil's Beach Beacon*. The headlines about Fab had been replaced with one about the primates here on the island. They were a never-ending source of fascination to newcomers and tourists.

"The monkeys? Well, they're mostly harmless. I say mostly because they do apparently carry a strain of herpes. And apparently they got dangerously close to a tourist last week."

Erica's eyebrows shot up. "Whoa, that's crazy."

It was Monday morning, just after the morning rush. Although it was more like a soft ebb and flow of customers, kind of like the waves of the Gulf of Mexico a few blocks away, which was concerning. Usually it was more like an open firehose: relentless for hours.

I was trying not to worry about it. Instead, I was bringing Erica up to speed on the island's monkey saga, telling her how my grandfather had opened a roadside zoo on Devil's Beach in the sixties. That's how the monkeys got their start.

In the seventies, animal rights activists had snuck onto my grandfather's property and opened the monkeys' cages. The primates fled to a nearby wildlife preserve here on the island. My grandfather then turned his attention to a kumquat farm.

The monkeys commenced their monkey business, and now here we were with a feral, herpes-infected monkey colony.

"You have a really interesting family," she said drily. "C'mon over and we'll practice some latte art."

I walked around the counter and ground some beans.

Erica asked, "So the monkeys have lived their best lives in that wildlife preserve for decades?"

First, I frothed the milk, then pulled the espresso shot. "A researcher from the University of Florida came to do a study last year. She's studying all the monkey colonies in Florida. Turns out they all have that strain of herpes, and the island's mayor went ape, saying they were going to infect tourists."

Erica drew in a breath. "I'm not sure I want to know the transmission methods of that."

I was silent as I focused on creating a fern pattern with the milk. Erica spoke as I drizzled the milk into the cup.

"Easy. Easy. Now run a line of milk up as the stem. Like that. Yeah. Oh, yeah!" She clapped her hands.

I stood back and appraised my work. "It looks like a fern!"

"Heck yeah, it does," she said. "You're doing so well that maybe we need to figure out how we can make a foam monkey. Uphold your family's legacy and all."

"I wouldn't go that far," I giggled. "Maybe a kumquat."

She frowned. "A latte art kumquat? But why?"

I was about to tell her about my grandfather's kumquat farm— he'd spent the last ten years of his life trying to brand the kumquat as the world's tiniest and tastiest fruit, a crusade that had failed miserably because the word kumquat is the silliest word in the English language—the bells attached to the door jingled. Erica and I both lifted our heads.

A tall guy with curly, golden hair came toward us. Lord, he looked familiar. He had the tanned skin of a longtime surfer, or perhaps someone who spent a lot of leisure time on yachts. He was broad-shouldered, sinewy, and casually gorgeous. Like most men on the island, he wore flip-flops. I guessed he said the word *dude* a lot.

He sauntered up the counter and grinned. "Hey," he said in a gravelly voice.

"Hey," Erica and I said in tandem.

There was an awkward pause as we sized him up. Okay, Erica sized him up. She had a skeptical expression in her eyes and yet, she greeted him with a chipper tone.

"Welcome to Perkatory," she said.

I admired his high cheekbones and full mouth. Then started to wonder if I was somehow going crazy from lack of touch or sex. It had been a year-long dry spell. Then a light bulb went off in my head. I knew this guy. He was Fab's friend.

The guy rested his big hands on the counter. "This was Fab's place," he said softly.

I sprang to awareness and leaned on the counter in his direction. "Yes. Well, technically, it's my shop. But sure, he worked here."

He nodded. "We were pretty close friends."

"I think you were here last week, right?" I asked.

"I was. Came in with my mother to see Fab. I don't recall seeing you, though."

"Oh, I was here. We both were." I motioned to Erica.

He grinned, revealing straight, white teeth. A dazzling smile. "Naw, really? I would've remembered."

I twisted a lock of my hair around my finger. Erica cleared her throat. "Would you like something to drink?" she asked, pointedly.

The guy glanced around, his curly hair flopping against his forehead. "Sure, dude."

There we go.

"Ahh, what do you recommend? Maybe a tea? Iced tea?"

"I can do that." Erica moved away, and I slid into her place. I was now eye to eye with the guy. Well, eye-to-chest. He was at least a foot taller than me.

"I'm sorry for your loss. I'm Lana. The owner of Perkatory."

He nodded and extended his hand. "I'm Lex Bradstreet. Fab told me all about you."

His giant hand swallowed my big one, then I let go. Goodness, his eyes were an electric blue, like the Gulf of Mexico on a particularly clear spring day. "He did?"

"Yeah. He liked working here. A lot."

"Odd, since he didn't give any notice when he left to work at Island Brewnette."

"Well, that move was a little beyond his control." Lex's expression turned uneasy.

"What do you mean by that?"

"Here's your tea," Erica said. "That'll be three-fifty."

"It's on the house," I said quickly. "Lex, would you like to sit and chat with me a bit?"

"I'd love to, but I really need to run." He grabbed the plastic cup of iced tea and took a long sip. "I'm on my way somewhere and passed by here. Just wanted to poke my head in because I was thinking about Fab. I miss the dude, y'know."

I murmured an mmm-hmm. Erica blinked.

"See you around, Lana. Thanks for the tea." He held it up as if he was toasting Erica. We studied him as he walked out. Well, Erica scowled. I noticed the way he strolled, casual and loose. I thought that one could learn a lot about a person by the way they walk.

"Interesting," I said.

"Sketchy," Erica countered.

"What do you mean?"

"That whole statement—it was beyond his control. What did he mean by that?"

"That was odd, wasn't it?" I chewed on my cheek. "I wish he would've stayed to chat. I wonder if he lives here on-island, or what."

Erica was silent as she wiped down the counter. I glanced at my laptop, which was open on a nearby table. I often did paperwork down here, instead of in the office upstairs because I liked the bustle of the café. I needed noise to work, probably a holdover habit from the newsroom.

"I've got an idea," I said, moving to my laptop and sitting.

Within a few keystrokes, I was on a public records search site. Erica stood behind me. "You're really going to spend fifteen bucks to find out where he lives?"

"No," I said, my fingers flying across the keyboard. "I still have the login from my old newspaper. Let's see if they've changed it."

Sure enough, they hadn't, and within a minute we had Lex's address. He lived on the other side of the island, not far from Erica's marina.

"I think that's the little cluster of bungalows that were once vacation cottages," I said.

"Oh, the ones that are painted the crazy colors?"

"Yep. That one." It was known as Devil's Village, and each cottage was a tiny shack, painted in either blue, green, or pink neon.

"And let's see if Mr. Bradstreet's been in the news lately." I was emboldened, the same way I'd felt when I reported a story. With a flourish of fingers on the keys, a few more clicks brought his name up in a single article.

"Whoa," Erica whispered, as I took in the headline. It was a long piece about the Tampa mafia, and it had been published five years prior in an alt-weekly.

"I dunno, this paper's known for being a little sensational," I said. I clicked and scanned the first few paragraphs. "This is all about some unsolved murder and how the victim owed some mobsters money. I wonder where Lex is mentioned. He's not in the first half. See?"

"Yeah, but his name must be in there somewhere. Right?" Erica asked.

My eyes skimmed the article, which was long-winded. Didn't this reporter have an editor? Jeez. I get it. Some gangster named Damon Carpenter sold drugs and then killed a guy. I could have written a better article in half the space. I sighed aloud. Sometimes I missed journalism so much it was palpable.

Then my gaze landed on the first meaty paragraph with Bradstreet's name. It described how Carpenter set up the murder.

Carpenter also asked his buddy Lex Bradstreet to come to the warehouse. Bradstreet was reportedly a foot soldier in the drug trade, a big, handsome lug who liked to brag about his bar-fighting and Miami Mafia connections.

The paper didn't implicate Lex in the murder, just insinuated that he was one of the many shady fellow travelers of the Tampa mafia. As a journalist, I thought it irresponsible to mention a man like that without backing up the claims or attributing the info to a source.

And if I were going to write an article about a suspicious death, I would find the information about Lex extremely interesting. I tapped my fingers on the weathered wood of the table and formed a plan.

*　*　*

I was still thinking about Lex Bradstreet's blue eyes and Mafia ties when I marched through town to the offices of the *Devil's Beach Beacon*. I held a fresh cup of coffee in one hand and a bag containing two Nutella brownies in the other.

The newspaper office was on the far end of Main Street, about six blocks from Perkatory. For as long as I could remember, the paper occupied the second and third floors of the sprawling, historic building that had once been a cigar factory at the turn of the last century.

The bottom floor was taken up partially by the paper's printing press, and also by a bar—the Blue Bottle Emporium, which was handy for the journalists upstairs. As I walked past to the *Devil's Beach Beacon*'s entrance, I waved to a few regulars sitting at the open-air counter, who were enjoying an early Monday afternoon cocktail.

"Hey, Lana," Rusty, one of the regulars, called out. He waved me over.

I took a few steps to the giant open window. "Hey, Rust," I said, smiling.

He leaned over and the smell of beer coming from his mouth made me take a half step back. "How's your dad?"

"He's great. Doing his yoga thing. How are your carved pelicans?" In retirement, Rusty had taken up two pastimes: sculpting pelicans out of sandstone and drinking. It was obvious which he was pursuing today, because his eyes were glassy and boozy. Like most beach communities in Florida, drinking wasn't merely a pastime. It was a way of life.

"Good to hear. I gotta do some of that exercise stuff, too. Get back in shape. By the way, what the hell happened to your guy?"

"My guy?"

"Your employee. Your coffee guy. I'm hearing all sorts of things around town."

I unclenched my molars. "Yeah? Like what?"

"That you pushed him to commit suicide. That he was in love with you. That maybe you even . . ." Rusty shrugged and took a long chug of his pint.

"I did not push him to do anything," I said, my tone rising an octave. "We were not in a relationship, and I did not kill him."

I stomped off. As much as I loved Devil's Beach, I was now reminded why I used to chafe when I was in high school. The rumor mill was brutal.

It had all become clear to me. I needed to pitch a story about Fab and find out everything I could about him, his background and his life—and maybe his death. It would clear my name and hopefully bring back business to the café. And the only way I could do that was by doing what I did best.

Telling the truth in a news story.

I bounded up the flight of stairs, excited. Just like I did when I first walked into the building in high school, the smell of ink in the air made my pulse quicken. It meant news and possibilities. No amount of layoffs or hedge-fund takeovers of newspaper chains would ever get that feeling out of my blood.

Inside the newspaper offices, I swept a gaze around the floor. It was a typical newsroom—covered in papers, files, and empty coffee cups—but there was no one in sight. It was Monday morning, and I figured I'd find an editor, at least.

"Hello?" I called out. "Anybody here?"

A shape shifted across the room, and then a figure came into view. It was Mike Heller, the editor. Awesomesauce. Exactly who I was here to see.

"Mike," I said warmly.

"Hey, kiddo, how are you?" He walked toward me with a smile.

By Devil's Beach standards, Mike was new to the island, having moved here twenty years ago from Atlanta to run the paper.

"Brought you a coffee," I said, extending a branded Perkatory cup. "And some brownies."

He chuckled. "The brownies aren't from your dad, are they?"

"No. Although that's an idea. Maybe we should sell those at the shop." I rolled my eyes. "Could bring business roaring back."

He accepted the coffee. From my intern experience, I knew he enjoyed it with a splash of cream, no sugar. "What's going on? What's up with the coffee shop?"

"Sales have dropped off since Fab's departure. The locals have been going to Island Brewnette."

He took a sip and studied me for a second. "Gosh, that's some excellent coffee. As always. As for the customers, I'm sure they'll come back. You okay, Lana? This isn't bringing back bad memories, is it?"

Mike was obviously referring to Gisela, but I wasn't in the right emotional state to think about that. I gave a half-hearted shrug. "I guess. Yeah. I'm hanging in there."

"Good to hear. What brings you here? You come by to tell me that you're headed to *The Washington Post* or *The New York Times*? Or did you just want to stuff me full of brownies because I'm competing in that marathon coming up?"

"Not exactly," I handed him the bag of baked goods. "I have a story pitch for you. A freelance idea. Juicy. Exclusive."

He tilted his head. No journalist worth their salt could resist the E-word. "Step into my office," he said, then turned and walked away.

His "office" was a cubicle, overflowing with papers, files, and power bar wrappers.

He cleared a yellowing stack of newspapers off a wooden chair, and I plunked down.

"This feels like every conversation I've ever had with an editor in a newsroom." My eyes flitted around the empty room, searching for the staff.

He chuckled and sat in a tired gray chair that someone probably once thought was ergonomic. "They're all out on assignment. We've got a reporter writing about the dustup with the town council. A feature writer working on a piece about a former bank robber who just got out of prison after a thirty-year stint—he's retired to Devil's Beach."

"Great."

"And of course, the monkeys."

"Yeah, that's a crazy story."

"So, what have you got for me? I do have a small freelance budget."

"I'd like to write about Fabrizio Bellucci. My plan is to do a deep dive into his life and death. He was a fascinating character." My voice took on that old excitement, the one I last used months ago when I pitched my editor back in Miami. "And I think I'm the perfect person to do it, given the circumstances."

Mike nodded slowly. "I've heard a lot around town about you and Fab."

"None of the rumors are true," I replied quickly.

"I didn't think they were."

I smiled. Mike knew me better than almost anyone, except Dad. "I don't want you to think there's a conflict of interest, which is why I'm pitching this as a feature. More of an essay, perhaps written in a first person POV. Think *The New Yorker*. I have details that might tie Fab to mobsters in Tampa."

I let that juicy tidbit hang in the air. Editors loved to be teased.

He folded his arms and tapped his finger on his chin, then stared thoughtfully at a small ceramic dolphin on his desk. Mike was a widower; his wife had been gone for years. I idly wondered if he was dating anyone. He'd be great for Barbara, my barista, who seemed a bit lonely. I mentally filed this away.

When he didn't respond, I leaned in. "Please? I really miss writing."

Mike turned to me with a grin on his face. "This damn business. You can never get it out of your blood, can you?"

"Just when I thought I was out . . ."

Mike and I recited the rest of the line in tandem. "They pull me back in."

"Okay, kiddo. Let's make a deal. You write that story about Fab and one other feature for us, and I'll pay you five hundred. We've got some new advertisers for the features page, and I need more stories to fill it out. I'd like to run local stuff, not just wire. And our features person is going on vacation soon, so I'm going to need more content."

"Sounds perfect!" I felt like hugging him. "What's the other story?"

"I'd love for you to do a piece on coffee."

"Awesome. I can do that." I could write something interesting about the origins of certain beans, or perhaps the history of coffee in the Caribbean. Two years ago, when our marriage was on life support, my ex and I had gone on a coffee tour in Jamaica. Coffee tourism! An excellent angle. My mind started to churn with ideas for both stories, and I almost felt like my old, creative self. A side of me that had been neglected for too long.

"What have you got in mind for the other feature? Or are you going to let me choose the topic?"

"How about," he swept his hand in the air, "Ten reasons your barista hates you."

*   *   *

Four hours later, it was late afternoon on that Monday. It was a sleepy time and day here on the island. Barbara was working the closing shift at the café. Everything in downtown Devil's Beach was closed or about to close, except the Blue Bottle bar (they had a popular happy hour), the Square Grouper, and Jack's Grocery.

I was in the latter, buying baking ingredients. Tourists and locals were filling their carts to the brim with cases of beer, enormous bags of chips, and watermelon. They were probably headed to their condos after a day of frying their skin and swimming in the Gulf, which was currently the temperature of bathwater.

For dinner, I had plans to bring Stanley over to Dad's, and we'd discussed having a cookout. He'd asked me to buy veggie burgers. First, I paused at the butcher's counter, but remembered that he'd recently bought a new grill and didn't want meat to ever touch it. Sighing, I plucked a couple of packages of Beyond Burger, thanking God that Dad still ate cheese.

Mmm. Cheese. I needed some brie to snack on while I baked. That led to a box of wafer crackers, and some grapes, and those spicy imported sausages from Spain. I was definitely not a vegetarian, no matter how much Dad lectured me about the evils of meat.

I then made a run for the cereal aisle, and bought three boxes of Rice Krispies. I snagged a few bags of mini marshmallows and enough butter to harden the arteries of every person on the island. My plan was to make tropical Rice Krispie treats because I had some dried pineapple and coconut flakes back home. I was standing in the checkout line when Paige Dotson came barreling down the main aisle with a full cart, with a sneer etched on her perfectly makeup-free face.

I immediately made eye contact, not wanting her to think I'd been cowed by her behavior the other night.

"Paige, hey there," I said, trying to sound warm and friendly. She had deep, dark circles under her eyes and a pang of empathy struck my chest. I'd never get over how she treated me in high school, but still. I couldn't imagine what she was going through. Even if Fab had been a cad to her pretty frequently, she didn't deserve this kind of suffering. She loved him, that much was clear. "How are you holding up? You poor thing."

She kept on walking, and clipped the corner of my cart with hers. Since I was at the front of my cart and was unloading the groceries onto the conveyor belt, I stopped.

"Excuse me, Paige," I said sharply, moving around the cart and pushing hers back a few inches.

"Don't ever say my name again."

I narrowed my eyes. The fury on her face was evident and obviously her anger had escalated since I'd seen her last. She seemed irrational.

"Listen, I'm not the enemy here. Why don't you come by and we can talk? Let's put the past behind us."

She inched closer to me, menacingly. "You'd like that, wouldn't you? Just the two of us. Why? Do you want to off me like you did him?"

I gasped, and out of the corner of my eye I noticed shoppers staring. Oh crap. There was the bank manager, and the gym owner, and my third-grade teacher. All staring. Even the woman at the register had stopped scanning the items of the guy in front of me and was gaping. Awesome.

"Paige," I said soothingly. "You've suffered an awful tragedy. Why don't we step outside and discuss it over coffee? Come on over to the café."

"Why don't I call the police and tell them how you wanted Fab dead?" she shrieked.

Oh dear. She really was unhinged. I moved a few feet away, putting my shopping cart between the two of us for safety. She continued to glare at me. My eyes went to the door and I peeped outside. If only I had someone here like Dad as a buffer.

"Paige, stop making a scene."

The man's voice snapped my attention back to her. It was Paige's father, Mickey Dotson. The owner of Island Brewnette. I opened my mouth to say something snarky but closed it when I saw him roughly clutch her elbow. He was the human equivalent of a throbbing head vein.

"Dad, ow. Stop." She tried to wriggle out of his white-knuckle grip, but he kept his big hand clamped on her. Something was wrong there, and I dragged air into my lungs.

"Shut up," he hissed. "Not in your condition."

"But, Dad, Lana—"

"I said shut it." While shooting me a dirty glare, he dragged her from the cart and a hush fell over the store. We all watched as she protested, screaming as he pulled her out of the store. It was a surreal, silent moment, and only then did I realize I was still clutching a bag of marshmallows hard enough to squash the contents.

In your condition. She seemed tired, but as fit as ever. According to what I read in the paper, she ran every 5K race held on the island. What was wrong with her?

Was she pregnant? Maybe with Fab's baby? I stifled a gasp. And what was with Mickey's roughness? I shook my head. With a father like that, no wonder she'd been so troubled all these years. Part of me wanted to call Noah and report Mickey for mistreating his daughter. Maybe I would, when I got home.

I set the marshmallows on the belt and mustered a smile for the cashier.

She regarded me warily and rang up my groceries.

"This summer heat really gets to people, doesn't it?" I said.

Chapter Twelve

I decided against going to Dad's, and called him to cancel. Paige's outburst put me in no mood to socialize, and I didn't feel like talking to anyone. My inner introvert reared its head, and I stayed inside with Stanley. Because I couldn't get Paige and her father out of my thoughts, I left a message on Noah's cell phone—and was promptly disappointed when he didn't immediately return the call. Did I want to talk to Noah for reasons other than the investigation?

Heck yeah, I did.

"Maybe he's not that into me, Stanley." The dog wagged his tail in response.

I threw myself into cooking, making dozens of batches of Rice Krispie treats and simmering a pot of chicken soup for the week's lunches. I also cleaned like a madwoman and then bathed Stanley with the puppy shampoo that Erica had given me. Now he smelled like jasmine and oatmeal.

I toweled him off, cooing. "Such a good boy," I said, carefully wiping his tiny face. He'd lived with me, what? Three days? And already I loved him with a fierce maternal instinct. My ex and I had talked about having children, and I assumed that someday, we would. I'd been robbed of that, along with my marriage.

I combed out Stanley's fluffy fur and thought about blow-drying him. But that seemed a little extreme.

He shook himself off and zoomed around the house for a solid five minutes, then plopped on a rug in the living room. Within seconds, he was snoring softly. Never had I seen anyone or anything fall asleep so quickly or so deeply.

If only I could be so lucky. Since Fab's death—well, since the night in Miami, really—I'd slept terribly. I tossed and turned, worry chasing my dreams. Or nightmares. I saw Fab in some of them, and in others, my ex-husband. Gisela also flitted in and out. Maybe it was time to admit that I had a lot of unresolved feelings about, well, everything.

I stared at the sleeping Shih Tzu and sighed. It was seven at night and my place was pristine. I'd eaten four Rice Krispie treats for dinner, and was contemplating a fifth when an idea popped into my restless mind.

Fab's apartment.

After my little dustup with Paige the other night, I hadn't returned. I'd been so shaken by her accusations that night, that I'd gone back home and drank a glass of wine, trying to forget about the altercation by bingeing something stupid on Netflix.

Tonight, though, I was determined. Plus, I had a news story to write.

Paige's outburst in the grocery store, along with my freelance assignment, meant I needed to be more focused than ever. Was there a clue to his death in his apartment? Had the police missed anything? I had to get going on the article. Mike hadn't given me a deadline, but I knew the sooner I could send it to him, the better.

And, I rationalized, I wanted Stanley's dog bowls. Plus, his shot records—I needed to bring him to the veterinarian and wasn't sure which one Fab had used. If he used one at all. If I recalled correctly, his girlfriend had given the puppy to him about a month ago. He'd posted a few photos of the dog on Instagram, then mostly kept him inside the apartment.

Poor thing. Well, now he'd have a better life. He'd have walks twice daily, proper health care, and his cute bandannas were on their way.

I grabbed my purse and walked the two blocks to the café building. This time, I was only a little out of breath as I climbed the stairs. At least I was getting a workout from all this. The hall light on the fourth floor flickered on—Dad had installed one of those motion sensors—and there was no one in sight.

Taking a huge breath and keeping my head down because it felt a little spooky to be up here all alone, I powered to Fab's door, key in hand. Looking to my left and right, I slid it in the lock.

I pushed open the door, snapped on the light switch, and shut the door softly. It was exactly as I last saw it while Noah and his detectives went through the place the morning I found Fab: messy and chaotic. The odor of the dog poop lingered in the air.

Fab was a typical bachelor. The secondhand, brown-hued furniture didn't match, dirty socks were everywhere, and there was a stack of empty wine bottles in the garbage. I glanced at the galley kitchen, and saw there were dishes in the sink. A fly buzzed around, and I sighed. Somehow it all seemed terribly sad—relics of a life snuffed out too soon.

"Gah," I said aloud, moving to the sink. There was no way I could sleep tonight, knowing there were moldering dishes here. I guess I could've thrown them out, but that didn't seem right either. I quickly washed the two plates and cereal-encrusted bowl, then wiped my hands with a paper towel.

All his stuff. It was so . . . here. I'd have to talk with Dad about hauling it out. He'd been Dad's tenant, after all. So, he should take care of this. I'd help, of course, as long as Noah gave the all clear. I tossed the paper towel in an overflowing trash can and glanced at the bank of windows. Thank goodness the police had closed the curtains—I wasn't forced to see the outside from the fourth-floor windows.

I quickly located Stanley's water and food dishes—they were powder blue and empty, which somehow saddened me even more, and I stacked them together. Now for Stanley's veterinary records.

I glanced around and saw something that passed for a desk. It was covered in papers, and I went over, sinking into the chair. I set the bowls down on the floor and started to rifle through the detritus on the desk. Aha! Here was Stanley's rabies vaccine certificate. Shouldn't there be other shots, too? I pawed around, looking for more vet records.

Business cards, all from women, were strewn everywhere. Doctors, realtors, shop owners. Half of them had cell numbers scrawled in pen on the back. A couple had smiley faces and hearts. I rolled my eyes. Had he bedded every woman on the island?

I shuffled through a few more papers. Most were routine bills for his cell phone, the electric company. Mundane stuff. Even sex gods had to pay the power bill. There was also a folder called "Training," and I opened it.

At first the words didn't register, then I laughed. "World Wrestling Federation School Application," I read aloud. I noticed that Fab had filled out half of the application in his blocky handwriting. Under "proposed stage name," he'd written "The Italian Stallion."

I snickered. Neither originality nor humility had been his strong character traits.

So Fab had wanted to become a wrestler. I frowned. Come to think of it, he did talk a lot about wrestling, and had asked for a weekend off so he could see WrestleMania in Tampa last month. He'd been so excited, like a little kid.

Considering his physique, he'd have had a good shot at wrestling school. I could've seen him as a showman on TV, muscles bulging, all oiled up and campy. Just one more reason it seemed strange he would kill himself.

I rifled through every drawer of the desk, searching for anything dog related. Or clue related. I was coming up empty, although in the back of one crap-packed drawer, I found two small photos. They were exactly two inches by three inches, and I knew this because I was familiar with the exact camera that had been used to take them—a Polaroid Snap Instant Digital Camera.

I'd bought one myself in Miami, back when I was nesting with my ex and was going through a craft phase. Every weekend I snapped photos of the two of us all over the city, and ended up with hundreds of little photos. I'd planned to make a scrapbook that our eventual children could cherish. But we had no children, only divorce papers, and now those photos were probably in some landfill now, because I'd trashed everything when I left the city, wanting to forever forget about that era of my life.

These photos in Fab's drawer were like nothing I ever took. They were nudes, of a woman with red hair. She appeared to be tied by her wrists and ankles to an X-shaped wooden cross. I flipped one over. Crystal, it said. Hunh. I wondered if Crystal knew that Fab was dead. I peered at the tiny photo. Crystal didn't look familiar, but part of her face was obscured with a mask and whoever had taken the photo was clearly focusing on her other assets instead. I peered into the drawer, reaching into the depths. My fingers found another photo.

It was of the same redhead, and Fab. They were both naked, and Fab was in a black leather getup. Were those leather boy shorts? Ew. I grimaced. He was into bondage?

Should I give these to Noah? Probably he or his detectives had seen them. I mean, if I found them after fifteen minutes of searching, surely they would have unearthed them. Perhaps they'd taken photos of the photos and written Crystal's name down. That must have been it. Or they weren't that interesting at all.

How would I handle this in the article? Of course I wouldn't identify Crystal, nor would I try to get the pictures published in the paper. Surely the curvaceous Crystal wouldn't want those floating around the island. I studied the pictures and crafted a paragraph in my mind.

Among the things Fab left behind: an application to a wrestling school, routine bills, and racy photos, more suited to an X-rated site than his usual fare on Instagram . . .

As I was about to extract a notebook from my purse to jot my thoughts, I heard a rattling noise. I swiveled my head. In years past, I'd heard Dad talk about rats in the building, but he'd claimed he'd gotten rid of them. I wrinkled my nose. Ew. Were they on the roof? I'd have to call him.

But it wasn't coming from the roof. The noise was in the direction of the door, and it sounded like someone was jiggling the doorknob.

Holy craparoni.

My heart jumped into my throat. With shaking hands, I dropped the photos on the desk and they fluttered to rest on top of the messy papers. I twisted my head over my shoulder. Yep, the doorknob was moving. It sounded like someone was picking it. Not the sound of a key, but a rattling noise. As if someone was trying to coax the lock open.

My eyes swept around the apartment. There was one way out to the hallway, and whoever was trying to get in was currently occupying that exact spot. I could flee to the kitchen, but there wasn't any place to hide in there, either. The bathroom was precariously close to the front door. Which meant there was one place left: the closet.

Moving with the stealth of a panther and the grace of an elephant, I tiptoed to the closet door, which was half open. I slipped inside, then shut the door, shrinking behind Fab's shirts that smelled overwhelmingly like CK One cologne. My eyes began to water, which was extra awkward because I was trying not to tremble or sniffle. Or sneeze. I pinched my nose with my thumb and forefinger.

My dive into the closet came in time to hear the lock tumblers release and the front door hinges creak open. I held my breath as I heard footsteps on the wooden floor. The steps came closer and sweat pricked the back of my neck.

I heard a man's gruff voice and a few choice swear words. The voice was unusual. Low and growly, with a hint of a southern twang. Possibly an old Florida accent, the kind that pronounced Miami "Miamuh." Then again, I was in no position to test my linguistics expertise.

"Idiot," he ground out. Fear flowed through me. What the heck? The guy, whoever he was, sounded enraged. But why? His voice was the audio equivalent of dark alleys. Who was he? Why was he in Fab's apartment? And most importantly, what did he know about Fab's death? The idea that I was hiding in a closet from a possible killer made those Rice Krispies treats in my stomach feel like ground glass.

Papers shuffled, and I knew the man was only a few steps from where I stood. I was breathing from the tops of my lungs. *Do not move. Don't even blink.*

Drawers opened and closed, and the man grunted. I pressed my hands into my thighs, trying to take up as little space as possible.

"Aha. Here they are." He swore again, saying something creatively filthy, then sighed. What was he looking at? And who was he referring to?

"That little tramp. Spreading her legs for him like that. And I thought we were friends."

Footsteps stomped across the wooden floor, making everything vibrate. Including my bowels.

And then the door slammed shut. Was he really gone? I couldn't be too sure, so I wasn't about to move. Another door slammed. Probably the one to the back stairwell, the one Fab routinely used and the one I'd taken to get here.

Out of sheer fear, I zoned out for several minutes. Then I inhaled loudly and my hands, which were stuck to my legs, relaxed. I moved my right hand along the back of the closet, or what I thought was the back. What was all this fringe? It felt like leather. Then I extended my other hand and came to something cold and metal. Weird.

My heart still pounding, I pushed out of the closet. I peeked out through Fab's shirts. The place was empty. Thank goodness. I emerged then turned back, peering into the closet now that there was light. I was curious about what my fingers had made contact with.

I parted the clothes. There, right where I'd hid, was a pair of handcuffs on a hook attached to the back wall of the closet. And on the other side, hung by a peg on a loop, was a whip. Okay, then. Christian Grey had a red room of pain and a walk-in wardrobe full of expensive suits, and Fab had a nondescript closet of mildly kinky toys and Hawaiian shirts doused in CK One. That latter fact was sadistic enough, in my opinion.

One thing was certain: Fab obviously shared many secrets with a multitude of women. Was there anyone on this island who knew them all? If so, how could I find that person? Because I'd bet if I did, I'd figure out how, and why, he died.

And my article would be incredible.

Backing away from the closet, my reporter's mind reeling, I rushed to the desk. What had that man seen? Stanley's vaccine certificate was still there, and I tucked it in my pocket. So were the business cards, and I grabbed as many as I could. I sorted through the papers once more.

Crystal's naked photos were gone.

Chapter Thirteen

I hauled butt down three flights of stairs and ran back to my house, shaking the entire way. Now that I was a dog owner, a fierce maternal instinct and irrational fear for Stanley's life welled inside me. I burst through the door.

"Stanley," I cried, slamming the door and locking it. He was okay! He bounded toward me and I knelt, allowing him to lick my face for several minutes. This was the love I needed after those terrifying moments at Fab's.

Crap. I'd forgotten the dog bowls. Whatever. I'd buy new ones.

My heart was still rattling against my ribcage. I swept my gaze around the house, and my cozy living room decorated in shades of gold and red suddenly seemed menacing. Stanley was panting from excitement, his silky gold tail wagging. I mopped the sweat from my brow. Gah.

"Let's go to Dad's, little dude," I said to the dog. The thought of staying alone gave me the creeps. Especially since whoever that was in Fab's apartment seemed to have a key to one of the downstairs doors. Or the expertise of picking locks. Who knows what else he had? Fab's keys to the cafe? The knowledge that I lived nearby, alone? What if that man was searching for Stanley?

Like I said, irrational.

I went to my purse and pulled out my phone, intending to call Dad and let him know I'd be over soon. Thankfully I'd kept it on silent during my sojourn to Fab's, and I said a little prayer that Noah had called.

No such luck. There was a message from Erica, however.

Hey, I'm getting down and dirty at the Dirty Dolphin. Want to meet me for a drink? This place is on fire! I think there's a cheesy Jimmy Buffett cover band about to come on.

I exhaled. *On fire* wasn't the phrase I'd use for the Dolphin. Dive bar with ex-felons was more like it. Still, it was one of the bigger bars on the island, always had live music, and sported an impressive waterfront deck that was a sweet spot for sunset watching.

Even though the sun had long since dipped below the horizon, maybe I should stop by and tell Erica what had just happened at Fab's. Dogs were welcome there, and I could use a cold one.

Maybe I was overreacting about the guy in Fab's apartment. After all, I'd been snooping around. Who was to say others wouldn't, too? I needed an outside opinion, and Erica was familiar with the whole situation. I'd grab a beer, chat with Erica, then go to Dad's.

Sure. I'll be there in fifteen. Bringing Stanley.

After tossing a few things in an overnight bag, I tried to steel myself as Stanley and I walked outside on the quiet street to my car, which was parked at the curb. Would I have to start parking in the garage? Or was I being paranoid? Devil's Beach was normally one of the safest places in Florida, and now it felt out of control. Threatening, even.

Ten minutes later, I pulled into the parking lot of the Dirty Dolphin. During the day, it was a serviceable, if a bit threadbare, restaurant that served decent grouper sandwiches. Tourists adored the place at sunset. After dark it turned into the cantina from *Star Wars*.

I walked in, and two bikers eyed me and the dog. Stanley growled, and the bikers chuckled. I did, too.

"Watch out, he's fierce," I said.

Erica was at the bar, and I slid into the seat next to her. Stanley was small enough that he sat in my lap, his tiny face peeking over the counter.

"Good lord, woman. What happened to you?" Erica eyed me and took a sip of her drink.

The bartender sauntered over.

"What'll it be?" he asked.

"Whatever she's having. And if you have a puppuccino for him, that would be great."

The guy cocked his head and grinned. "Puppuccino?"

I smiled, for what felt like the first time in forever. "Cup of whipped cream."

"Puppuccino and a Sex on the Beach, coming up."

I rolled my eyes. Guess I'd only have one drink tonight, or I'd have to leave my car here and Uber to Dad's.

Swiveling my chair to face Erica, I groaned.

"Yikes, what happened?" she blew a blue strand of hair out of her face. "You're sweating like a hog."

"Thanks. That's attractive. I'm dying over here. Somebody fan me."

She reached to scratch the top of Stanley's head.

"I went into Fab's apartment tonight. Again." I'd told her about the confrontation at Fab's door with Paige the other night.

"What?" She snatched her hand back and grabbed her drink.

"Yeah. Thought I'd go up and get Stanley's dog dishes. And find his shot records."

"Bull crap. You were there to snoop around."

"Oh. I didn't tell you. The editor at the paper wants an article. So, yeah, I was doing research."

"That's great news," she squealed. "And is that what they call breaking and entering now? Research?"

The bartender brought my drink and I scowled.

"Kidding. Here's to research!" She held her plastic cup in the air and I touched my drink to hers. Stanley whimpered, and I rested my drink on the bar so I could give him the treat. He lapped up the whipped cream with gusto.

"I found something."

"Oh my God. What?"

I leaned in. "Naked pictures. Of a woman named Crystal. Fab was in one. I think he was into bondage."

Erica blinked. "Hunh. Wouldn't have thought he'd be into that. So? You going to put that in the paper?"

"Crystal? No. I won't name her. I might mention that he was into some sex games. How can I write the article without mentioning how he was the town's bicycle?"

She cracked up, slapping her knee. "The town's bicycle. Everyone rode him. That's hilarious."

I shrugged. "Fab probably received tons of naked pictures from women."

"Okayyy . . . so what's the big deal? People do that these days." She put the straw to her lips.

"Someone came in while I was snooping around, and I had to hide in the closet."

Erica's eyes bulged and she started to cough, so much that a little liquid leaked out her nose.

"You okay?" I stopped feeding Stanley the whipped cream and handed Erica a paper napkin.

"Someone came in?" she wheezed. "Did they see you?"

"Nope. I hid in the closet. Where there was bondage gear. Whips and chains and stuff."

"Okay, this escalated quickly."

"You're telling me. And I was almost drowned in his stupid Calvin Klein cologne that was on all the clothes in the closet. I can still smell it on my hair."

Her nose wrinkled. "So, what happened with the person who came in?"

"The guy stomped around for a few minutes, swore a lot, then stomped out. When I finally climbed out of the closet, I saw that he'd taken Crystal's naked photos."

Erica shook her head. "Whoa. Are you thinking this has anything to do with Fab's death?"

I took two long swallows of my Sex on the Beach. "I guess? I have no idea. I'm going to have to run this by Noah. Although he probably won't be pleased that I was probing around, considering he gave me explicit instructions not to snoop. But that was before I got the assignment to write the article."

"I don't think the article excuse will matter much to Sheriff Hottie."

"Chief. Not Sheriff."

We grinned at each other, and I waved my free hand excitedly. "Oh, and I found this, too: Fab was applying to a wrestling school. He'd talked about how much he loved wrestling. That means he had something to look forward to. Why would he kill himself? It still doesn't make sense, and I refuse to believe it."

Erica held her plastic cup up, signaling to the bartender that she wanted another. "So, let's say he was killed. Who are the suspects so far?"

I wriggled closer to her and unstuck Stanley's little snout from the cup. "Okay. Let's assess. There's the unknown man in the apartment. He had a deep voice and southern accent."

"Deep Voice Burglar," she held up her index finger.

"There's Paige Dotson, his girlfriend. She was upset that he was screwing around."

"Paige." Erica held up her middle finger, so she looked like a Boy Scout. "Paige has accused you, so that might mean she's trying to divert attention away from herself."

"Right! And there's Mr. and Mrs. Clarke, the swinger couple who also bought Fab a scooter. Although they're on a cruise." When Erica blinked, confused, I quickly explained. "Rumor has it that Fab had given Mrs. Clarke some private latte lessons, if you know what I mean. The Clarkes have been on the island forever. Pillars of society. Kinda weird."

"Ah. Okay. Mr. Clarke, weird spurned husband." She held up three fingers. "What about Lax?"

"Lex? The sexy surfer?" I raised an eyebrow.

"Yeah. Him. He said he was a friend, but is he really? And he has Mafia ties, allegedly."

I shrugged. "Who knows? I mean, it's Florida. Who isn't hiding something? There's also Fab's uncle. I spoke with him on the phone and he sounded super sketchy. Can't even make it here to claim the body or plan a funeral."

"When's the funeral, anyway?"

I was silent for a beat. "I'm not sure. I kind of assumed Paige and her dad would arrange something. Since she was closest to him and he was technically working there when he died. I forgot to ask her while she was accusing me of murder this morning at the grocery store."

"She accused you publicly?"

"Oh. I didn't tell you about that." I gave her the rundown of what had happened at the market.

"Hmph. She sounds like a loose cannon. I'd keep an eye on her, if I were you."

Erica and I drank in silence, and when Stanley started to get wriggly, she held out her arms. I handed him over. "I have to pee," I said, sliding down from the chair and wobbling a little. "Whoo-ee, that Sex on the Beach really packs a punch." I'd never been good at holding my liquor.

I made my way through the now crowded bar. It was filled with people wringing the final drop out of their summer vacations, doing shots and slurping down fruity frozen drinks from tall plastic glasses. Of course there was a line for the restroom, and I stood in a dank, dark hallway, waiting for whoever was in the women's room to finish.

There was already a guy slumped against the wall, waiting for the men's room. He nodded at me, his sandy hair dull in the dim light.

Eons passed. The jukebox started to blare a Doobie Brothers song. I hummed along. What was taking the person in the bathroom so long? I checked my messages. Nothing. I crossed my legs and sighed.

"Come on," I groaned aloud, rolling my eyes.

The guy next to me chuckled. "Yeah, what are they doing in there? Same with the men's room. Been in there for freaking hours." The guy pounded on the men's door, and I looked up.

He was lanky, with a thin, beak-like nose. His skin was overly tanned, a burnished leathery texture common among some Floridians who work outside a lot. He wore the unofficial male uniform of Devil's Beach: white T-shirt, khaki cargo shorts, flip flops.

No wonder I liked Noah—he was so well-dressed. Even that night on the beach when he'd come from the gym, he seemed like he'd jumped from the page of a Crossfit ad. I crossed my legs and tried to think about more pleasant things, like what Noah would look like in a tuxedo.

"Hey, jerks. Snort your last line and get the eff out." He swore out loud. "Some folks just have no manners. What happened to being courteous, dammit?"

I froze. That swear word. That *voice*. Growly and with an old Florida accent. No. It couldn't be. A chill ran down my spine.

The door to the women's bathroom opened slowly. An elderly lady hobbled out. I practically knocked her over to get inside and latch the door, and not just because my bladder was about to burst from fear.

I'd have recognized that man's voice anywhere. After all, it was imprinted in my brain after hearing it echo through Fab's apartment.

* * *

You need to get in here right now, I texted Erica while I peed. Through the flimsy walls, I heard a toilet flush and the door slam from the men's bathroom.

In where? I was about to order us another round of drinks. Can Stanley have more whipped cream?

No, he may not. I'm in the bathroom. Now! It's important. I wondered if this was too much to ask of a new friend. But if anyone understood quirkiness, it was Erica. She had an eccentricity that I admired.

Okay, okay. I'll put the drinks on hold. You're buying the next round.

I hyperventilated. What were the chances of running into the guy who'd broken into Fab's apartment (while I was breaking

152

into it)? Pretty high, actually. Devil's Beach wasn't that big, and the Dirty Dolphin was the only bar with live music tonight, if you didn't count that hoity-toity lounge at The Sands, the luxury resort on the other end of the island. Had I run into the sketchy guy at The Sands? *That* would have been odd.

Running into a burglar and possible murderer at the Dirty Dolphin? I snorted out loud. Probably a quarter of the men in this bar had been charged with at least one, if not both, of those crimes. Another quarter were probably on probation. (It was another reason why my love life here stunk, but I wasn't ready to unpack that particular detail tonight).

After about a minute, there was a sharp rap on the door.

"Lana?" Erica's throaty voice wafted through the flimsy wood. I flung it open ushering her and Stanley inside.

"What's up?"

I peered out into the hall. It was empty.

"Quiet," I hissed, shutting the door and locking it.

"Hey, if you want me to snort some toot, just so you know, I don't do that crap anymore," she said, putting Stanley on the floor. He wandered to the corner and hiked his leg on a discarded paper towel.

"Stanley, no," I sighed. Whatever. We had bigger problems. At least it was on a towel. "Erica, no. I wasn't asking you in here to do coke. I've never done drugs."

She peered into the mirror, checking her ruby red lipstick. It was somehow still bold and perfect. I'd have to ask her later for the brand. "You didn't seem the type, but you never know. What's up?"

"The guy from Fab's apartment. He's here in this very bar." I paused for dramatic effect. Blergh. Could I sound more like a bad extra from *CSI: Miami*?

I explained how I'd been waiting for the bathroom when the guy standing next to me spoke and I recognized his gravelly voice.

"I felt ice through my veins," I hissed. "I know this is the guy. I'd know the voice anywhere. I swear to God it was him."

Erica turned, leaning against the lavatory. "Well, this is an interesting dilemma. What are we going to do? Do you want to call Sheriff Hunk?"

I grimaced. "Chief Noah Garcia?"

She waved her hand dismissively. "Chief, Sheriff, whatever. Yeah. Him. Hunk. Dude who wants to get in your pants."

"Now's not the time to think about that, unfortunately." I ran my tongue across my teeth. Admittedly, I hadn't thought of getting Noah involved. "What would I say if I called? Hey, I broke into Fab's house tonight to snoop around, and I think the other burglar is here so come arrest him for murder because I have a funny feeling?"

"Not optimal," she agreed. "You'd have to come up with something a little more concrete."

I sighed. "I think we need to talk to the guy, somehow. Get more evidence."

"We absolutely need to talk to him. What does he look like?"

"Tall. Thin nose. Sandy brown hair. Wearing a white T-shirt and cargo pants."

She lifted an eyebrow. "You've just described half the dudes in this place. Unfortunately."

"I know, right? It's pretty slim pickings on this island, man-wise." I paused. "He had tattoos on both arms."

"That doesn't narrow it down at all. I think you're the only one without ink here." She studied my bare arms, pale as skim milk. Hers were liberally decorated with seafaring scenes.

"Are you saying I'm a prude?"

"No, I'm saying that you could use a little art on your skin. Maybe I need to take you to my guy in Orlando." She held out her freckled arm, showing a sleeve with a cat and a sailboat.

Like that was going to happen, with my fear of needles. "I'll think about it." I tapped my foot on the floor.

"Okay, I've got an idea. Let's go. Let's hope he hasn't left."

I scooped up Stanley and followed Erica out of the bathroom. Since someone had taken our seats at the bar, we migrated to the far corner of the room. Several guys sized us up, and it was no small feat to avoid eye contact while I searched the place for the mystery man. Finally, I spotted him. He was standing at a high-top table, alone, drinking a beer and seemingly absorbed in whatever was on the television. *Matlock*, I think.

Boy, he was going to be disappointed when the Margaritaville Maniacs—a popular Jimmy Buffet cover band on Devil's Beach—started up. The guitar player plugged in his amp and the singer tapped the microphone, sending an ear-splitting hum of feedback into the air.

I leaned toward Erica. "That's him. By himself. Nine o'clock. Tattoo of a machete on his left arm."

Her eyes flickered up and down, scanning his entire body. He was about ten feet away, and we could only see his hawkish profile. "Got it. Follow me."

Before I could ask her what she had planned, she marched up to the bar. "Three shots of tequila," she said to the guy behind the counter before handing over her credit card. "And keep the tab open."

I cleared my throat and poked her with my free hand.

"I'm driving," I muttered.

"Don't sweat it," she said. "Leave your car here."

"Tomorrow's a work day."

"Who cares?" she hissed. "We're trying to get some answers tonight."

Yes, we were. Emboldened by her certainty, I decided to follow her lead.

Erica collected the three shot glasses then gestured with her head. "You get the lime and salt."

I grabbed the salt shaker and stuffed it in a plastic cup, along with three lime wedges. Like a laser, Erica focused on the guy and strutted up. Catwalk models had nothing on her, and several men glanced, whistled, and murmured in appreciation. I scurried to keep up with her, Stanley tucked under one arm and holding the condiments with my free hand.

We stopped at the guy's table.

"Hey there," she said with a giant grin, setting the three glasses down. "The bartender accidentally poured too many shots for me and my friend here. Since the dog doesn't drink, I figured you looked like a man who could use some free booze."

The guy's eyes went from Erica, to the shots, to me. I was wearing jeans and one of Mom's old Tom Petty tour T-shirts. A grin spread across his face. "Maybe tonight's my lucky night after all. Make yourselves comfortable. Here, put the dog on this chair."

He pulled up a high-top chair for Stanley and scratched his head. "How's it going, buddy?"

Stanley wagged his tail. Probably because he was a young and innocent dog, he wasn't too discerning between good strangers and serial killers. We'd have to work on that in puppy kindergarten.

"Cute little guy," the man growled. Aww, he was a dog lover. Well, he might be a murderer but that sure scored points with me. Stanley settled in. I placed the cup of limes and salt in the middle of the table.

The guy licked his hand, then grabbed the salt shaker, coating the skin between his thumb and forefinger on the back of his leathery hand. Erica did the same, and I followed. We all took limes.

Erica slid us each a shot and held hers up. "To new friends."

I paused. This was a situation that called for thinking on one's feet. How was I going to get any details from him if I was drinking and didn't have a way to take notes? I'd never drank with sources as a reporter. I knew many reporter guys who did, but as a woman, I walked the straight and narrow.

"Lana?" Erica said with a warning glance.

"Oh, right. To new friends and the end of summer," I said cheerfully.

"To free booze and island girls," the guy said in that southern accent, chilling me to my core.

The guy's tongue darted out of his mouth, lapping his hand. Erica and I locked eyes, and I watched her lick her hand. This seemed like a terrible idea, because tequila was almost always a poor choice in any situation.

In this circumstance? Tequila had the potential to be an incendiary device. Or a truth serum. Oh well, I had no other options of investigating this man and his connection to Fab. Wincing, I put my tongue to salt.

The liquor burned during its journey down my throat, giving me prickles of confidence along the way.

Chapter Fourteen

Approximately ninety minutes, six Jimmy Buffett cover tunes, and two more tequila shots later, I was cracking up at one of Gary's stories. I had to admit, if you moved past the tattoos of the violent scenes, his one gold tooth (left incisor) and his habit of scratching his jaw with the spout of his Corona bottle, he was a pretty good guy.

Yes, we were old friends by now. Drinking buddies. Gary was a shrimp boat captain, and he seemingly had an endless supply of stories about damaged shrimp nets, fishing in tropical storms, and shark attacks.

"I had no idea shrimping was so exciting," I admitted. It was true; I merely snarfed shrimp every chance I could get without giving so much as a thought about where they came from.

"I was even thinking about writing a book called *Big Shrimpin'*," he said, holding up his giant hand and skimming it through the air. "I can see it now. *Big Shrimpin'* with Gary Leon Knowles. I think it would be way better than that *Tiger King* crap."

"Oh, is that your full name?" Erica batted her eyelashes. She'd been doing that a lot, and was so convincing that I could've sworn she was flirting with him for real. It was a little disturbing to watch, but considering I was getting a treasure trove of info, I didn't mind all that much.

"Yep, that's my name. Gary Leon Knowles. I go by three names. Like a serial killer." He and Erica dissolved in laughter, and I tittered. Oh dear. His little joke reminded me of why we were really here at the table, drinking with this random man. *Because he probably has clues about a murder!*

"In speaking of death," I said brightly, while Erica and Gary's grins faded, "How about that barista who died? Fab. That was quite a shock, wasn't it?"

In my drunken state, it occurred to me that Gary might actually know who I was—there weren't any other Lanas on the island as far as I knew. But he seemed to be oblivious, and I pressed on, inspired by Jose Cuervo.

"Sure was," Gary said, suddenly sober. "Quite. The. Shock."

"Did you know him?" I probed, while wobbling a little.

He stared at me without blinking. His eyes were a clear green, like sea glass, and a current of fear went down my spine. "I did. We're friends. Well, were friends. Used to hang out. Did you know him?"

Was he trying to intimidate me? My boozy bravado reared up. "He worked for me. I own Perkatory, the coffee shop."

Gary nodded slowly. "He lived in that building, too, didn't he?"

You and I both know he did because you were there a few hours ago going through his stuff, I wanted to say, while pointing accusingly as if we were in a courtroom drama. But I didn't. "Sure did. My dad rented him the place. I didn't hang out with him much outside of work."

"Hmph. Guess you're about the only woman on the island who didn't." Gary took a big slug of his beer, then focused on

Erica. Goodness, this man could drink. "How about you? You ever hook up with Fab?"

She shook her head. "Only met him once, at Perkatory, right before he died. I just moved to the island a few weeks ago."

The two of them started talking about Erica's liveaboard sailboat, *Eek*. That wasn't good. He seemed quite interested in her. Not cool. There were three marinas on the island, so it would take time for him to figure it out. But still. She shouldn't roll out the red carpet for a probable killer. The more I drank, the more convinced I became he was behind Fab's death. Why would he change the subject so abruptly?

Three names. *Like a serial killer.* I glanced at his tattoo. It was of a machete, slicing through an anatomically correct heart. There was a snake somewhere in there, too. Lovely.

I grabbed my phone and waved it at them. "Erica," I said shrilly, nearly losing my balance. I clutched the back of her chair to steady myself. "My dad's coming to pick us up."

Gary roared with laughter. "What are you, Cinderella? You sure you're old enough to drink? You two have curfews?"

"No," Erica said.

"Yes," I blurted. "Work, you know. Gotta punch the clock for the man. I mean, I'm the man." Good lord, I was ridiculous when I was drunk.

He chuckled and Erica rolled her eyes.

"You two are too much. I'd love to hang out with you again." I figured he'd rather hang out with Erica only, but I nodded enthusiastically anyway, glad I'd steered the conversation from where she lived.

"Anytime," Erica purred.

I turned to my phone and tapped out a message to Dad.

Hey you. I've been drinking. Can you come and get me and Erica and Stanley at the Dolphin?

My dad texted back: *Can't Stanley drive?*

I blinked. Sometimes my dad's texting skills were questionable. *No, he's a dog. He doesn't drive. Yet. Are you high?*

Oh, right. I thought Stanley was some guy you two picked up. Sorry! Laughing out Loud. Be there soon. No, I haven't been smoking tonight.

Dad still didn't grasp the concept of LOL, no matter how many times I'd explained it to him.

"How about we grab a drink next weekend?" Gary said to Erica. "I'm going out on the boat for a few nights, but I'll probably be back by Saturday afternoon. We could meet here that night. Normally that's date night, but screw it. Time to find some new playmates."

"Date night? Playmates?" I piped up. "You're spoken for?"

Erica snorted.

Gary lifted his hands, palms up. "I've got an old lady. But we got a real unconventional situation. It's complicated. An open kinda thing. We've been having some troubles lately."

I frowned and pressed my hand to my chest. "Are you married?"

"Well, a Florida marriage. Crystal and I have been living together for a while. She'd probably get jealous of you two. Or maybe she'd like you. Could go either way, she's a little freaky." He grinned menacingly.

"Crystal?" I said weakly. "Freaky?"

"That's her name." He took a sip of his beer.

"Do you have a photo?" Erica asked.

"Why would she be jealous if you have a freaky open relationship?" I swayed on my feet. Nothing made sense. My vision was swimming, as if I was just under the water's surface. Erica jabbed me hard in the ribs with her sharp elbow.

"She's got a nasty streak, but I don't give a damn. She's got it coming, anyway. Made me jealous one too many times." He rapped his knuckles on the table, enough to make the empty shot glasses rattle. Erica and I exchanged alarmed glances.

He looked up. "What's good for the goose is good for the gander, right?"

Erica mustered a tight-lipped smile. Now she wasn't flirting, thank God. "Absolutely. Well, we'll see you probably over the weekend!"

He leaned in and gave her a peck on the cheek. "It was a pleasure, my dear," he said gallantly.

I extended my hand, not wanting to get that close to him. I was already quaking a little, mostly from the excitement of finding out that Crystal of the nude photos was his *old lady*. The pieces were falling together! He'd killed Fab in a crime of passion. I could practically write the article tonight, solve the crime, and call Noah to make the arrest.

Of course, I wouldn't, because I was so drunk I probably couldn't turn on my own computer.

"Thanks for the free drinks, ladies! It feels nice being objectified for once." He laughed at his own joke, stretched and scratched his chest. "I think the band's going to start their second set. Gonna move a little closer and get my dance on."

"You do that. Nice meeting you, Gary," I said, scooping up Stanley.

"Bye, little fella," he said, extending a thin hand to Stanley's ear and scratching. Stanley squirmed with glee. No, Stanley was not a good judge of character at all.

Erica and I practically tripped over each other trying to leave the bar. We burst out the front door, and by that time, Dad was already there in his Prius.

I dove into the passenger side with Stanley, and Erica into the back.

"Good lord, you two smell like a tequila distillery," Dad said.

"Holy crap, did you hear that?" Erica shrieked.

"Hear what?" Dad asked eagerly.

That was my dad for you. Even though his thirty-year-old daughter was drunk on a Monday night with a random woman she'd recently met, toting along a new Shih Tzu puppy acquired from a crime victim, he was willing to ignore those details to get the gossip.

No wonder I'd become a reporter.

"I think we found Fab's killer," I replied.

*　*　*

Business the next morning at Perkatory was tepid, like a cup of instant coffee left on the counter for an hour. But my hangover was a full-on roar, made worse by the pit of shame that had formed in my stomach. I wiped down the tables in the nearly empty café, my limbs heavy.

I had to turn this around, and fast. It had been Mom's dream to open this coffee shop, and while she was alive, it thrived. Dad had let it get a little frayed around the edges, but I had turned it around—until Fab died. If Perkatory failed on my watch, my heart might not take the fracture of destroying Mom's vision.

It would also mean that I'd failed at not one but two careers by the time I was thirty.

Sighing, I scooped up a stack of newspapers and brought them behind the counter. It was old habit to peel open the paper, while I sipped my coffee, going through the stack. Comics, sports, supermarket flyers.

I scanned the headlines while thinking of the article on Fab. It gave me a little satisfaction that with a week of reporting, I'd be able to write an article like the *Devil's Beach Beacon* hadn't seen in decades. At my old paper, I was known for writing investigative long-form journalism. I'd also penned the occasional quirky feature, and, of course, articles about Florida Man, the oft-cited reference to any guy stupid, crazy, or wacky enough to get into the news.

Today, the *Devil's Beach Beacon* sported a full page spread of the wild monkeys—including one particularly eye-catching photo of a monkey diving into a pond at the wildlife preserve in the middle of the island. I skimmed a boring city council meeting story and read every word of a brief about a man who had a screwdriver lodged in a very private place.

I turned the page, thinking I'd check the "Community" section. It was where the island's births, deaths, and weddings ran. Like the society pages for Devil's Beach, only instead of Town and Country, most folks here were poor to middle class service workers, and named their kids Kyzer, Jax, Amor, or Stoddard.

Most of the people I'd went to high school with had moved away, but the few who hadn't were already past the wedding stage and well into the baby stage of life. And as a fourth-generation island resident, I usually knew more than a couple of folks in the obituaries, too.

Today, the Community page's top headline jumped right into my line of vision.

Memorial Service Scheduled For Popular Island Barista.

I sipped in a breath. Guess Paige had organized something after all.

Next to me, Erica slid a gallon of milk into the fridge.

"Did you see this?" I asked her in a quiet voice. No need to rile up the few customers we still had.

She came next to me, her hand on her hip. "Hunh. You planning on going?"

"It's next week. A few days before the barista contest. I should go, at least for the article, I guess." In between snooping for clues about Fab and learning to care for a puppy (which as far as I was concerned pretty similar to having a newborn dropped into one's home, only with barking and four paws), I'd been fretting about that Sunshine State Barista Championship. I wasn't sure if I still had the bandwidth for it.

"I think you definitely need to be there," she said. "Show that you're not intimidated. Let's put it this way: if you'd met him in passing, say, as a bartender at the Dolphin, would you go?"

I considered this for a moment. "Of course. If anything, out of respect for him as a fellow service worker. I feel like hiding, for some reason. Even though I haven't done anything. Stupid, isn't it?"

"Well, don't hide."

I closed the paper and folded it into a rectangle. "I'm not sure I feel like doing the barista contest, either."

"Shut up. We're doing the contest. Your latte art has gotten so much better."

I lifted my shoulders. "I guess."

It was true. In our spare time—which was often because the café hadn't been busy—I'd been practicing my foam hearts and palm trees under Erica's tutelage. Just this morning, I'd made one so pretty that I'd Instagrammed it myself.

"You and I will compete in the championship and . . ." I followed her line of sight, to the counter. It was Mickey Dotson, owner of Island Brewnette. Why hadn't I heard the bells? I glanced to the door. The bells were gone. Crap. Had someone stolen them?

"And what?" he asked, a smirk dancing on his face.

"And we're going to win," I snapped. Ugh. Probably a bad idea considering he was the father of Fab's girlfriend. And his boss, for a few hours. Still. His snarky expression and creeping up on our conversation irked me.

"We'll see about that. Paige and I are a pretty good team."

They didn't seem that great of a team at the grocery store, but I let that slide. Truth be told, I'd felt a lingering sympathy for Paige since that day.

I'd always been wary of the Dotsons, ever since Paige and I were in high school. They were such a perfect family—at least that's how they portrayed themselves to the island in between infrequent public outbursts. She'd been consistently mean to me. That behavior of his in the grocery store was a crack in their shiny façade and explained a lot about her attitude.

"How can we help you?" I asked.

"Well, I'm certainly not interested in your coffee," he sniffed.

I narrowed my eyes. Jerk. *That's because it's real coffee, unlike the generic sludge you serve*, I wanted to say. But I couldn't bring myself to be nasty.

"I came to invite you to Fab's memorial service," he said stiffly. "I figured your employees would want to attend. Tell your father, too."

My nostrils twitched.

"I appreciate the invite. Thank you."

We stood, staring at each other, in kind of a face-off.

"Why'd you hire him away?" I blurted. "That wasn't very neighborly to steal him away like that. Who knows what would've happened had you left things alone."

He snorted and shook his head. "I was trying to make Paige happy. She thought that she could keep an eye on him if he worked there . . ."

I nodded slowly, getting the impression that there was more to this story. ". . . but?"

"But he'd broken her heart one too many times and then the damned fool had to go and die, okay?" His dark eyes blazed with fury.

I reared back. Clearly Mickey was someone who had a flash temper. The hair on the back of my neck stood up. Just when I was about to ask more questions, Mickey's phone buzzed. "Gotta take this. It's the health board."

I frowned. "The health board?"

"Yeah, didn't you see today's story in the paper? I was recently appointed. There was a vacancy when June Smith moved up north. I thought you'd know, since you're a newshound and all." There was that snarky grin again.

Blergh. I'd insulted a guy who was on the health board. Someone who had the power to shut my business down. I smiled, tight-lipped. I was an idiot. "Congratulations. And hey, thanks. I appreciate you telling us about the funeral."

Just as he was walking out, Noah strolled in. The two men passed, and I watched as Mickey didn't say hello to Noah. He flung open the door and didn't allow Noah the courtesy of entering. Instead, he huffed out.

With a half-smile, Noah approached the counter. "What's up with him?"

"He's a meanie," Erica said.

"Something to do with his daughter," I muttered.

Noah scrutinized me with those whiskey colored eyes. *Tell me everything*, his eyes said. *Okay*, my man-starved heart replied.

He grabbed for an individually wrapped Rice Krispie treat, and I poured his hot water.

"How's the case going?" I asked, sliding the hot cup to him.

"Which one?" He grinned lazily.

I rolled my eyes. "You know the one I'm talking about."

He took a deep inhale and by the way his cheeks, nose, and eyes pinched, I guessed that he was sick of me pestering him about Fab.

"We're leaning toward ruling it a suicide," he said in an even tone. "I'll make a determination in a day or two."

"What?" I cried out. "That's ridiculous."

Erica stared at me with wide eyes. "I'm going to check inventory in the back room," she said, jerking her thumb over her shoulder. "I think we're running low on the house blend." She scurried away.

"Well that was quite the reaction," Noah said, unwrapping the Krispie treat. "Why are you so adamant about it not being suicide?"

"I think there's . . . more. More that you don't know. I'm writing an article about Fab in the *Devil's Beach Beacon*."

He raised an eyebrow. "Oh, really?"

"Yes. I've been doing some research." I ignored his warning stare.

"Didn't I ask you not to investigate?"

"I'm on assignment. I'm a professional journalist. You might not be used to those here on Devil's Beach." I folded my arms.

He sighed. "Okay. Want to share any of your research with me? Or do I have to wait to read it in the paper?"

While he demolished the sweet, I told him about my night of drinking with Gary. I explained everything except the part about me breaking into Fab's house. Noah narrowed his eyes and folded the plastic wrap into a neat square, then rolled it into a ball.

I held out my hand. "I'll take that," I said.

His fingers brushed my palm as he dropped the plastic into my hand. My skin felt like it had been singed.

"Yeah, so Gary was an interesting guy, and a bit strange, too," I said, rolling the plastic ball between my palms.

"Back up. What about Gary the shrimper is strange? That's kind of random, you picking some guy out in a bar."

I wrinkled my nose. "You're a good cop, you know that?"

"No, I just know an incomplete story when I hear one."

Aiming at the wastebasket, I tossed the balled-up plastic and made the shot. "You're right. There is more to the story."

Noah's eyes widened when I told him how I'd gone into Fab's apartment. About the naked photos of Crystal. About Gary going into Fab's place. His mouth set in a hard line and he shoved his glasses up his nose, looking cuter than ever.

"It's interesting, but I'm not sure what it means," he said, running a hand through his shock of dark hair. "Other than there's more than one person on this island willing to break into Fab's apartment. I don't think that's an ethical reporting tactic, Lana."

"I didn't break in. I had a key. And anyway, he's my tenant. I'll have to clean the apartment out eventually." Well, he was really my dad's tenant, and he would have to clean the apartment. But those were unnecessary details. Ones that Noah was well aware of.

"And the other guy? Did he have a key?"

I shrugged. "He got in somehow. It didn't sound like a key, though. It took him a while to get the door open."

"And we don't know for certain that the man who walked into Fab's was the same man you talked with in the bar."

I smirked. "Whoever it was took Crystal's photo. And Gary Leon Knowles said he was involved with a woman named Crystal. Seems pretty solid to me. Plus, their voices matched."

"Did Gary tell you where he lived?"

"Actually, he did. Well, he told Erica. Why? You thinking about going to chat with him?"

"Possibly."

"He's not here. He's on a shrimp trip. Or whatever you call it. Said he was leaving today and coming back Saturday."

Noah nodded. "I might swing by his house anyway, in case he hasn't left."

"To talk with Crystal?"

"Perhaps."

"Can I come?"

Noah stared at me incredulously, a look so hilarious that I laughed. It made me want to tease him.

"I mean, why not? I used to tag along with cops all the time when I was a reporter in Miami."

A grin slowly spread on his face. "You're a pest, you know that?"

"I'll go get my purse and notebook."

Chapter Fifteen

On the drive to Gary and Crystal's in the police cruiser, I studied Noah's profile. His features—ears that stuck out slightly, dark brows, a nose on the big side—weren't all that remarkable if taken individually. They were possibly even ugly, on another man. But on him, the entire package was irresistible, alluring in a dark and brooding way that made my stomach squeeze.

Yes, Chief Noah Garcia was more interesting-looking than my ex. And probably way less narcissistic, too. In the confines of his police car, he wasn't as friendly as he normally was in the café, and we rode in silence for a couple of excruciating minutes.

"How do you like these dash cams?" I asked.

He grunted in response.

My gaze landed on a little medallion stuck to the dashboard. It was about an inch in diameter and etched with a winged figure.

"What's this?" I asked.

"St. Michael."

"Oh. Your patron saint?"

"Patron saint of police officers, paramedics, and the military."

Interesting. He didn't strike me as the superstitious or religious type, but I guess every little bit didn't hurt when one was dealing with Floridians.

"Why'd you become a policeman, anyway?" I asked casually as we drove Beach Drive, the road that rings the island and hugs the coast. On one side, giant mansions loomed. On the other, there was the impossible blue of the Gulf of Mexico.

"I was kinda born into it. Father, grandfather, great-grandfather, great-great grandfather. All cops in Tampa. I was my parents' only son, the firstborn."

Impressive. In my time in Florida I met few people like me whose roots were in this state.

"It must have been hard to leave Tampa and come here all alone."

Yes, I was shamelessly fishing for personal information.

He shrugged and slowed the car, flicking his blinker and smoothly taking a right on Spruce Street. This was the less-nice part of the island, where a cluster of trailer parks and apartment buildings sat. Mostly the island's service workers lived in this neighborhood, as it was the last affordable area left.

"I'd gone through a bad breakup and had enough of the city. Had enough of a deeply dysfunctional department that wasn't changing with the times. I wanted change. And lots of it. I also wanted to wake up in the morning and see the water. Take out my kayak on my days off. Do some fishing. When I was in Tampa, I lived downtown in a condo a few blocks from the station. I never got away. Wasn't healthy."

Now we were getting somewhere. I thought of my life in Miami, and it was much the same. "Understandable. How did your family take it, coming here?"

"My mom wasn't pleased. She loves having family around and had hoped for grandkids. Dad passed last year, and that was another impetus for me to leave."

"I'm sorry," I said softly. "I thought I heard something around town about you being Cuban-American? When did your family come to Florida?"

"My great-great-grandfather came to work in the cigar factories as a teen. He eventually became Tampa's first Cuban police officer. My mom's side is also Cuban, they came in the sixties."

"Fascinating. I don't meet many people who were even born here, much less have any significant family history here."

"Yeah, I guess we're kinda the same, you and I, with those Florida roots." He finally cracked a grin and my heart melted a little. We had common ground. If only I could get over my hang-up about older men and convince him I wasn't a murderer, perhaps we'd have a shot at a relationship. *Yeah, right.*

We were close to Gary and Crystal's street. "There," I pointed. "Mariner Avenue. On the left."

Noah turned the car, and I peered out of my window. "I think that's it. He mentioned that he had a black truck."

There, in the driveway, was a monstrous truck with big, jacked-up wheels. My heart fluttered a bit. I'd forgotten how exciting it was to be out with an officer doing their job.

Noah pulled in behind the truck. "You stay here."

"Why?"

He stared at me.

"You think it's dangerous?" I asked. "Wouldn't it be better if I was there to casually introduce you to Crystal? Or Gary, if he's here? Tell them that we were driving around together and stopped."

Noah burst out laughing. "Lana, I don't need an excuse. I'm the police chief."

"It's a small island. Might be friendlier. You are considered a newcomer here," I pointed out.

Noah grunted adorably. "Fine."

We both got out of the car, and I followed him down the long driveway to the trailer door. The yard was barren, save for some odd metal contraptions that looked like they were tangled in rotting nets.

"Wonder what those are," I muttered.

"Shrimp trawl nets," Noah replied casually, without breaking his step. "I spent four months undercover on an illegal seafood ring some years back."

"Oh, so that's how you knew the eyeball was from a swordfish," I said.

"Exactly. I suspect that eyeball came from an illegal fishing expedition. You need a permit to catch 'em."

I was about to ask him why he didn't become a fish and wildlife officer—I was actually thinking about how he'd look shirtless, on a beach—but before I could open my mouth, he was bounding up the two white steps leading to the trailer.

The white door was adorned with a pretty wreath made of cream-colored and sparkly gold bows. A small hand-lettered plaque was tucked amidst the frill. It read, "Dogs welcome (People tolerated)."

"At least Gary wasn't pulling my chain about that," I muttered.

"About what?" Noah glanced at me, his eyes flashing dark.

"He seemed to genuinely like Stanley, and I'd wondered if he was putting on an act." I gestured to the door. "Guess he wasn't."

Noah rapped on the door, a short, staccato sound. Even his knock was efficient.

No one answered.

"Did Gary happen to say where Crystal worked?"

I shook my head. "He didn't actually talk much about her. He only told us that Crystal was his old lady," I used air quotes, "much later in the conversation. I think he didn't want to lose the chance at a date with Erica."

Noah knocked again, but there was no answer.

"No one home," he said cheerfully. "Guess we'll get going."

We climbed back in the car. "You going to come back to question them?"

He shrugged. "Possibly."

"Did you come out here to humor me?"

"Lana, I don't do investigations to humor pesky coffee shop owners, no matter how pretty they are."

Flirt alert! I beamed. "So, you'll check it out? You agree with me that Fab didn't commit suicide?"

"Are you quoting me for your article?"

I tilted my head. "No, but I was hoping for an exclusive."

"Yes, I'll check it out. I'm not going to comment on Fab's cause of death."

That he believed my story about Gary—and the fact that he called me pretty—seemed like a huge win. We rode back to Perkatory, and my entire body was bathed in a warm glow, something I hadn't felt in a long time.

*　　*　　*

Later that night, Erica and I were in my kitchen, drinking some Perkatory house blend spiked with Kahlua.

"How were things today with Sheriff Hunk?" She reached for the can of whipped cream and squirted a giant ball into her coffee.

"He's not a sheriff," I said primly.

"Did he ask you on a date?"

"No." She handed me the whipped cream and I squirted it on a spoon, then opened my mouth and took it like syrup. "He called me pretty, though."

"How gallant! How old fashioned!" Erica hooted and raised her right hand in the air. She gave herself a high five with her other hand, which made me giggle. "I was right. Let's get this show on the road."

I shook my head. "It was nice to flirt and all, but I should take it slow. Or not go down that road at all. Could be a dangerous one for me."

"Bull crap," she said, leaning in. "You are thirsty. For Sheriff Hunk."

"Naw. He's too old. And he's a chief."

"How old is he? Forty? Forty-five? He's not married, right?"

"Nope. Not according to what Dad told me."

"Not engaged, right?"

"Doesn't seem so. Said he went through a bad breakup in Tampa then moved here. He's only been here a few months, and so far no one's seen him with a date. Dad discreetly asked around."

"Your father is a reliable source. He gave me the rundown on every City Council member the other day."

I smirked. "I just can't go there with Noah."

"Go where? Down the pants of Sheriff Hunk?"

"Crass." Laughter erupted out of my mouth.

She shrugged. "You're single. He's single. He's stopped considering you as a suspect for Fab's death, right?"

"I think so. Hope so. He's leaning toward suicide. I think he's wrong on that, though."

"Is that why you can't date him? Because you disagree with his investigative tactics?"

I slurped my drink, the alcohol sliding smoothly down my throat. "He's too old."

She frowned. "How old are you?"

"Thirty."

Erica held her mug halfway to her mouth. "There's a ten-year age gap at most. So?"

I lifted a shoulder. "He's around the same age as my ex-husband."

"There are millions of dudes the same age as your ex. Can you not date any of them? Are you swearing off an entire generation?"

"I want to make sure Noah's not on the prowl for younger women."

Erica took a gulp. "Okay. Fair enough. Doesn't seem like it, though. I noticed that he didn't even take his eyes off you when those three college girls came in wearing string bikinis the other day."

"That's good to hear. I'm just really hesitant about older men. My ex and I started dating when I was twenty-one. Then right before my twenty-ninth birthday, he left me for a twenty-two-year-old. I want to avoid a repeat of that."

She shook her head. "Men."

"See why I'm wary of Noah?"

"I get it, girl. But are you still in love with your ex?"

I let out a snort. "Hell, no. He taught me a valuable lesson: that I couldn't change someone by loving them more."

"There you go. So, don't let that stop you from having a little fun." She took the can of whipped cream and squirted it directly into her mouth. Stanley ran in from the kitchen and reared up on his hind legs, pressing his front paws into my calf.

"Only a little for you." I squirted a dab on my finger and allowed him to lick my finger clean. "I don't think I can do fun.

I'm not wired that way." I didn't want to let on that I'd lost my virginity to my ex and that he'd been the only guy I'd ever been with. Even though Erica was around my age, she was much more worldly. I'd been a news nerd for my entire adult life.

And now? I didn't know what I was. A café owner who was trying to solve a murder, and trying not to fall for the wrong man all over again.

* * *

As if things couldn't get any stranger on Devil's Beach, the devil himself appeared on the island the following morning while I was eating my oatmeal.

"And we've got a special report from Florida, with our own Miles Ross."

My ex-husband. He was on my morning news. It was Thursday, and because I'd scheduled a veterinary appointment for Stanley, I was going to the café a little later. Erica and Dad were handling the morning rush. Which meant I'd been able to sleep in. It had been a lovely morning.

Until this.

I swallowed a thick lump of steel-cut oats just as my ex came on the screen. "Oh, come on," I gurgled loudly. Stanley was next to me with his new toy, a plush gray seal. He looked at me, his brown eyes alarmed.

I stroked his fur, to calm us both down. What was my ex doing on my island? This was the risk of watching his network. Usually I watched a different channel, not wanting to take the chance of seeing him, but I'd been alerted in a Facebook group to a segment about five-ingredient cookies and didn't want to miss that.

"I'm live here on Devil's Beach, a sleepy island in Florida about three hours west of Miami," Miles intoned in that Have-I-Got-A-Story-For-You-Martha folksiness. Back when he worked for the local station in Miami, I'd helped him perfect this. I'd joked that it was his "Boy- Next-Door Authoritative Voice," but he'd clearly taken it to heart.

I squinted at the television with a simpering expression. He was doing his live shot from the North Beach sand dunes, which was arguably the most popular spot on the entire island. He should know—we got married on that beach, at sunset, six months after we'd met.

Today, the morning sunlight kissed his face and a soft breeze ruffled his hair. Almost as it did when we were married. Only today I felt no softness, no love. Just a deep, seething annoyance.

Wasn't there enough news in Miami to cover? Corruption, murders, celebrities—Miami had it all. What did we have on Devil's Beach that could possibly be of interest to a network TV morning show?

"The Italian consulate in Miami is investigating the death of Fabrizio Bellucci, a well-known Instagrammer and coffee barista who lived here on Devil's Beach."

A photo of a shirtless Fab, holding a Perkatory coffee mug, flashed on the screen. Then an Instagram video of him at the cafe, working the espresso machine with a grin and a flex of his muscled forearms. Then a third, of him on the beach flanked by two bikini-clad women.

As a former journalist, I had to admit, Fab was a made-for-TV story. Too bad he never got the chance to be a wrestler. Still. This wasn't going to be good for business. Or the island.

"Authorities have ruled the death a suicide, sources tell us."

An image of Noah flashed in my mind and a corresponding flutter of desire appeared in my stomach. Wait. Had Noah told Miles the cause of death before sharing it with me? Or had he phoned the consulate? My competitive reporter instinct kicked in.

"But an official from the consulate told me exclusively that they have their doubts whether it was suicide."

At least someone agreed with me.

"I'll be speaking with the island's police chief later tonight, so stay tuned. This is Miles Ross." He paused, giving viewers a smoldering glance, "reporting from Devil's Beach, Florida."

I stabbed at the remote's off button, then snatched my phone. Didn't I, as the owner of the café where Fab had worked, deserve some say in this? Any publicity about his death would reflect on Perkatory, and none of it would be good. Ugh. Being on the other side of the news wasn't pleasant.

I dialed Noah's number, rolling my eyes when I realized that Erica had somehow gotten ahold of my phone when I wasn't looking and saved him under the name *Sheriff Hunk* in my contacts.

"Lana, I was just about to call you," Noah said.

"Why did you give him, of all reporters, the scoop?"

"Hang on, let me shut my door." I heard the phone clatter to a hard surface, and a door slamming. "Lana, you there?"

"Yeah," I grumbled. God, I loved the way he said my name.

"Do you know Miles Ross?" he asked.

"Do I know him? I was married to him." I said.

"Oh."

There was a pause.

"Yeah. Oh. So why did you give him the scoop?"

"I didn't. I think there's a leak in the department. Someone else told him we were leaning toward suicide. Probably the new guy on patrol; he seems to like publicity. I still haven't made a final determination on the case. But Miles ran with the off-the-record info, and says I'll be on the network news tonight."

"That's his tactic," I cried, pacing my living room. Stanley, who was on the floor chewing on a toy shaped like an eggplant, looked up in alarm. "That little weasel does that to people. Because if you don't show up for the interview, you're the one who seems like you're evading him. Well, he didn't always do that, not when I first met him. He was once an ethical journalist."

I spared Noah the story of how Miles and I had gotten in a huge fight when he told me about that particular interview tactic. That was in the final year of our marriage.

Noah groaned. "He'd left a message early this morning, and I wanted to check with you before I called him back. He said he was from Miami and I figured you might know him and give me some intel."

"Sadly, I know him all too well."

Noah cleared his throat.

"What should I do about Miles?"

I sighed. "If you're feeling particularly salty, don't show up. He'll insinuate you're avoiding him, but it will also take the wind out of his sails and he won't have as exciting of a live shot. Or show up and correct his reporting. Depends on your mood."

"I'll think about it. And, hey, Lana?"

"Yeah?"

"That guy doesn't seem like your type."

I huffed a little laugh. "No kidding. I made a huge mistake."

"We all have. Can I ask you a question?"

"Sure."

"Why'd you break up?"

"He cheated on me with a woman half his age, an intern. Humiliating, isn't it?"

Noah pushed out a breath. "For him. Not for you. But he looks like the type to do that. You're better off. You deserve better. Chin up, cupcake."

A smile spread on my face. "Thanks, Noah."

"You're welcome." I could tell he was grinning from the sound of his voice. "I'll let you know what I decide about the interview. You at the café this afternoon?"

"I'll be there after about eleven. Gotta bring Stanley to the vet."

"Give him a scratch for me, okay?"

When I hung up, I somehow didn't feel so bad.

Chapter Sixteen

"Clean bill of health, pupper."

I set Stanley in the back of my car and buckled his harness onto his special doggie car seat. I'd ordered one online and it had arrived the other day, and this was the first time I'd been able to use it. Seeing him in his tiny plush seat, his little tongue lolling out of his mouth, I felt a maternal swell of my heart. I was a responsible dog owner. Me!

Because Stanley was probably exhausted from the stress of the vet visit—he'd gotten two shots—I planned on dropping him home first. Dad said he'd stop by to take him for a potty break, and I was grateful for that.

Today, the sun was high and bright, and the sky a brilliant azure. I rolled down my window so Stanley and I could get some fresh air. There was nothing better than the smell here in the summer—salty and tinged with suntan lotion, with a hint of earthiness from the humidity. The scent of home.

A few blocks from my house, while I was driving down Main Street, Carly Simon's *"Nobody Does it Better"* came on. Not sure what it is about that song, but it always inspires me to croon along.

The light at the corner of Main and Oak turned red, and I was midway through belting out the chorus and laughing like a maniac because Stanley howled when I hit certain notes.

A police car with its windows down glided next to me.

"Nobody does it betterrrrrrrr . . ." I belted out the chorus and as I crooned the last word, Stanley howled in sync.

It was Noah. He was laughing, hard. I spotted his dimple and everything. Oh blergh. The light turned green and I drove off, my face hot as scalded coffee.

Once I got Stanley settled at home, I power-walked to the cafe, still smarting from the embarrassment of the car karaoke. Just when Noah had flirted and called me pretty, I went and did something dorky.

I pulled open the glass door to Perkatory and the first thing I saw was Miles, my ex. Ugh. He was a bout of instant indigestion, and just as welcome.

He stood, smoothing the lapels of his dark blue suit. "Lana, so good to see you."

I rolled my eyes and went behind the counter, donning an apron. Erica came up to me. "I tried texting but you didn't answer."

"I was busy with Stanley. Where's Dad?"

"He had to go show a condo. Said it was some new, rich lady who also does crystals."

I glanced at my ex, who stood near the temporary display of album covers that graced the back wall. It was a funky addition to the coziness of the café, and I'd plastered the space behind the sugar and creamer station with the square covers. Miles would probably launch into a discourse about how many of the bands he'd seen back in the day.

Erica and I locked eyes. "I take it that he showed up after Dad left."

"The timing was uncanny. About five minutes after Peter walked out, he waltzed in. Was super picky about his order."

"Small, not-too-sweet, half-decaf mocha latte with caramel drizzles on the bottom of the cup?" I asked while staring at the back of my ex's head, shooting him with invisible daggers of hate.

"I can't even picture the two of you together. How did you endure that?"

"I endured his crap taste in coffee and a lot more." I sighed. "Believe it or not, he was once a good guy. Although I have to dig deep to remind myself of that."

"Why's he here?" she hissed.

"Didn't you see the morning news?"

"No. Don't have a TV on the boat."

I inhaled as Miles turned around. "He's doing a story on Fab. The Italian consulate is looking into his death."

"Oh Lana," Miles said warmly. "Do you remember when we saw The Vapors together?"

I rolled my eyes. "No," I answered truthfully.

He advanced on the counter, a frown crossing his too-perfect face. "You don't. Oh, maybe that was before your time. Must have been back in the day when I was in college. You were a baby then."

"Just as you like 'em," I said.

He paused, blinking. "Now, I wouldn't have come here to say hi if I knew you were going to be bitter."

I folded my arms across my chest. "Miles, you left me for a woman barely old enough to drink."

"Babe, we need to talk."

I shot him a sour glare. Babe? Talk? Us? Yeah, right. "Why'd you come into Perkatory?"

He blinked at me as if I'd thrown a hot demitasse of espresso in his face. "This place was so special for me. It had been your mother's. I wanted to stop by and say hello. To her and you."

The tips of my ears burned. How dare he mention Mom. She'd have been devastated by our divorce, and thank God she was gone by the time he left me for Yasmin. I glared at him.

"And I also wanted to talk with you about a few things."

"I'm not going on camera for your story on Fab." I folded my arms.

"No, no, I'd never ask that of you. Couldn't do that, since we're friends, er, have a personal relationship."

"Had. Had a personal relationship. And we're not friends. We're not anything,"

He licked his lips. "Well, I'd like to share something I heard about Fab. Thought you might want to know. And talk to you about stuff."

He knew I'd never be able to resist an interesting tidbit of information. I lifted a shoulder, feigning boredom. What could he possibly know about Fab? He'd been on the island for what? Six hours?

"I mean, I know you're not a reporter anymore, but I can't imagine that old fire isn't still burning inside, right?" He unfurled that trademark flirtatious grin of his. "Yeah, I know all about that flame inside you."

My face contorted as if in pain. Although I hated his innuendo, he knew exactly which buttons to push. Which irked even more. I pointed to an empty table in the far corner. "Fine. Want to chat over there?"

"I was thinking more like lunch. I'm doing this new paleo diet where I eat every three hours, and I need protein. Can't live on Rice Krispie treats and coffee. Well, you can, but those of us who are in the public eye have to be more careful not to pack on the pounds."

I turned to Erica, slipping off my apron. "Against my better judgement, I'm going to take him to Bay Bay's. But there's a fifty-fifty chance I might be arrested on homicide charges for real."

"I'll make sure I have the bail money ready," she said, glaring at him. "Ride or die, babe."

Yep, I'd found a true friend in Erica.

*   *   *

I held my head high as Miles and I walked into Bay Bay's, a Devil's Beach mainstay. Although it was two blocks from the actual beach, it still retained a waterfront vibe, with walls that were covered in dollar bills "donated" and signed by patrons.

Its slogan was: *As Casual As The Beach*. Sure enough, most of the people inside were wearing flip-flops and beach coverups. Or they were in bikinis and board shorts, and drinking piña coladas.

In jeans and Perkatory T-shirt, I was overdressed. In his suit, Miles stuck out like a porcupine in a nudist colony.

Like nearly every restaurant on the island, Bay Bay's specialty was seafood. We were greeted by Emmy Botwin, a waitress and a lifelong friend of my mom's. She'd been to our wedding.

When she saw us, confusion washed over her face. I was certain Dad had told her all about the divorce.

"Hey there, Lana. And . . . Miles?"

My ex-husband sprang into anchorman mode. "Hi, good to see you again," his voice a half-octave lower than usual. He probably didn't remember her at all. I rolled my eyes.

"We're here for a quick lunch. He's here working on a story." I smiled, tight-lipped, hoping to exude a breezy, yet slightly pained attitude.

"Of course," Emmy said, grabbing two menus.

She led us to a booth in the back of the restaurant. "I already know what I want. The grouper chowder," I said.

"That's all?" Miles asked. Usually I ordered that and a salad. It was a little shocking that he even remembered.

"I'm in a hurry," I said briskly. "I'm a business owner, and I have a lot to do this afternoon."

"Miles, do you need a minute?" Emmy asked my ex. She'd probably seen him do his morning live shot from the beach, since the TVs at the bar were tuned to his station.

"Ahh . . ." Miles studied the menu.

"No. He doesn't need a menu. Can you bring him something paleo caveman friendly? No carbs, no sugar? Meat and a piece of lettuce. Thanks."

"Sure thing." Emmy hustled off.

Miles tilted his head. "Lana, baby, you don't need to be so bitter and hostile."

I leaned in. "Miles, baby, stop calling me *baby*. I'm not your wife. And yeah, I'm still a little hostile, considering you left me for a woman half your age. We haven't talked since that day in divorce court."

He waved his hand in the air. "I thought we were friends."

"For the second time. We are not friends."

He reached for my hands and I snatched them away. "What did you want to tell me about Fab?"

"In a minute. First, I need to apologize."

I crossed my arms. "For what?"

"For Yasmin."

My eyes were rolling back in my head so hard that I could almost see my brain. "Please. Spare me the song and dance."

"We've broken up."

"What? You all were so lovey-dovey at the banquet last week." I grimaced at the memory of them smooching, and yet didn't feel triumphant.

His shoulders slumped as his entire body sagged against the back of the booth. "She's pregnant."

I blinked, and I'd be lying if I said I wasn't startled. "Wow. Well, congrats."

"It's not mine."

The tension left my muscles. Somehow, I fought back a smirk and pasted on a sad expression. "I'm sorry. I know you always wanted to be a dad."

"I wanted to be a dad for your child, Lana. Our child. This whole drama with Yasmin made me realize that. She told me this past weekend and moved out. I made a mistake with you. A terrible one."

Oh boy. Miles was up to something here. I inhaled deep. No way was I in the mood for his shenanigans. He fiddled with his napkin and I stared at his long, tapered fingers. I felt no attraction to him whatsoever. A little surge of triumph went through me.

Progress!

"I've been doing a lot of thinking, and I'd like to see if we could give it another try."

Here we go. My eyes narrowed to slits. "You want to get back together because you found out your barely legal girlfriend was knocked up by another man?"

"No. I mean, yes. I mean, I miss you, Lana." His voice was a pathetic wail.

I groaned. "No. Absolutely not. Gah."

Emmy arrived with glasses of water. Seeing the sour expression on my face, she scurried away. I took a long sip, marveling at the uncomfortable tension between us. Small droplets of sweat had formed on Miles' graying temples. My skin was as cool as one of Erica's iced lattes.

Probably I should get up and leave, but watching him squirm was too enjoyable.

"I didn't think you'd say yes. I figured I should share with you my thoughts, that's all." He seemed offended, as if I was the guilty party for turning him down. Typical.

"You broke my heart when you had the affair with Yasmin. That's why I divorced you. I'm only now getting my bearings. And you come waltzing in, wanting . . ." I threw my hands up in the air.

"I was kind of hoping we could spend the night together, because I miss you," he murmured. "You look hot."

If my gaze could kill, Miles's heart would have stopped.

"Sorry, Lana. I meant pretty. You look pretty today. You haven't aged a day since we met."

My gaze snagged on a dark splotch on my T-shirt, where I'd earlier spilled hazelnut syrup while juggling three drinks. "Yeah, right. You came to my island wanting a booty call?" I tossed my napkin on the table. "You are unbelievable. No. I'm no longer available for people that make me feel like crap."

"Fine. Forget I said anything, okay? You can't fault me for trying."

"I can, and I do."

"Are you seeing someone? Is that it?"

Laughter bubbled out of my mouth. "Stop. Let's change the subject. Do you have anything to say about Fabrizio, or was that a lie to get me to have lunch with you?"

"I do have something to tell you, actually."

"Then let's get to it. I'd rather talk about a death investigation than rekindling our romance. If you say one more thing about getting back together or hooking up, I'm leaving. I'm a busy woman. I run a business now." I glared at him while drumming my fingers on the table. What a jerk.

Miles sighed. "Fabrizio Bellucci a big topic of discussion at the Italian embassy in Miami. And among the Italian expat community, too."

"Italian expat community? Didn't know you were so plugged in there. You've really expanded your range from The Shore Club's pool lounge parties," I sneered. That had been another thing he'd done in the waning months of our marriage. Instead of hanging out at home and playing board games with a few close friends like we used to, he started spending hours at "lounge parties" with c-list celebrity DJs. I'd gone exactly twice, declared it ridiculous, and never went again. He'd continued on without me, declaring me "a fun sponge."

Miles cleared his throat. "Yasmin's dad is a bureaucrat at the Italian embassy."

I let out a chuckle. Now it all made sense. This was likely a favor to the bigwigs at the embassy, probably in exchange for theater tickets or party invites or some stupid crap. His speed was viral video of toddlers, dolphins doing tricks, and reuniting long-lost siblings. He'd never been good at hard news, and the first couple of months we were together, I'd been convinced he was sleeping with me just to get story leads.

"Of course," I smiled. "But why do you care about impressing her dad now that she's scooted off with someone else? Oh, I forgot. You never met a powerful person you didn't want to butt-kiss."

"What?" he yelped.

"Nothing." My phone, which was on the table, vibrated. I turned it over to see if it was Erica.

SHERIFF HUNK, it said. I stifled a laugh and turned the phone over. I'd read Noah's text later.

"So, what do you know about Fab?" Miles said, using his professional voice.

"Don't use the anchorman tone with me," I said.

He groaned. "Can you help me with this? Please? I'm trying to impress my editors."

"I don't know much," I said, feeling a little sorry for him. "He worked for me. Dad hired him. I only knew him for a few months. He was an incredible barista. He'd gone to work for his girlfriend's dad shortly before he died."

Shortly, as in, hours. But I wasn't about to give Miles the full timeline because I didn't feel like answering more questions.

"Anything else?"

I twisted my mouth to one side and turned away, pretending to think. "He was a hit on social media; everyone loved him."

"Some people on the island said you were quite nasty to him the day before he died."

"Me, nasty?" I pointed to myself.

"You do have a temper. But I liked that feistiness when we were in bed—"

"Stop." I shut my eyes for a second, then opened them.

"Fine." He smiled. This was a flirting tactic to wear me down. No way was it working today.

"I might have a temper, but do you think I'd kill someone?"

"Doubtful. You're too conscientious."

"Thanks. Anyway, I was in Miami the night he died, at the awards ceremony. Remember? You and Yasmin and I posed for photos together. Hey, was that her baby daddy, the old network executive who kept leering at her?"

Miles squirmed. "I'm going to ignore that remark. What do you know about this man?"

He reached for his phone, tapped and swiped, then held it up for me to see. A frisson of awareness went through me as I studied the photo.

It was of Lex Bradstreet and Fab. They were shirtless and on a boat. Both were grinning and doing that stupid thing that certain bro-dudes do—holding up their index and middle finger. What did that mean, anyway? Peace? Victory? I'm a playboy whose brain is located in his genitals?

"Hmm, he doesn't seem familiar." I wasn't about to tell my ex anything.

"Lex Bradstreet's his name. I think he and Fab were friends."

"You think? They appear to be having a bromance in that photo," I responded.

Ignoring my sarcasm, Miles tapped again on his phone and studied the screen, "Someone told me he works at the Devil's Surf Shop here on the island. They were closed when I stopped by this morning."

"What's unusual about any of that?"

"I've heard some extremely interesting things about Mr. Bradstreet." Miles set the phone down.

"Like what?" I studied my cuticles. Maybe Miles had finally learned how to use the Interwebs for reporting and had stumbled on the story about Lex's mafia ties.

Anyway, I had a solid idea of who was the most likely suspect in Fab's death: Gary Leon Knowles. And I wasn't telling Miles that.

"Lex is close with a known mafioso in Tampa."

Bingo. I almost wanted to praise Miles for his progress. That was probably what he wanted though, and thought it would impress me enough to invite him back for an afternoon romp between the sheets.

"Hmm. Really?"

"And my sources at the consulate say Lex has ties with some drug dealers in the Keys. Jeez, Lana. I'm surprised you're not all over this. I half-expected you to have begged the local paper to write a story."

I clenched my fists under the table. "Lots of people have ties to drug dealers in the Keys. This is Florida, for God's sakes. How does that factor into Fab's death?"

"Apparently Fab went with Lex on one of the drug smuggling missions. There was an Italian on the boat, leaving the island. He said Lex threatened to throw someone overboard during the journey from Havana to the Keys. Fab saw everything."

I sat up straighter. This was interesting, if Miles's reporting and sources were correct. Which were questionable, to be sure. But if Fab saw Lex threaten someone, maybe Lex didn't want Fab to tell anyone . . . Still. It was a threat, not an actual murder. Maybe I needed to investigate Lex a little more.

Emmy bustled over with our food. "Enjoy." Her brow furrowed, because enjoying anything didn't seem on the cards for me or Miles, not with the way my mouth was set in a slash.

"Have you talked to Chief Garcia about this?" I asked.

"You know how I do that thing where I say on live TV that someone will be appearing later that night, even though they haven't confirmed?"

"Mmm-hmm." I slurped my chowder.

"Well, I did that with the chief, and I expected a call. Expected to be yelled at, then he'd agree. That's how it usually goes. But this guy here told me no and hung up."

I shoved more chowder in my mouth, not wanting to chuckle in Miles's face. Noah had taken my advice. That's my man.

My man. A little flush of happiness rippled through me. Then I eyed my ex across from me, primly cutting into a naked chicken breast. He never used to be like that. His eyes went to my creamy, fat-laden chowder and flashed with a hot, hungry leer that used to be reserved for me when I wore the white lace lingerie he liked.

He sighed and speared a dry hunk of chicken. I stirred my soup slowly, savoring the rich, milky scent, then scooped up a hunk of grouper.

"Too bad. I'll bet he could have really helped on this story." I slowly ate a spoonful while letting out a pleasurable little moan. This lunch wasn't all bad, not when grouper chowder was this tasty.

"Yeah, and I was called off tonight's live shot because he cancelled. New York wants me to do a taped stand-up here, then get to Naples. It's been a crappy reporting day. Crappy day all the way around, now that I know you don't want to take another chance on us."

"What's in Naples?" I took another heavenly spoonful into my mouth and ignored his plea.

Miles's face brightened. "The botanical garden. There's a corpse flower and it's supposed to bloom tonight or tomorrow. They want me there until it opens. It's supposed to stink like hell. Why don't you come with me? We'll get a hotel."

He looked positively thrilled to be covering such fluff. I smiled. Poor Miles. He'd tried so hard to put on his big-boy reporter pants and break a story about a dead Italian.

"The answer's still no."

He gazed at me with sudden focus. "Hey, you don't happen to still have one of those gas masks you had to cover those protests at the Republican National Convention in 2012, do you? Wouldn't it be funny if I wore one of those for the live shot?"

"Sorry. I think I left that behind in Miami when I moved. I didn't think anything on Devil's Beach would stink, unlike my life in Miami," I said, happily tucking into my soup.

And happy was the best way to describe what I was feeling, because for the first time in years I realized I didn't love Miles Ross anymore.

Chapter Seventeen

After calling Erica and telling her I didn't need to be bailed out of jail for committing an act of violence, I cruised on over to the Devil's Surf Shop, a place I'd driven by several times but had never actually been inside. While I loved to dog paddle around the Gulf, I wasn't much for watersports. A surfer, I was not. Intensely curious? Absolutely.

I wanted to know the deal with Lex, and whether Miles's sources were correct. After all, I was working on an article, and I hoped I could find him at his place of employment.

I knew so little about surfing, in fact, that it came as a shock when I strolled in and asked a muscular young woman behind the counter for the owner—who turned out to be my sixth-grade history teacher. Mr. Johnson emerged from a back room, grinning. He had to be sixty, at least, but a robust sixty.

"Lana," he said warmly. We hugged.

"I had no idea you owned this place."

"Took it over last year. You in for a surf lesson? Want to rent a paddleboard?"

I chuckled. "Not really. I was in the neighborhood. I'm doing an article." I glanced around, but there was nothing but paddleboards and surfboards and those shorter boards. Boogie boards? I had no clue because I was under the impression that people didn't surf in the Gulf of Mexico unless there was a hurricane approaching that kicked up the swells.

"For the local paper?"

I grinned and nodded. "It's a longer feature on Fab, the barista who died. I'm sure you heard about it. Apparently, he and Lex, your employee, were friends."

A shadow crossed Mr. Johnson's face, and he took me gently by the elbow and steered me toward a rack of what appeared to be extraordinarily long canoe oars. Probably they were for paddle boarding.

"Lana, please tell me you're not mixed up with Lex. I know you always liked a certain kind of guy—"

"Hey, just because I went to the junior prom with a guy who was later on the FBI's most wanted list for bank robbery doesn't mean I like bad boys. I'm doing an article, not angling for a date."

He shook his head. "Okay. Lex used to work here. But I let him go. He's involved with all sorts of shady things."

Like drug smuggling, I almost asked. "Like what?"

Mr. Johnson rubbed his bald head. "I mean, I have no proof. But the signs were all there that he was dealing in pot. Or what's that new drug? Spice? He had two phones. And he got a lot of calls. And once, an extremely unsavory man came here, asking for him. I hope you're not dating him."

I pressed my lips together, trying not to laugh. Of all that I'd heard about Lex Bradstreet, none of the things Mr. Johnson listed as "signs" seemed all that bad. But maybe I'd gone soft since I left reporting.

"Mr. Johnson, I'm single and definitely not ready to mingle after my divorce."

"I'm so sorry." He put a hand on my shoulder. "Your dad told me about your breakup."

Him and the rest of the island. "Right. Well, it's for the best. I was searching for Lex because I thought he could give me some insight into Fab's past."

"Well, that does make sense, doesn't it? In that case, let me give you Lex's address. I think he lives in those beach huts at Devil's Village."

Mr. Johnson hustled over to the counter and scribbled on a piece of paper. "This was the address he gave on his application. He's a nice kid, but I couldn't have someone dealing weed here. I'm not against it for medical reasons. All for that, in fact. But I can't risk illegal business in my own shop."

"Of course not. And thanks. See you around!"

"Come on in and I'll give you a free paddleboard lesson," he cried as I walked out.

That would happen exactly . . . never.

*　*　*

It took me about ten minutes to get to Lex's house. Devil's Village was a cluster of brightly colored cabins on the island's south side. It was once a hippie commune in the seventies. Dad liked to tell stories about how he and Mom would hang out there before I was born.

Now it was something of low-income housing for service workers, albeit with a prime beachfront view. Rumor had it that the property's owner was militant about height restrictions of buildings on the beach, so he maintained the cabins and refused every big shot developer's offer that came his way.

Lex lived in a tiny pink cabin closest to the water. It was a million-dollar view, and he probably paid no more than eight hundred a month, if that. As I parked my car and studied the miniscule home, a pang of envy went through me. I imagined cute potted flowers, a beach-themed flag, a tiny fenced yard for Stanley.

I didn't have anything rehearsed as I walked to the door and knocked. Sometimes I'd done this as a reporter—winged it during interviews and asked whatever came to mind. Not during the important interviews, mind you. Just the ones where I was on a fishing expedition.

The door swung open. Lex's eyes registered surprise, but his mouth spread into a wide grin.

He was shirtless, and wore only blue swim trunks. No shoes. I swallowed. He was definitely easy on the eyes.

"Hey," he said warmly. "Lana, right?"

I grinned. "Yeah. Hey, Lex. I thought I'd stop by and say hello."

What the heck was I doing? Stop by and say hello? I was flirting with a drug dealer. A possible murderer. "I mean, I'm doing an article for the local paper and thought you could help."

"Sweet. Well, I'm glad you came by."

We paused and stared into each other's eyes. They were so blue and clear.

"Wanna come in?" he asked.

"Sure." Was this a good idea, going into his house alone? I'd done this dozens, if not hundreds, of times, as a reporter. Don't know why I was worried now.

He wandered inside and I followed. Part of me was curious what his tiny home looked like from the inside, and I wasn't disappointed.

I walked over gleaming wooden floorboards, past an expensive looking, modern sofa that looked like it was crafted out of butter. His house was decorated like a surf shack, with a couple of gleaming, waxed boards leaning against one wall. Everything else was blonde wood and white, and I could see through a door that there was a bedroom back there. Unlike Fab, Lex seemed to value a clean home.

I cleared my throat.

"You want some water? A beer?" He asked. "I just got back from paddle boarding."

"Water would be great," I said.

He took a pitcher out of the fridge and poured it into a plastic cup. He gulped from a green glass beer bottle.

"So . . ." he said. "How'd you know where I lived?"

Should I tell him? I didn't see any reason not to. "The owner of the surf shop told me. He was my sixth-grade teacher."

He nodded, but didn't say anything.

"I wanted to come by to ask you about Fab for an article I'm writing."

Lex came around to the sofa, an overstuffed brown sectional. He scrunched up his face and looked like he might cry, then pointed. "Have a seat."

I did.

"What did you want to know?"

"Mind if I take notes?"

He shook his head, which was my cue to grab my pen and notebook. Sometimes I recorded interviews with my phone, but I preferred the old-fashioned reporting method. "Tell me how you met Fab."

He was silent for a second, staring at the remote on the coffee table. "I met him the first week he came to Devil's Beach. So, about a year ago. I was drinking at the Dirty Dolphin, at the bar. He came in and we started to talk about surfing. I invited him out to paddleboard and we just, I dunno. Bonded. We loved a lot of the same things. Boats. Water. Fishing, Paddling . . ."

"Women," I added.

Lex grinned and stroked his chin. "Yep. Women. Dude, we had some good times together."

"I was wondering about the last time you saw him. Fab and I ended things on a bad note. And I wanted to try to piece together his last days."

He nodded. "I get it. You want to try to get over the guilt."

I winced. "Yeah. I guess that's it."

"Fab really liked you. He felt bad about leaving your café without giving notice. But he didn't have any other choice."

That hardly seemed possible. Two weeks' notice wasn't that difficult. "I don't understand. What do you mean, didn't have any other choice?"

Lex ran a hand through his mop of sun-streaked, dirty blonde hair. "Paige. She wanted him close by at all times."

"His girlfriend." I nodded, hoping he'd elaborate.

"It was complicated, the two of them."

"He had quite the reputation with women."

"I told him he was going to get himself in trouble, but . . ." he shrugged and sipped his beer.

"Trouble for what?"

Lex turned his blazing blue eyes on me. "Fab had some unusual tastes."

"Meaning?" My mind went to the pictures of Crystal.

"Let's just say he was sexually liberated. More than me. The guy was insatiable and really liked ah," Lex cleared his throat, "does this need to be in the paper?"

I tapped my pen against my mouth. If this were Miami, I wouldn't hesitate to say yes. Here on a small island?

I pondered for a beat. "What's the harm of telling me things on the record?"

"Fab knew a lot of powerful people on the island. I don't want any blowback. I'm trying to stay clean here." Lex shifted uncomfortably in his seat.

"Understood," I said slowly. "What about you? When was the last time you saw him?"

He sighed. "We were supposed to hang out that night, the night he died. But I'd gone out surfing that day—remember it was raining and a little windy? There was a decent light surf and I was bitten while out on the water."

"Bitten?"

"Yeah, by a shark. A small one. But I went to the hospital to get it checked out. Hurt like hell. They kept me there overnight so I never went over to Fab's." He extended his leg, and sure enough, there was a large bandage on the shin. His long fingers went to the bandage and peeled it aside to reveal three puncture wounds. "That's where it clamped down on me. See the teeth marks?"

"Yikes," I said.

"It's not so bad now." He reattached the bandage.

I nodded. This sure did seem like an alibi.

"Hang on. I want to show you something." Lex set his bottle on the coffee table, next to a phone, and rose. He ambled into the bedroom.

I sipped my water as I waited. His phone, which was about a foot from my knee, lit up. My eyes went to it immediately, because a photo flashed on the screen.

"ONE HOT MAMA," the text read.

It was Paige, in a crop top and shorts, her hand resting on her stomach.

I almost gasped. What was that about? I flashed back to how her father had used the phrase *in your condition*. She was almost certainly pregnant. The question was, who was the baby's father? It had to be Fab. But why was she texting Lex?

"Here it is!" he called out.

I swiveled in my seat to meet his voice and pasted on a smile. Had he been sleeping with Paige? Why would she send a sexy photo to her dead boyfriend's friend?

Lex sat next to me. He held a photo in his hand. It was of him and Fab, on the beach. They were both flashing hang ten hand signs, and I wondered if the two of them ever were captured on film without making some sort of gesture. I had to admit, though, they both appeared extremely handsome in the shot.

"My best friend," Lex said, his voice husky.

"You two look like GQ models," I said.

"You think?"

I glanced up and Lex's blue eyes were wet.

"I do. It's a photo to cherish," I said. "Thank you for sharing it with me."

"I'd love to send you a copy, but I don't want my face in the paper. I've probably said too much. I don't want to be quoted after all."

We both stared at the photo as my mind spun over the other photo on Lex's phone. And at the fact that my best quotes had just come from someone who no longer wanted to be part of the article.

"Could I quote you anonymously? Identify you as a friend?"

He stuck his index finger in his ear and twisted. "That could work. Let me think about it and I'll get back to you. How's that?"

This interview wasn't going as I'd hoped. Was I losing my touch?

"Well, you've already gone to the trouble of talking with me."

"I've had some problems with the law in the past, and I don't want any attention. I've got a good thing going here and don't want to screw it up."

Probably I should ask what kind of troubles, but I'd deal with that later when I searched his criminal record online. I finished my water and stood. "Fine. Let's talk in a couple of days. Do you think Fab killed himself?" I asked Lex. His broad shoulders slumped.

"No. I don't. And I don't think he lost his balance, either. You should've seen him on a paddleboard. Fab had wicked balance skills." He wiped a tear from the corner of his left eye.

"Then what happened?" I chewed on the inside of my cheek.

He shook his head and set the photo down next to his phone, misery clouding his expression. "I'm sorry. I don't think I can talk about this anymore."

The poor guy appeared so sad that I squeezed his shoulder and left.

* * *

The next morning, I was still thinking about Lex and Paige and Fab—*why did they all have such hip names*—when I grabbed a copy of the newspaper off my walkway. It was Saturday, and Dad was working at the café. Which meant I could spend the morning reading the paper and drinking coffee while lounging in bed with my main man: Stanley.

He seemed to be a dog after my own heart. I allowed him out to do his business in the front yard, and he was already done and waiting at the door by the time I picked up the paper.

We went inside, and I grabbed a cup of Perkatory's house roast, then shuffled back to the bedroom. It was 9 AM, and I was still in my pajamas. Stanley's little legs were too small for him to jump onto the bed, so I gave him a boost. He immediately flopped down and resumed sleeping.

Not a bad idea . . . but. A leftover instinct from journalism meant I had to read the headlines first thing. I'd actually already scanned *The New York Times*, CNN, and *The Miami Tribune* on my phone, but checking the physical paper was a compulsion.

I slid the *Devil's Beach Beacon* out of its plastic sleeve. A sip of delicious coffee warmed my throat, and I unfolded the paper. There was the usual small-town fare on the front page: a hot debate over sewer rate increases, a feature about a dog who body surfed, and yet another article about the barista championships.

Today's story had the entire line-up of competitors from around Florida, and my stomach tensed with nerves as I scanned the list. I recognized the names of some of the baristas and their coffeehouses; many were from larger, better known shops in Orlando and Miami. There was no way Erica and I would place, much less win.

"Crap," I muttered, turning the page to the crime blotter. This was more my speed.

Today's best story: Man Tells Police Wind Must Have Blown Cocaine Into Car

I chuckled and scanned the article, followed by the rest of the paper. I thumbed through, skimming stories about the island's parks and rec board, the engagements, the births, and the obituaries.

The Lifestyle section held my interest for a while because there was a detailed story about a vegetable pickling class at the community center. I was about to close the paper and fall back asleep next to Stanley, who lounged on his back, showing his chubby puppy belly.

Then I saw a photo of a familiar woman.

Island Resident is Mer-Mazing With Her Mermaid Tail Business, the headline read.

Who was that? I moved the paper closer to my face, then away. That severe ponytail . . . where had I seen her? Definitely at the café.

The day before Fab died. She was the woman who'd asked for him that morning. And who was in Island Brewnette when I had my spectacular meltdown. Hmm.

I read the article. Apparently her name was Brittany Yates, and she'd recently moved to the island and opened a mermaid tail business. At first, I wasn't entirely sure what that was, but the lengthy profile told me all I needed to know—apparently young women and girls had a huge desire to dress, swim, and act like mermaids, and the comely Brittany was filling a gap in the marketplace by making mermaid fins.

Some sold for upwards of a grand, which seemed excessive to me. But what did I know? My salary standards were obviously low after years of being a reporter and now as a small business owner selling coffee. Maybe I should have gone into mermaid fashion.

The article said Brittany was single, but she said that she'd recently lost someone close to her. That had to be Fab. I ran through a mental list of the people I'd chatted with about Fab. Lex, Gary, Paige (reluctantly), Paige's dad, Mickey. Maybe Brittany could shed some light on Fab's final weeks on earth.

At the very least, I'd get a quote and some context for the article from one of Fab's adoring fans.

I reached over and scratched Stanley's floppy ear. "I think we're going to pay Mermaid Lady a visit today, buddy."

Chapter Eighteen

Mer-Mazing Creations was located in a strip mall on the eastern edge of the island, near the bridge leading to the mainland. Situated between a sandwich shop and a nail salon, it was a place easily overlooked.

I tucked Stanley under my arm and walked to the front door. "Buddy, you're gaining weight," I murmured. He'd lived with me just over a week. He felt like a small lead football. Could he have gained an entire pound in the time I had him? A question for the vet. Still, he was so darned cute with his puppy fur and his new blue harness.

Unlike when I paid Lex an unexpected visit, today I was prepared with interview questions.

I opened the door. Brittany was at a long table covered in fabric, and she raised her head in greeting. Today she wore bright pink, plastic-rimmed glasses and her silky, blonde hair loose. She had on a lime green sweat suit that accentuated her curves. She looked like the stripper version of a Lilly Pulitzer model. Odd, but it worked in her favor. Sometimes I wished I could pull off interesting outfits like that.

"Hello," she chirped, grinning. "How can I help you have a mer-mazing day?"

I had to give it to her, she had her branding down. The walls were lined with photos of people in various mermaid tails—including men, which surprised me a little, but hey, equal opportunity fantasies here on Devil's Beach—and mannequins in mermaid tails and matching tops.

"Hello!" I paused at a particularly unique creation, a tail that appeared as though it was made from sea junk. It was a deep green, with pieces of shells, fake seaweed, and small plastic bottles sewn into the material. The top appeared to be risqué and see through, made of some kind of mesh fabric.

Brittany came to my side. "I made this for an Earth Day event. It was a protest piece to stop polluting our oceans with plastic," she said.

Ohhh. Now it made sense. "Impressive."

She leaned in and scratched Stanley's head. His back end started wiggling. "You're such a doll," she cooed. Then she straightened her spine.

"That's Stanley." Her voice had gone from bubbly to stone-cold in a matter of seconds. "Fab's dog."

"Yes." A chill flowed through my body. It was a stupid idea to bring Stanley here. What if she'd been the woman to give Fab the puppy? What if she wanted him back and we ended up fighting over him? I tightened my grip on the dog.

"I'm Lana," I said, extending my hand.

She shook it, warily. "I know. The café owner."

"Yes. My dad was Fab's landlord."

She nodded.

"I thought I'd come by to tell you personally about Fab's memorial service next week. Not sure if you saw the notice in the paper. And I'm also writing an article for the *Devil's Beach Beacon* about him. I was hoping to get a quote or two from you. You know, as one of his customers. You spoke so highly of him the other week."

I watched as she swallowed hard, and my heart tugged for a second. Now that I studied her face, the dark circles under her eyes jumped out at me.

"Thank you for telling me about the funeral," she whispered. "I didn't know. I don't read the paper."

I almost sighed but stopped myself. *Who does read the newspaper anymore?*

"It's so sad all the way around, isn't it? Such a shock. He was full of life, wasn't he? I'm sorry for your loss."

A watery smile spread on her face. "Thank you."

"Were you two close? Oh, and do you mind if I record the interview on my phone for the article?" Normally I preferred to use pen and paper, but I couldn't write and wrangle Stanley at the same time.

She shook her head. "Don't mind at all."

I put the dog down and held tight to his leash while holding my phone about a foot from her frosted-pink lips.

"We met years ago, Fab and I. In New York City."

"Really?" I perked up.

"Yeah. We both worked at a café called Pane e Cioccolato. Bread and Chocolate. In the village. We were both baristas. We weren't close back then. We lost touch when I moved to the Keys for a few years, then I came here. That was a month ago. I ran into him at a party."

"What a coincidence. You were a barista? And what kind of party?"

Her eyes flitted around. "It was kind of an exclusive event. For adults only."

Uh-huh. Probably some sort of swingers thing. Before I could ask another question, she spoke quickly. "We started to hang out a bit, just friends. I'd asked him if he wanted me to pet sit Stanley."

"Yes, another of his girlfriends, er, friends, had given Stanley to him. I'm told she's no longer on the island, so he's staying with me." It was a little white lie, but I didn't want to open the door for her to claim him.

"If you don't want him —"

"Oh, I do," I interrupted, then added quickly, "I was about to get a dog anyway."

"I see. Well, thank you for coming by."

"You're so welcome. I have a few more questions. I was wondering, when was the last time you saw Fab?"

She walked behind the counter and unfurled a roll of fabric. I followed along, holding my phone out so I could record her answers. "Let me think. Probably about a week before he died. We paddle boarded to Beer Can Island."

That wasn't really an island, it was a sand spit a few hundred yards from Devil's Beach. It was known for being a party spot—or a make out spot for couples, at least back in high school. Kids would take their families' boats there and hang out. As I didn't kayak, canoe, paddle, or boat, I hadn't been there since my return home.

"I see." I paused. "Wait. The day he died. At Island Brewnette. You saw me confront him."

Her eyes widened. "Oh! Yes. That's right. I did. Stupid me. And I was supposed to see him the night he died but he texted and said something had come up."

"Oh?" Fab seemed to have a lot of plans that night, between Lex and Brittany. Unless one of them was lying.

"Yeah, so I ended up staying here and sewing all night." She held up the fabric. "I had an order for a mermaid costume for a stripper up in Jacksonville."

I blinked, trying to imagine how that would work from a physical standpoint.

Brittany laughed, a pretty, tinkling sound. "You're confused, right? I was, too. We think of mermaids as having no feet."

I giggled. "Exactly!"

"See, I'm going to have more of a gown that hugs the lower part and kicks out in the back, like a tail. It's open like a skirt, kind of like a Morticia Addams dress." She ran her hand over a sequined swatch. "It will be held together with Velcro so it's easily removeable on stage."

"So clever." I peered over the counter. "You think of all these patterns and designs yourself?"

"I do," she said proudly. "I went to FIT in New York. But I figured this was a better place for a mermaid tail company than the city." She glanced at a clock shaped like a clamshell that was attached to the wall. I'm so sorry, I have another appointment soon and must get ready. It's a custom fitting. Is that all you wanted to ask?"

"I had one more question."

"Shoot," she smiled.

"Do you think Fab committed suicide?"

She licked her lips. "That's what police say, right? I saw that on TV."

"Pretty much."

"Is there any reason not to believe them?" She blinked a few times, and I wondered how she kept those long, false eyelashes on so well. Every time I'd tried to use them, I felt like my eyes were covered in spiders.

"I guess not. It appeared as though Fab had everything to live for. And so many people are asking about him, I thought I'd write an article to try to shed some light on his life, and troubles."

Brittany swept her hands over the fabric. "What is it that they say? Appearances can be deceiving?"

"True." I paused, letting that sink in. I pushed the STOP button on my phone recorder. "Well, I'll be sure to hit you up if I need a tail. Or a stripper outfit."

We both smiled at each other and said goodbye. I hoisted Stanley in my arms and toted him to the car. Maybe Fab's death had a silver lining—it had forced me to go out into the world and talk to actual human beings again.

*   *   *

Sundays were usually hopping at Perkatory, and thankfully today's steady flow indicated that regulars were returning. Dad and I worked the counter together, then paused during a lull at around ten-thirty.

"I heard Miles was in town the other day," Dad said. He was clutching a thermos of his gross green juice that he'd brought from home.

"He came to do a story on Fab." I reached for my espresso and took a sip. Talking about my ex was the last thing I wanted, especially after the relatively normal morning, the first we'd had in days.

"Heard that, too. Someone at Bay-Bay's told me."

"Of course they did."

"He didn't try to talk you into moving back to Miami or anything, did he?"

I snorted, thinking about what Miles tried to talk me into. "Hardly. And even if he tried, I wouldn't go back to Miami."

"Really?" Dad's eyebrows lifted. "Any reason you prefer it here on Devil's Beach now? There was a time when as a teenager you couldn't wait to leave."

It was true. I wasted no time in getting out of here when I graduated from high school. I shrugged. "Pfft. No. Even if Miles said he'd support me, and I could just hang out and go to the spa every day on Miami Beach. I'm done with him and that lifestyle."

"Interesting. Might it have something to do with our handsome police chief?"

"Dad, no," I protested, wondering who had been gossiping about Noah and me. "I want to make this work here. Just wish I could nail this article on Fab I'm doing for Mike at the paper, though. It's the only thing I miss about my old life. Writing."

"How is that story coming along?" Dad took a big slurp of juice.

I wiped down the counter and paused, shooting a judgmental glance at a green blob clinging to his mustache.

I'd woken at four this morning and tried to sketch an outline of the story but came up short. "My article is crap," I mumbled, finishing my espresso.

"I find that hard to believe, pumpkin. Not with that shrimp boat captain having the criminal record that he does."

I scowled. "Gary?"

"Yep. Gary. You need to get the official records of course, but rumor has it, he's quite the felon."

"Hmph. He was supposed to return from his shrimping trip last night. I wonder if he's around today and available for an interview."

I thought about calling Erica, since he'd been so flirty with her. Maybe we could go chat him up for the article and try to find out more about his relationship with Fab. And Crystal's relationship—although from the photos, that connection was pretty obvious.

Erica. Come to think of it, I hadn't heard from her since yesterday. She'd claimed to have a lot to do around the sailboat. Something about swabbing the deck or something. I didn't know if that was a euphemism for something kinky or illegal, or if she was actually going to clean her boat.

I reached for my phone and texted her.

Mornin'! How are things with you?

My anxiety grew every second she didn't reply. "Tell me more about Gary's criminal record," I said to Dad.

"From what I hear—and this is coming from the police department secretary—he was in a lot of trouble up in Louisiana."

"What kind of trouble?" I hissed. Now I was exasperated. Dad sometimes did this, doled out the gossip in drips and drabs for dramatic effect.

"Oh, you know. Shrimp smuggling. That sort of thing."

"Is that a thing? I've never heard of that criminal charge."

Dad raised his shoulders. "That's what I heard. Oh, and disorderly conduct. And I think an aggravated assault."

My eyes widened. Dear God, I hoped Erica didn't somehow hook up with him. Was she strange enough to do that? I didn't know her all that well. They had talked about hanging out when he returned.

"Do you think he had anything to do with Fab's death?" I lowered my voice.

"Hard to tell. You have any other possible suspects?"

"Not really," I said. My phone vibrated and I lunged for it.

Oh God I'm barely alive. Send help.

I gasped. "I think Erica's in trouble."

Dad frowned. "How so?"

Where are you? Where is he holding you? I'll call Noah and we'll come save you.

My phone rang almost immediately. It was Erica.

"Why are you calling the chief?" she said in a raspy voice.

"Oh my God. How badly hurt are you?" I yelled.

"I'm not hurt at all," she replied. "And thank God no one's holding me right now."

"Then why did you say you were barely alive?"

"Because I'm hungover."

I paused. "Oh."

"I went out last night with a couple of women I met at the marina. You've gotta meet them. They're fun as hell."

"Oh."

"What did you do last night?"

"Baked cookies." Suddenly I felt about eighty, not thirty.

"Cool. Save some for me." I was surprised Erica didn't make fun of my geekiness, but it was probably because she was moaning in pain.

"I'm just glad you're okay."

"Why did you think I wasn't okay?"

"Well, because I thought you were with Gary Leon Knowles, and I was worried he'd hurt you somehow . . ." my voice trailed off. It sounded kinda stupid when I said it aloud.

"Nah. He never even called or texted like he said he would."

"Probably a good thing."

She yawned. "I'm going back to bed. See you tomorrow."

We hung up and I drummed my fingers on the table. I needed to do more reporting. Wanted the thrill of writing an amazing story. Wanted to shed light on Fab's brief life, and mysterious death. He'd sought the spotlight, and now that he was gone, might gain a bit of recognition if I could craft a great story. I owed that to Fab, after how I'd treated him on his last day alive.

"I'm going to do some sleuthing," I said to Dad.

He slurped his green juice. "That's my girl."

* * *

I hadn't asked Lex about Gary. They both knew Fab, but did they know each other?

It honestly hadn't occurred to me—the two seemed like they were from different planets. One was a sexy surfer with ties to the mob (allegedly) and the other was a rough-hewn southern boy who looked like he might be a good candidate for casting in a remake of *Urban Cowboy*. Lex said "like" a lot, and Gary preferred "y'all."

Still, unlike nearly everyone else, Lex had been kind to me. He'd practically cried on my shoulder. I needed to press him more about going on the record for the article, and to question him about Gary, so I headed back over to his cabin.

I pulled up under a palm tree, two homes down from Lex's place. While walking to his front door, I worked up a sweat. Even though it was August, it was hotter than hell and all of Florida. If it got any warmer, I'd have to take off clothes I should really keep on.

The main door was open, and the screen door shut when I walked up the three steps. I gently rapped on the wooden side of the screen door. No answer. I pulled at the edge of my blue T-shirt, which was stuck to my back. My skort—yes, a skirt-shorts combo—had adhered to even more uncomfortable locations on my body.

I peered inside, but saw no one. Since his backyard faced the beach, I figured maybe I'd find him there. Sunning himself shirtless, probably. As terrifying as it was to think of Lex being part of the Mafia, I had to admit that he was nice to gawp at. Although he was no Noah Garcia, who was the full package of hot and smart.

Lex was pure guilty pleasure. Like a romance cover model.

There was a path with cement pavers along the side of the house, and I followed it toward the beach. It was heavily overgrown with foliage, and I could barely see a foot in front of me. Every few inches I shoved aside a tropical fern or palm frond. Lex was not keeping up with the gardening.

I nearly tripped over an uneven paver, and righted myself. The beach had to be here somewhere; this wasn't a never-ending path. I could hear the surf and see the sand, but before I parted the foliage to emerge, like Indiana Jones, I heard a woman's cry and paused.

"Being pregnant sucks in this heat. Sucks with everything else going on," she wailed.

"I know, girl. I know." Lex's sympathetic voice was easily recognizable. "Are you drinking enough water?"

"I am, but my feet are swelling something fierce."

"Maybe you need a foot rub."

"Oh God, I would love that."

Using only my index finger, I eased a giant leaf aside. Then nearly gasped. It was Paige! In a bikini. Sitting on a beach chair. Lex was on the sand, working his fingers into her bare foot.

Paige was definitely pregnant, I could figure from the small swell of her belly. I carefully let the leaf flutter back into place. Surely the baby was Fab's.

"Babe, that feels so good." Her moan was nearly orgasmic. Or perhaps her baby wasn't Fab's.

She moaned again. How good were Lex's foot rubs, anyway?

"You deserve a little pleasure; you know that, Paige?"

Maybe things were more complicated with Paige than I knew. She groaned again. Oh my God. This sounded so nearly pornographic that my face grew hot. I needed to get out of here. I carefully turned.

"I think I'd like some water," Paige murmured in a baby voice. "But I don't want you to stop."

"I'll fetch you some, then I'll keep massaging."

I tried to tiptoe quickly down the path, but tripped about half-way. Fortunately, I caught myself before I fell, and when I got to the front of the house, I sprinted to my car and peeled away. My heart hadn't stopped racing ten minutes later when I pulled up to my house.

I needed to call Noah with what I'd just found out. What if the baby was Lex's? What did it all mean? Sure sounded like Paige was cozy with Lex, the way they carried on.

Could it be that Fab was killed by the people he trusted most?

Chapter Nineteen

Noah wasn't answering my calls. Of course, he probably had actual police business to attend to, and wasn't eager to hear my theories about Fab's death.

I was positively bursting with the details I'd seen and heard at Lex's house earlier. Since Noah wasn't around, I texted Erica.

I found out some really sketchy stuff, potentially impacting the Fab situation. I need to tell someone. Can you come over?

I'm on the mainland at the boat store, she responded. How about I come over when I'm done? Two hours?

I let out a sigh. *Sounds good. Bring wine.*

To control my shaking hands and overactive mind, I set about making up a cheese plate as a snack. Like me, Erica couldn't resist cheese. And I happened to have several kinds. Plus, crackers. And those little cocktail pickles. I arranged everything on a pretty blue platter, slid it in the fridge, then started to fidget. What the heck, I might as well make more cookies for the coffee shop. I donned an apron and pre-heated the oven.

I rooted around in my cupboards, thinking about cookies and murder. Flour, sugar, baking powder. What if Lex was the father of Paige's baby and Fab had confronted them? What if he'd gotten into a fight with Lex and somehow Fab was thrown off the roof? I could almost see it happening as if a movie were unfolding in my mind. Maybe the two men had been drinking.

But that dashed my Gary theory.

Crap. I was out of chocolate chips. I did have raisins and oatmeal, though. I was in the mood for something more substantial than cookies, so this was good news. As I was mixing the flour for oatmeal raisin bars—the kind that are chewy and dense and give the illusion that they're healthy like energy bars but are actually full of sugar—there was a knock at the door. Erica must be early.

Stanley barked twice—short, sharp woofs. Wiping my hands, I went to the door and peered out the side window.

It was Noah, and he wasn't wearing his uniform. No, he was dressed similarly to that night on the beach, in workout clothes. A blue T-shirt and black shorts. Sneakers. Delish. I flung the door open.

"Hey," I said.

"Hey." He gave me the once over, and I fidgeted with the pocket of my apron. "Are you okay?"

I glanced down at my flour-covered, red-and-white polka dot retro apron. "Oh. Sorry. I was baking."

"I can see that." His dark brows drew together, and he seemed a little out of breath.

"Come on in." I led him inside and shut the door. "Want water? I don't have lemon."

"Yes, please. That's fine." He slid onto a stool at the kitchen counter and I grabbed him a bottle of water. He gulped it down. Lord, he looked supremely sexy with that little bit of sweat on his dark brow.

"Did you jog here or something?" I cracked an egg into a bowl.

"I did, in fact. I was at the gym and checked my phone. You'd called about a million times and I was worried. Then you didn't answer your phone, so I thought I'd come by since the gym's down the street."

Weird. He sounded either peeved or . . . concerned. A triumphant warmth spread through my body. "Sorry. I was caught up in my baking."

"Why'd you call so many times, Lana?"

"I didn't mean to alarm you. I'm fine."

"And I'm glad for that." He paused and we stared into each other's eyes. A smile spread on his face and corresponding goose bumps raced down my arms. My gaze skittered to his hand, which was holding the water. He had the most masculine hands I'd ever seen.

"At least I get to see you in that 1950s apron."

I bit my lip. Oh, dear. Is he flirting? *I think he's flirting.* "Uh. Thanks. I, uh, really called you about Fab. About some things I found out today."

"Doing some more investigating?" His eyebrow quirked upward. "I thought I told you—"

"Research for my article. I was visiting Lex Bradstreet—"

"You were what?" His dark eyes flashed.

"I figured he'd give good quotes for the article." Plausible. He nodded. "And?"

"And I stumbled upon him and Fab's girlfriend, Paige. Did you know she was pregnant?"

By his split second of stunned expression, I guessed he didn't. "Go on."

"They were quite cozy together." I leaned over the counter. "Like foot rub cozy."

"Foot rub cozy? Am I supposed to know what that is? Is that like Netflix and chill?"

I giggled. "No. It's my own phrase. He was giving her an actual foot rub while sitting on the beach. They didn't know I saw them. That's a pretty intimate thing, foot rubs."

"So, you were spying on them?"

"No. I wasn't," I tried to sound indignant. "They were out in public, on the beach. I was, ah, behind a tree. With large leaves. You know the kind."

"Sounds like spying to me."

"Okay, maybe it was unintentional spying. Whatever. I didn't set out to do that. I didn't wake up this morning and think, "I'm going to hide in the bushes and perform surveillance on a sketchy surfer and a dead man's girlfriend."

He snorted, and I guessed he didn't quite believe me.

"Seeing them canoodling like that made me wonder if they wanted Fab dead for some reason."

"Canoodling?" He scratched his square jaw.

"That's what it seemed like, yes."

Noah took a deep breath. "Lana, you have an extremely overactive imagination. Paige has an alibi for the night Fab died. I've already checked it out. Maybe she and Lex are just friends."

Just as I was about to tell him not to ignore my clues, there was another knock at the door. "Yeah, right. Excuse me, I said daintily.

It was Erica. "Hey. The chief's here," I whispered. "We were . . ."

"Going down to bone town?" She arched her right eyebrow.

"You're a perv. We were not—"

"Lana was telling me about her latest theory about Fab's death." Oh dear, I hadn't realized he was right behind me and heard that entire exchange. "I was just leaving."

"Great!" I said brightly. "Thanks for coming over. Check that tip out, willya?"

"Sure thing. Hey, are you going to Fab's memorial tomorrow?"

I grimaced. "Yeah, I probably should."

"I've got the café covered," Erica piped up. "So, if you two want to go together . . ."

I shot her a hard stare. Was she trying to set us up on a date . . . for a funeral?

He inhaled and nodded. "Pick you up at twelve thirty?" he asked.

Well. Maybe this was a date. Was this a new thing, funeral dates? It seemed inappropriate, but then again, if anyone would have made a move on a member of the opposite sex during a funeral, it would have been Fab. Might as well seize the moment.

"Sounds great," I replied. Erica beamed.

Noah smirked and nodded at Erica, sliding by us on his way out and squeezing my arm in the process. He paused at the door. "Oh, and Lana?"

His eyes bored into mine and my face burst into flames. I'm certain my skin was as red as my apron. Awesome.

"Yes?" With the back of my hand, I mopped a rivulet of sweat above my left brow.

"Don't go over to Lex Bradstreet's house again. At least not without me. You got that?"

My jaw dropped. Two simultaneous thoughts went through my mind.

You're not the boss of me.

Dear God, he's sexy when he's possessive like that.

Still, since he and Lex were both from Tampa, I figured he might know something about him that I didn't. Something that I'd try to pry out of him on the way to Fab's funeral. So, I cooed in agreement, and he turned and jogged down my walkway.

Erica shot me a lusty smile. When she shut the door, she turned to me and made a growling noise.

"Geeky Sheriff Hunk has a jealous streak," she said in a sing-song voice.

"What. Ever."

"He was totally checking out your butt, you know. I was watching him as he stood behind you."

"Oh, come on, no way," I cried. Still, the scorching sexual tension between me and Noah, along with Erica noticing that he'd checked me out, was enough to make me a bit giddy. "Get in here and eat some cheese with me."

*   *   *

The next day was overcast and oppressively muggy, perfect for a Florida funeral.

I was at my usual corner table at Perkatory, wondering whether to order a smaller shipment of beans for our cold brew. I'd crunched the numbers and discovered that business had taken a thirty percent hit since Fab's death. Hopefully we were on the upswing, but many of the customers who hadn't abandoned us adored the cold brew. It was the second most popular thing on the menu, after the cappuccino, which meant I should order the beans.

Each night, I made a small vat of the cold brew in a food-grade plastic bucket. Because it was still infernally hot outside, cold coffee sales might stay steady, or even increase. The organic Guatemalan volcano roast was so heckin' delicious, with its full body, heavy sweetness, and medium acidity. My mouth watered while thinking about brewing a new vat.

Decisions, decisions. This was what being a business owner was about. It was far different from working as a reporter, when

I had to make choices about stories and writing, and little else. Definitely not about the bottom line and money.

"Good morning," came a chirpy voice.

I lifted my eyes from the spreadsheet on my screen. It was Brittany, the mermaid tail maker.

"Hey," I said. Unlike the other two times I'd seen her, she wasn't wearing bright colors. Today she was in black, a sleek sheath dress, and she looked formidable. Her hair was pulled back in a severe ponytail, and huge, dark sunglasses covered her eyes. Extremely pretty, in a severe way. Then it hit me.

"Aww, you're going to Fab's memorial?" I asked sympathetically, making a tsk sound with my tongue.

"I am. I had to run a few errands first and wanted to stop by."

"Oh, nice. Have a seat." I shut my laptop and gestured to the chair across from me. "How are you holding up, anyway?"

She lifted a shoulder but didn't sit. "I have good and bad days. Hey, I came by because I wanted to ask you a question."

"Sure."

"I saw that you entered that barista championship. Your café, anyway. I finally read the local paper, first time since I've been here. Saw an article about it."

I blew out a breath. "I think so. I mean, it had been the plan, but Fab had quit the day before he, ah, died. Erica wants to do it. I need two people. Barbara, our afternoon person, would be great but she already has an art fair in Fort Lauderdale that day, and she can't get out of it."

"Ohh," Britt said in a breathy voice.

"And my dad isn't great with latte art, and I'm pretty questionable myself. I'm trying to get better. I've mastered the heart and the fern and am working on some other designs." I thought back to the heart-shaped latte I had made for her that day before Fab died. When I went and studied her tag on Insta, I realized my latte that day had all the aesthetic appeal of something Picasso pulled out of his butt.

"Well, that's where I come in." She slid her sunglasses off and her blue eyes glittered. "I'd love to compete for your café."

"Hunh? You're a mermaid tail maker." I squinted.

"That's my profession now. I told you. I was a barista while in college. Remember? It was how Fab and I met."

"I remember. New York, of course." I nodded as if I was intimately familiar with the city, which I wasn't.

She leaned down, almost in my face, and spoke in a low tone. "Fab never wanted to admit it, but I was better than he was when it came to latte art. Well, at least with the tulips. I can also do mermaids. And palm trees—those are super cute. Want me to show you?"

She sounded so excited that I didn't have the heart to tell her that we'd probably lose against Paige and Mickey Dotson anyway. Both had gone to culinary school.

Unless Paige was arrested for Fab's murder before Saturday . . . but no. Noah said he'd confirmed Paige's alibi, something I wanted to ask him about when I saw him later today. Gary was the killer. Right? Gah. I was all mixed up.

I eyed Erica, who was working the espresso machine like she was one with the metal and steam. She'd become part of the café's fabric so quickly. She grinned at a customer, who stuffed bills into the tip jar. Even with her punk rock fashion sense, people seemed to love her.

It would be best to consult with her before I brought anyone else into our orbit. Given how wry and snarky Erica was, and how bubbly Brittany appeared, it might be a recipe for a piping hot mess.

"Let me think about it, okay? I need to study the rules. See if I could hire you as a temporary worker or something. I think there are regulations about the number of people on a team." If I recalled correctly, there were two people to a team and one alternate. Maybe she could be on the team and I'd become the alternate . . .

Brittany's eyes were wet with tears. "Thank you. I'd love that."

Poor thing. I glanced around nervously and spotted Mike entering the café. Must be a doozy of a day, since he'd already come in for one cup a few hours ago.

"Excuse me, I've got to chat with someone. I'll text you or stop by your shop, okay?"

She slid her glasses on and straightened her spine. Good lord, her heels were tall. I had to crane my neck to peer up at her.

"Sounds great, Lana. See you later?"

"Yes. See you at the funeral. Take care, okay?"

She nodded and strutted to the counter, her glossy ponytail swishing against her narrow shoulders. It was clear that Brittany had that New Yorker attitude, that "*don't screw with me*" aura.

What I wouldn't give for an iota of her confidence.

I tried to harness some of that and sashayed over to Mike.

"Hey, kiddo," he said as he accepted a cup of Americano from Erica. Brittany stepped up, and I heard her ask for a flax milk latte.

"No can do, hon," Erica said jovially. Normally I'd step in, but I figured she could handle it.

Mike moved away from the counter, gesturing with his head for me to follow him a few feet.

"How's the article coming along?" he asked while gingerly removing the top of his piping hot coffee.

"Pretty good. I've talked to a bunch of people, and just this morning did an outline for it." A bit of an exaggeration but all writers did that when talking to editors at this stage of a story.

He nodded thoughtfully. "Good. Because I'd love to run something sooner rather than later. Considering his funeral's today. I'm afraid it'll be old news pretty soon."

Spoken like an editor. Okay, I could do this. After all, I produced better copy on deadline. I was a last minute kind of writer. "I was hoping to gather more details at the funeral. What if I got it to you Saturday, and you could run it Sunday?"

"That works. If we can't run it Sunday, I think we'll have to kill the idea. I still want that other feature, though."

Ugh. I hadn't even thought about *that* story. "I promise you'll have the article on Fab first thing Saturday morning." I'd have to call Dad in to work a shift while I talked with more people and wrote the article.

"Good. And try to keep it under twelve-hundred words."

"Twelve hundred? That's nothing. I was thinking more like two thousand." I pressed my hand to my chest. Like I even had two thousand words of content. "Sorry. That was an automatic reaction. I get that way with editors. Or did, at my old paper."

Mike grinned. "I know how you writers are. Can you try to keep it at a reasonable length?"

After agreeing, I watched him walk out, then turned to the counter. Erica and Brittany were still talking. Oh, good. Maybe they were getting to know each other. Maybe I could hire Brittany temporarily and she and Erica could compete in the barista championship, and I could watch from the sidelines. That would make life so much easier over the next few days.

"Flax milk does foam just as good as cow's milk. I've tried it myself," Brittany huffed.

"It absolutely does not. And it tastes like crap." Erica crossed her arms and smirked. She was a coffee purist, like me.

Brittany turned on her four-inch black heels. "Witch," she said under her breath, and stalked out.

My eyebrows shot up to my hairline and I approached Erica. "So much for asking the two of you to be a barista team."

Chapter Twenty

Noah was ten minutes early in picking me up for Fab's funeral. A zing of desire went through me when he walked in, and even Erica let out a little impressed grunt under her breath.

"Your date is here," she whispered.

"Stop it. We're going to a funeral," I hissed in response.

"You seem . . . more formal than usual," I said, pointing at Noah's midnight blue ensemble. He wasn't wearing his glasses today.

"Dress uniform," he said. "And you look quite nice yourself."

While I wasn't as sleek as Brittany, I'd worn my cutest black wrap dress and plain black kitten heels. And the only strand of pearls I owned; they were once Mom's. Okay, and maybe my most supportive push-up bra. Fab would have approved of the cleavage, I was sure of it.

Erica waggled her fingers at us when she waved goodbye, as if she was a proud mom, sending her daughter off with the town's most eligible bachelor. Once in Noah's cruiser, I was about to seize the opportunity to grill him when he spoke first.

"Lana, about Fab. I think we're pretty close to declaring his death a suicide. I know it's not what you want to hear, because suicide is difficult to accept." His voice was exceedingly gentle.

"I think you're making a mistake. Surely there must be some other evidence tying someone to Fab's death. What was Paige's alibi?"

"She and her mom and dad were off island, spending the night with family friends."

I squinted at him. "And she didn't take along Fab, her boyfriend? The father of her child? Seems odd."

Noah shrugged.

"What about the autopsy? Any results from that?"

He took a deep breath. "He had alcohol in his system."

I snorted. "That goes for ninety percent of the island."

"Exactly."

"Did anything else from the autopsy or the evidence stand out? Anything at all? Just try me."

"There was one thing that struck me, but I didn't think it meant anything considering his body was found by a garbage dumpster."

"What?" I couldn't believe how breathless I was.

"It was fabric of some sort. Found next to his body. It looked torn. Almost like a bra."

I stared out the window for a few beats as we passed the beach. "Weird."

"Yep. A woman's bra. Well, not a traditional one made of lace or silk. I've never seen one that looked like this."

"How familiar with lingerie are you?" I side eyed him, and he bit his lip. "Don't answer that."

"It was made of netting."

I scrunched my nose. "Netting. Like a fishnet?"

"Kind of, but not a commercial one. Similar to one of those 1980s fishnet shirts. Remember those?" Noah glanced at me.

"Not really. A bit before my time. Do you happen to have a photo?"

"Got it right here on my phone. I'll text it to you."

He tapped and swiped, and my phone pinged. We took off and I stared at the screen of my cell. The photo was of a greenish-hued fabric caked with dust. It looked more like a bralette, one of those that provide virtually no support. In the photo, it was almost an abstract pattern against a stark white background. I glanced up. "Interesting, don't you think? It might not be a bra. It's hard to tell from that photo."

"Lana, there were other small pieces of garbage in that alley. That happens a lot—we collect all sorts of stuff we think is evidence, but it turns up nothing. We also found cigarette butts, a paper cup—"

"A shrimper net," I said excitedly. "What if it's not a bra and it came from Gary Leon Knowles?"

"Doesn't look like a net used to catch shrimp." Noah said, pulling into the funeral home parking lot. "And besides. Would Gary have brought a net to push Fab off the roof? Seems implausible."

Probably not, but perhaps Crystal had worn something like that . . . "Have you had a chance to speak with Gary? Or his wife?"

"I haven't. We're dealing with department recertification this month and I've been swamped."

We climbed out of the car and walked into the funeral home. Everyone stared as we entered, probably wondering why I had the guts to show up at Fab's funeral when my last conversation with him was so nasty. But because I was with the chief, people were too polite to say anything. Instead, they shook my hand, nodding and murmuring about how sad it all was.

I spotted Dad on the far side of the room. He was talking animatedly with a gaggle of women who appeared to be drinking wine. It was two in the afternoon. I waved, and Dad blew me a kiss.

Thankfully, it was a closed casket. Father John O'Halloran, the island's Catholic priest, took the podium and cleared his throat. Everyone in the place found a seat, and I perched next to Noah.

"Fab was Catholic?" I hissed to Noah.

He leaned in, his lips near my ear. I shivered. "He was from Italy, so I'm guessing yes."

Ugh, there was so much I didn't know about him. I needed to get moving with the article. I reached a hand into my bag and discreetly took my phone out of my bag and opened it to a notes app. Noah glanced at me.

"It's for the article," I whispered.

The priest began to speak, and his voice was a droning monotone. I stealthily tapped a few notes and details as he talked.

"Our Father in heaven, we thank you that, through Jesus Christ, you have given us the gift of eternal life. Keep us firm in the faith, that nothing can separate us from your love. When we lose someone who is dear to us, help us to receive your comfort and to share it with one another . . ."

I tuned out, instead doing what I used to as a reporter: count the number of people in the room. I'd covered dozens of funerals and that was always the first thing I did. Find out how many people were in attendance.

I began counting heads and came up with two hundred people. Bored, I counted again, realizing I recognized nearly all the islanders here. I spotted Brittany and Paige (sitting on opposite sides of the room, I noted), Lex, Mickey Dotson, and Mr. and Mrs. Clarke (she was sobbing softly, while her husband had a grim frown on his face). Many of our customers were also in attendance.

After I counted the crowd a third time, that was when it hit me: Gary Leon Knowles and his girlfriend Crystal were nowhere in sight. Was that significant? I wasn't sure.

* * *

I was near silent on the ride back to the café. All I could think of was how few people spoke at the funeral. Other than Lex, who dissolved into tears during a story about the two of them on a fishing trip, no one gave up any details about Fab.

It seemed that he knew everyone, but no one really knew *him*.

Noah pulled up to Perkatory.

"I'd love to hang out more, but I need to be back at the station. We've got a meeting with the fish and wildlife folks about those dang monkeys. They're really turning into a PR nightmare for the island," he said, turning in his seat.

"No worries." As much as I'd have liked to sit here in his police cruiser and stare at him in his snappy dress blues while discussing wild primates, I had other things to do. My fingers found the door latch. "Thanks for the ride."

The corners of his mouth lifted. "Wasn't quite the first date I'd hoped for."

"Well, maybe we can fix that and go out on a real first date." Holy crap. Did I say that out loud?

He chuckled. "I'd like that."

That stunned me into silence. At least until I blurted what was on my mind. "You would? You don't mind dating a one-time possible suspect in a death investigation?"

He frowned. "Are you talking about Fab? Or were you a suspect in another investigation that I don't know about?"

"Fab."

"Lana, you were never really a suspect. Not to me."

"I wasn't?" A grin spread on my face.

He shook his head. "I got the parking lot videos from the Miami hotel you stayed in the night of Fab's death. There was no way you could've been responsible based on the ME's time of death. You were on the road. Plus, your car was captured coming across the toll bridge in the Fast-Pass lane from the mainland at about, oh . . ." He fixed his eyes out the window moved his head from side to side, "Five forty five that morning. You might want to slow down when you go through those toll-booths, by the way."

"You knew all this and didn't tell me?" I playfully punched his forearm.

"There's a lot you don't know about me, Lana."

We stared into each other's eyes. The temperature in the cruiser ratcheted up about ten degrees. "We can change that."

He nodded. "Yes. We can. Dinner on Friday?"

Dammit. Figures the first time I'm asked on a date since the breakup with my ex, I'm busy. "That's the night before the barista championship. Erica and have plans to prepare."

"That's right. The competition. I was planning on stopping by. Okay, Saturday, then? Dinner at my place? I'll cook."

Whoa. This was a serious date. I did some mental calculations. The barista contest went from nine until three. Which meant I'd have time to go home, lick my wounds from losing, and get ready for the date. "Saturday sounds perfect."

We stared at each other until I blurted a question that had been on my mind for weeks. "Why don't you drink coffee?"

His chuckle was low and gentle. "You're suspicious of people who don't drink coffee?"

"No. Well. A little." I shifted in my seat.

"My entire family drinks Cuban coffee. You know, the little shots of sweet jet fuel?" He held up his thumb and forefinger an inch apart.

"I drank gallons of that in Miami. It was an entire food group."

"I'm sure you did. I used to, as well. Especially when I first started on patrol. I had to stop at a certain point. It made me too jittery and my thinking was impulsive. I like things to be," he made a line in the air with his hand, "on an even keel."

"Perhaps I could introduce you to some blends that might be a little kinder on your nervous system. Cold brew, for example. It's sixty-seven percent less acidic than regular coffee. So, you don't get that harsh, bitter taste. The low acid's also better for your teeth and your stomach. You might really enjoy it."

"Perhaps. If anyone's able to persuade me into drinking coffee, it's you."

My resolve to not date older men flew out the window of his police cruiser and sailed off into the distance, carried by the wind over the Gulf of Mexico and to the Land of Swoon. I giggled softly.

His police squad radio squawked, interrupting our flirtation. "We got a 10-54 by the nature preserve. Caller says there's a crowd of tourists feeding a monkey on the side of the road."

"Uh-oh," I said. The crackling tension between us dissipated. "You have to take care of some monkey business. See you this weekend."

"Sounds good, Lana." His smile and the way his eyes flickered over my face made tingles race down my arms.

I grinned all the way into the café. At least until I opened the door and saw Crystal—Gary's *old lady*—sitting in the corner with mascara-streaked cheeks.

Chapter
Twenty-One

Erica was wiping down a nearby table and she sidled up to me. "That's Gary's main squeeze," she hissed.

"I recognize her from the photos in Fab's desk. Why is she here?"

"Not sure. She came in, ordered a latte, then started crying when I handed it to her. Mumbled something about Fab and then sat down. She's been over there for about twenty minutes." She blinked several times. "That's a great business model. Come to Perkatory and weep."

"I'm going to chat with her. I wonder what she wants."

"Try to get her to stop crying."

I padded over and approached with a nonthreatening smile. She regarded me and dabbed the corner of her right eye with a napkin.

"Hi there. I'm Lana Lewis. I'm the owner here." I paused. "Can I sit?"

She nodded and gestured to the chair across from her.

I sunk down. "You okay?"

"Do I seem okay?"

"Not really. That's why I wanted to come over. Our barista Erica said you mentioned Fab."

A fat tear rolled down her cheek. "I miss him," she whispered.

I took a long, thin inhale through my nose. Okay. Now we were getting somewhere. But if she missed him so much, why wasn't she at the funeral?

"We all do."

"I met him here in this very café."

"Really?" I scowled. Odd that I didn't recall ever seeing her here.

"When he first started. 'Bout a year ago. Right when your dad gave him the job and the apartment. I'd drink lattes in here all morning, then, after his shift, he'd take me upstairs." She paused and wiped a tear.

I nodded. Years of being a reporter meant that I didn't react when people told me unusual or salacious details.

"I stopped coming in here because it was too obvious to everyone. That hussy found out. Paige." She practically spat the last word.

Ah, so that was why I'd never seen her.

"Oh." I paused. "So, you and Fab were together, in a relationship kind of way? Sorry I'm asking so many questions. In addition to being the owner here, I'm also writing an article about him for the paper."

"You are?" She fixed a wary eye on me.

"Yes. A feature story."

"Like a tribute?"

I nodded. "Something like that, yes. Would you like to be quoted?"

"I dunno." She let out a sigh, and I studied her. With her long mane of red hair and a smattering of freckles on her face, she appeared a lot younger and prettier than in the photos in Fab's desk. "I cared for him. He was such an amazing lover, you know?"

I didn't, and stopped myself from grimacing. If by amazing lover she meant, possibly exposing half the island's female population to chlamydia, then yeah, I guess she had a point. "Your name's Crystal, right?"

She eyed me suspiciously. "How did you know?"

I leaned in and lowered my voice to a whisper. "I saw some, um, photos of you in Fab's house. I had to go upstairs to gather some things for Stanley. Your name was written on the back."

"What?" Her eyes widened.

"Sorry. Maybe I shouldn't have said anything. I'd gone upstairs to look for vet records for Stanley, his dog, and stumbled across them."

She sagged back in the chair. "He told me he'd destroyed those."

My opinion of Fab, which had risen in the days since his death, plummeted. "Wow. What a jerk."

She nodded slowly, and stared at the table as if in a catatonic state. I needed to get the conversation back on track.

"I actually wanted to meet you because I was curious about your thoughts on Fab."

"About what?" she was definitely nervous now, shifting in her chair and balling up tissue after tissue. "Oh, for the article. Right."

"I didn't know him for long, but it seemed really out of character, the idea that he'd commit suicide."

She nodded and more tears fell from her eyes. "He betrayed me with the photos and now he's dead. Just great. And I don't think he committed suicide."

"Do you think he was murdered?"

She lifted both her shoulders. "It crossed my mind."

I was racking my brain and trying to think of the best way to ask the difficult yet obvious question—*did your husband Gary kill him*—when she leaned in.

"I can think of one person who wanted him dead," she said.

"Who?"

She pressed her pink lips together.

"You?"

"No!" She paused. "Well, not until just now, when you told me about the photos."

"Right. Then who? Gary?" I prodded. "Your husband?"

"Fiancé." She scrunched her eyes shut and nodded once. *Bingo.*

"Where was he the night of Fab's death?"

Her eyes snapped open. "I don't know. It's pretty common for him to leave and go places without telling me. He has a ton of drinking buddies and knows a lot of people. He even hung out with Fab a few times. But Gary and I haven't had a good relationship in a while. All I know is that when I got home from work, Gary was still gone."

"What time was that?"

"'Bout five in the morning. I work at a bar, and we close at four. Takes us a while to clean up and for me to get home."

I mulled this for a few seconds. "Do you think you should talk to the police about Gary?"

"Thought about it. But I'm still trying to decide. Part of me thinks Gary wouldn't have killed him."

"But another part does?"

She stared down at the table.

"Why are you telling me all this?"

She sniffled. "I don't know. There's no evidence against Gary. Not really, I suppose. I can't believe he'd kill a man out of jealousy. He knew what I was doing with Fab. We had, well, have, an open relationship."

Blergh. "That sounds messy."

"It doesn't have to be, but I let emotions get in the way. Gary's had his flings, too."

I reached for her hand, then swept my eyes to the counter, hoping to get Erica's attention. I needed backup here. "Are you okay at home with him?"

"I believe I am. He's never laid a hand on me."

I worried my lip between my teeth. "You sure you don't need help getting somewhere safe? Is he back from his shrimp trip?"

She shrugged. "Yeah, he came back this morning. I'm the one who screwed up by falling for Fab. Gary and I had a pact. We could have other lovers, just don't fall for them. And I fell hard for Fab. He was so darned attentive, you know? Like I was the only one he cared for. And that Italian accent." She pronounced it *eye-talian*.

I cleared my throat. Theirs was the definition of a complicated relationship.

"Of course, I wasn't the only one who was smitten with Fab." She dabbed at her eyes. "Gary was jealous that I had feelings for him."

"Sounds like you and Gary have a lot to work out," I offered.

"True." She sighed heavily. "I'm sorry. I need to run. My shift starts soon. If you want to talk more for your article, you can call me tomorrow. I'd ask you to visit me today at work, but we've got a big group coming tonight. There's a coin collector convention in town. I'll be there every afternoon this week."

"Oh, where do you work?"

"I recently got a job on the mainland at the Pink Pony."

"The . . . strip club?"

"Yeah, I'm a bartender. I work there six days a week. Great tips. Normally I work during the day, but the night Fab died, I was filling in on an overnight shift. We're only closed from 4 AM until 10 AM."

"Oh." No judgement. Work was work. "Good for you."

My phone buzzed from the abyss of my bag. "Come on back any time you want a free coffee," I said. "If it makes you feel better about, you know. Everything. Fab. And I'll call you tomorrow."

We both stood, and my phone buzzed. She pointed at the cell in my hand. "You'd better get that. And thanks. It does give me some bittersweet memories to be back in here. You're a sweetheart. Put in your article that Fab was the eternal bachelor. He never wanted to grow up. That he was a big kid who liked to laugh and love. With the emphasis on love."

Finally, a decent quote. "Will do."

She scooped me up in a hug, and I was awash in an intense, floral perfume. Poor woman.

We disentangled and said our goodbyes.

"Wait," I said. "One more question. Why didn't you attend Fab's funeral?"

Her eyes once again filled with tears. "I couldn't say goodbye. Not in public like that. Not with Paige there. I was worried that she'd start something. She's mean as cat poop."

I nodded slowly. Crystal had a point. I squeezed her shoulder, then watched as she sashayed out of the café. My phone buzzed again, and I reached for it.

"Hello," I said.

"Lana, it's Brittany. The mermaid tail maker."

"Oh, right. Yes. Hey."

"Beautiful service today, wasn't it?" Her soft voice was at odds with what I'd seen of her at the service—she'd mostly glowered at Paige the entire time.

"Yes. It was. Fab would have been pleased that so many came out for him."

"Definitely. So, I was thinking. And I wanted to apologize for getting into an argument with your barista. That was totally my fault and I'm sorry."

I glanced at Erica, who was wiping down the espresso machine. "No worries. Seriously. Emotions are high around the island today."

"They sure are. And I didn't get a chance to ask you at the memorial because you left so quickly with the police chief. But have you decided about the barista competition yet? Can I join in?"

Goodness. So pushy. I barely had time to deal with the competition because I was writing an article and on the verge of solving a homicide. Maybe we wouldn't enter at all. This was getting too much.

I decided to evade her question and tell a little fib. "Our team's set for the year. I can only have two people in the competition, and Erica and I are the team. Sorry, Brittany, maybe next year. Listen, I'm in the middle of something, and I have to run."

She made a little huffing noise, and I imagined her stamping her tiny feet. "Fine," she grumbled.

"See you around."

I hung up and went to Erica. "You're not going to believe this," I said.

"Try me. We had a dude come in today with a parrot who had a more colorful vocabulary than me. The mayor was here enjoying a latte and the parrot called him a name that rhymes with the word rock."

I pressed my fingers to the bridge of my nose and shut my eyes. Great. He was a regular, and had stuck with us through the Fab situation. Did every day have to fail in some spectacular way? Couldn't one thing go smoothly? The last thing I needed was an offended small-town public official going to the health board—namely, Mickey Dotson—and shutting me down for a violation over having birds in the café.

Normally, I tried to have a pet-free establishment, but I'd been lax in recent days because of Stanley. Fortunately, he was home today, so I could apologize without a shred of hypocrisy. I dialed City Hall and asked for the mayor.

"Mayor, I'm so sorry about the bird," I cooed into the phone.

"Oh, dear. It's fine. At least that bird doesn't vote."

The mayor thought that was way funnier than I did, but I laughed along. "Free coffee for you next time you come in."

At this rate I'd be handing out free coffee to the entire island. Gah.

"Well, thanks for that, Lana," he said warmly. "And I'm excited you're representing the island this weekend at the barista championship. Read all about that in the paper. I'll be there watching you and the Dotsons. That'll be quite the battle, especially considering your two coffee shops had that issue with the dead barista."

"No issue, just a little misunderstanding."

I cleared my throat and thanked him for not holding the foul-mouthed parrot against Perkatory. Then hung up. I didn't have the heart to tell the mayor that I was leaning toward canceling on the barista contest.

I wasn't in a competition mindset, not after listening to Crystal's sadness, the mourners at Fab's funeral, and Brittany's weird insistence on helping out. It was all too much—and that was on top of the probability that Gary Leon Knowles was most likely a murderer who committed a crime of passion. One who would get away with his crime if Noah didn't start believing my theories.

How was I going to even write the article? I had little hard evidence proving anything, and my story about Fab was turning out to be a tale of his sex escapades and his loneliness. At this rate, the article would be a thousand words of me retelling stories of him making lattes. Not exactly great reading.

I must have seemed pretty dejected because Erica came up to my table with a cappuccino. "Spill the tea. Or, uh, coffee. What's wrong with you?"

I shrugged. "Thanks for making this. Hey, this is a unicorn!"

She'd created a perfect foam replica of a unicorn in the cup. It was almost too pretty to drink.

I told her everything, from how Gary and Crystal weren't at Fab's funeral to how Crystal doubted Gary's innocence to my waffling on entering the competition. Everything was so damned overwhelming at the moment.

"Okay, first things first. We're entering the contest. No more waffling or discussion." Her hand sliced through the air, a gesture of finality.

"But—"

"No buts. We're a team. You're good enough, and I'm amazing. We're giving it a shot."

"Wish I had your confidence." I mustered a smile. At one time, in Miami, I felt invincible. Where did that woman go?

"What were you going to do when Fab was here? Weren't you the second barista on the team?"

I nodded. "But things seemed way less complicated back then. I thought people would overlook my incompetence with latte art. He wanted to compete to show off. I wanted publicity for the shop. Now it seems like the pressure's on."

She scowled. "Screw the pressure. We're doing this for fun. And the judges aren't from around here. I did some research. So they're not going to care about Fab or any scandal. And you aren't incompetent. Your foam hearts have improved in the time I've been here. I'd advise you to stay away from any abstract patterns, because that's when your lattes take on a blob-like quality."

"You really think we should be in the contest?" I sipped from the cup. Man, she made delicious coffee. It was as if the beans came alive for her.

"Heck yeah, we should. Let's hold our heads high and do it. Mickey and Paige aren't that good. They're okay. Before you hired me, I spent a few hours there, drinking coffee and reading a book. I watched them work. And there will be others from around the state, too. But it's great publicity for the café, and isn't that what you want? Let's just get out there and rock it to the best of our ability."

I smiled. "Okay. Fine. You've talked me into it."

"Awesome. One problem solved. As for the other thing. Do you think Crystal's in danger? Do you think you're in danger?"

"Me? Why me?"

Erica shrugged. "What if Crystal tells her old man that she spilled her guts to you?"

I winced and took another sip. "Oh God. I don't know."

"Listen, I've had some experience with this."

"With what?" I must have appeared alarmed because she held up her hands and lowered them in a calming motion.

"With abusive guys. I dated one, up north. Probably why flirting with Gary came so easy for me."

I nodded slowly. "I'm sorry."

"It's behind me. But I also wouldn't put it past Gary to do something."

"What do you suggest?"

"I'd tell Sheriff Hunk about it. Maybe stay at your dad's for a night or two."

"You think it's unsafe for me to be in my own home alone?"

She pressed her lips together. "I don't know. Did Crystal say when Gary was getting back?"

"He's back, apparently."

We stared at each other and nodded. "Erica, what about you? Do you feel safe staying on board your sailboat? Gary's familiar with all the marinas on the island and can probably figure out where you live. And who knows what Gary's telling Crystal to make her jealous. Their relationship seems pretty messed up. Toxic."

She curled her lip and rolled her eyes.

"Why don't you stay at Dad's with me and Stanley?"

She nodded. "Probably a good idea."

"We could bake," I said, trying to brighten the mood. "Maybe some cake pops."

* * *

The cake pops turned out fabulously. They were chocolate, with vanilla frosting, and Erica carefully stabbed them with wooden popsicle sticks, then rolled them in sparkly pink sprinkles. Dad ate four of them, and was about to plow through another when I playfully smacked his hand.

"We need some to sell tomorrow," I said.

"Fine," he groaned. "I'm going to change the record."

As we were baking, Dad had been playing DJ, spinning albums on his old record player. He'd introduced Erica to the deep cuts of Fleetwood Mac, and we were now into Grateful Dead territory.

"Don't get him started on how he followed their East Coast tour in 1978," I muttered, handing a finished cake pop to Erica.

"How'd you get into real estate, anyway? Seems weird for a Deadhead," she said to Dad, who had put on Terrapin Station and was cracking open a kombucha.

"My father was a realtor here on the island. I'd met Lana's mom and fell in love hard, and wanted to do right by her. She didn't want a bum. Lana's mom was a few years older than me, and she already had this swashbuckling job, traveling all over to buy coffee beans. I had to step up and be a man."

"So, you settled down into suburban bliss," I joked.

"Hardly," Dad said. "Your mom and I were pretty freaky."

"Okay, moving on." I shot Dad a warning stare while Erica cracked up.

"We were going to live in Miami, but felt like it was better to raise our daughter here on Devil's Beach. My parents were still alive back then and they adored Lana. And Lana's mom loved it here. It was always her goal to open a coffee shop. She came up with the Perkatory name decades ago. Thought it was hilarious."

"She'd be so proud to see it now," I muttered sarcastically.

"Lana, hush. Your mother would be proud."

My eyes snapped up to Dad. His voice was sharper than usual, which was odd since I knew he'd smoked some of his medical marijuana, which usually made him sound like he had a mouth full of oatmeal. "She'd be mortified if she knew what was going on with her café."

"Not true, LeLa. She'd have been offended by Fab jumping ship at the last minute. And she'd be behind you one hundred percent in trying to write your article to seek the truth about him." He turned to Erica. "Lana and her mother were carbon copies of each other. Sharp as tacks, patient as all get out. But when they feel there's justice to be had, watch out. Like pit bulls with facts."

"Too bad the Miami paper didn't feel the same way," I said.

"Oh, screw them," Erica said. "There's this thing called the Internet, and it's available to you. You can do great work here. Freelance articles, like you're doing. Or maybe a podcast. Write true crime novels. You don't need a stupid paper. Heck, I'll help you start a blog or do a podcast with you. The three of us can do a podcast."

"Erica, you are brilliant," Dad cried.

As the two of them chattered on about the mechanics of starting a true crime podcast, my phone pinged.

It was Noah.

Just checking to make sure you don't have a fish allergy. I'd like to make my special Key Lime grilled grouper for you on Saturday.

Grinning, my fingers flew across the cell phone screen. *There are few things I love more than grilled grouper.*

I waited a few seconds while three dots flashed on my screen. Then, a message from him.

Can't wait to find out the others.

"Who was that?" Dad said. "Why that sly little grin?"

"Noah. He's making dinner for me Saturday night."

Dad and Erica high-fived each other, and I rolled my eyes.

* * *

At the crack of dawn, Erica and I returned to her boat so she could change. We'd left Stanley with Dad for the day—Dad was taking him to his first Doga class—and we made our way to Perkatory. I opened the back door and was hit with a funny odor.

"Do you smell that?"

Erica sniffed loudly. "I'm a little congested. Allergies have hit me hard this month."

"Weird." I walked around, turning on the lights, taking deep inhales into my lower lungs. Nothing seemed out of place. My apron was as I'd left it the night before. The espresso machine gleamed, since Erica had given it a good scrub.

I set the plastic tub with the cake pops on the counter and rested my hands on my hips. What was that awful smell?

Usually the café in the morning was faintly scented from the previous day's earthy, roasted coffee, and the lingering smell of cinnamon from either the baked goods or a cinnamon candle I sometimes burned.

Today it was more of a rotten egg odor.

Something in my brain clicked. Back when I was a reporter, I'd covered an explosion at a Cuban restaurant. I recalled what the owner had said to me: *olor de huevos podridos*. I'd asked the paper's photographer to translate for me.

Odor of rotten eggs.

"Erica, crap, we need to get out of here. It's gas. This is bad."

I grabbed the Tupperware container and we ran out. We stood across the street and dialed 911.

"I think there's a gas leak of some sort at my café," I said, noticing one of my regulars walking toward the front door. I moved the phone away from my ear so I could shout. "Hey! We're closed. Gas leak! You'd better stay back."

The guy jogged away.

Within a half hour, the island's fire chief came over with the news. "Somehow the gas line leading to your oven was cut," he said. "That could've been deadly, Lana."

Chapter Twenty-Two

Perkatory was closed all day so we could air out the gas fumes. We threw open every door and window, and the fire chief graciously brought over two giant fans. That kindness was a definite perk of living in a small town.

Erica, Dad, Stanley, and I sat drinking iced coffee at one of the café tables outside, listening to the whir of the oversized fans.

"I can't believe the luck I've had lately. First Fab. Then my ex comes to town. And now this," I said morosely. My inner worrier had come out to play.

My phone pinged. It was Raina, the woman who owned Dante's Inferno, the yoga studio next door. I considered her a close acquaintance—not exactly a friend, since we enjoyed different things. Still, she'd been welcoming and warm when I took over the café.

I'm in the airport about to fly home from Costa Rica. Just read my emails for the first time in days. I'm gutted about Fab. And the gas leak? I got a message from the utility company. What is going on there? Is everything okay? I leave for ten days and Devil's Beach has imploded!

Raina had been in Central America leading a yoga retreat. She'd missed everything. Probably for the best, since she and Fab had hooked up (or so I'd heard). I hoped her retreat was relaxing, because she was about to return to the world of weird here on Devil's Beach.

It's complicated, but pretty tragic. I'm fine, the building's fine, your studio is fine. I'll tell you all the deets when you return and get settled. Safe flight. xo

I raised my eyes from the phone and sighed. "We've lost an entire day of business. Between this and the slight downturn after the Fab situation, it's going to be a tough month."

"You'll make it up," Dad said, ever the optimist. "There's an ebb and flow in business. Isn't that right, Erica?"

She nodded. "We'll get back on track after we win the barista championship. You'll see." Erica seemed to share my dad's sunny nature, at least on this point. Or they were high; I'd seen them giggling in the alley together a couple of hours ago.

"Even if we win, will we get back on track? I feel like as long as there's a cloud over the café because of Fab's death. Bad juju."

"Does Noah have any news about cause of death?" Dad asked.

"Sort of. Says it was suicide and I need to accept that."

"What do you two think?" Dad looked at me, then Erica.

I leaned in. "I have my suspicions. But I'm not finished with my reporting for the article. Maybe instead of sitting around here, I should get to that."

"We can hang here with Stanley for a while," Erica fiddled with her phone.

"You're sure you two have this under control?"

Dad and Erica assured me that they did, and I took off.

*   *   *

It was probably a bit stupid to knock on Gary's door in the middle of the day. Crystal had said she had to bartend at the strip club today, which meant Gary would be alone. In theory. Hopefully he wasn't entertaining any of his other ladies—or under the impression that I wanted to be a part of his harem. The very idea made me shudder.

As I waited for someone to open the door of the trailer, I eyed the net in the yard. It didn't look anything like the photo Noah had showed me of the evidence found near Fab's body. Or did it? I walked a few paces and inspected it. Nope. This was black. The net near Fab's body was green. I went back to the door and knocked again.

Ugh. What did it all mean? My stomach churned. The flimsy door flung open.

"Hey Gary," I said brightly.

"Hey girl!" he sounded casual and pleased, like it was the most natural thing in the world for me, a near stranger, to stop by. His overly tanned skin was especially leathery today, probably because he was shirtless. I studied him as he scratched the tattoo of a large, faded phoenix on his chest. If there was an entry of Florida Man in the dictionary, it would be accompanied by a photograph of Gary Leon Knowles.

"I was in the neighborhood," I said, feeling stupid. I'd used that excuse with Lex, too. What was I? Someone who roamed the neighborhoods of Devil's Beach, visiting people I'd met once?

Actually, yes.

"C'mon in, it's good to see you. I just woke up." I followed him inside. The place was tidy and comfortable, and the only thing that stood out was a large photo portrait of a Rottweiler on the wall. I saw no evidence of a dog, though.

"Beer?" He asked. It was two in the afternoon.

"Nah." I waved him off.

He shrugged. "Suit yourself." He ambled to the fridge and extracted a can of Busch Light, popping it open with a fluid motion.

"Listen, Gary. I'm gonna be honest here." I dug deep and tried to conjure the bravado I used to have while doing stories in Miami. "I'm writing an article for the *Devil's Beach Beacon*. And I wanted to talk with you about Fabrizio."

"What about him?"

"You'd said you were friendly with him. Where'd you meet?"

He shrugged. "Around the island. Mutual friends. Saw him at the Dolphin now and then. Went fishing once together on a buddy's boat. We hit it off pretty well. He liked to party."

I nodded sagely and took my notebook out of my bag. I wrote down *liked to party* in cursive. Unoriginal, but it was something.

"I figured you'd be able to give me some quotes and details about his life. And death."

He paused, the can of beer in mid-air.

"You want to know where I was the night Fab died. And if I killed him."

My heart skidded against my ribs. Yikes. If he really murdered Fab, what would stop him from killing me? Well, I was here, and he brought it up. Might as well try not to show fear.

I looked him dead in the eye, recalling how he'd broken into Fab's house and taken Crystal's photos. "The thought crossed my mind."

"How'd I guess. The answer is no." He inhaled deeply. "That's not to say I didn't want to kill him after I found out how Crystal fell in love with him. And how he treated her. But I didn't murder him, and I have an alibi. Just not one that I wanted to share with Crystal."

"I see." I paused. "What's your alibi?"

"Why should I tell you? You're going to put it in the paper."

"No, I won't. Promise. And I won't tell Crystal. This is off the record. I don't care what you do. I want to know about Fab. Don't care about your business."

"Hm. Dunno if I want to be quoted."

"You don't have to be. I can guarantee anonymity."

He licked his lips. "See, I'm involved in some sketchy stuff."

"Who isn't? It's Devil's Beach," I tried to appear casual.

"Not drugs or any of that crap. I, well, hell. Don't tell the chief, okay? And you can't put this in the paper. You gotta promise."

"Fine." I crossed my arms.

"I do a little alligator stuff on the side."

I squinted. "What?"

"Alligator meat. Sometimes I go out on hunts and catch some gators. Also some swordfish and, on occasion, pythons. But not always during hunting season, if you get my drift."

"Oh, you hunt and fish illegally?" I flashed back to the eyeball Stanley and I found on the beach.

"Yep. There ain't no shortage of gators in Florida."

He had a point. "So, you hunt gator and sell it somewhere. Is it good money?"

"Every little bit helps. The folks who want gator meat pay top dollar out of season. They want fresh, not frozen. Frozen tastes like crap, y'know?"

I didn't, since I drew the line at eating cold-blooded reptiles. "So, you were out gator hunting when Fab died?" It seemed like the most Florida of all possible alibis.

"No. I'd just picked up some of the processed meat. In fact, Fab came with me to pick up the meat. I dropped him at his building."

He took a long swig and my heart sped up. "So, you were with him that night."

"Yeah, until about nine. Fab said he had a hot date. But he always had a hot date. So, I dropped him off and went over to see the guy I sell the meat to. I brought over a shipment and him and me and a couple of guys he works with had beers and played cards."

"So, Fab knew about your gator business?"

"He used to help me. We'd drive to the Everglades and hunt, then drive the carcasses to the processing plant in Arcadia. We'd then pick up the meat and sell it."

So that's why Fab had that gator processing business card. "Did you sell meat to someone here on island the night he died?"

"Yup." I racked my brain, trying to think of which restaurant in town served gator meat. The only one I could think of was the Square Grouper.

"Was Crystal with Fab the night he died?"

Gary shook his head. "Nope. She was working. She called me from the club's phone at four. I was still playing cards, but left soon after she called."

"Hmm." I tapped my pen on the notepad. This was not going the way I planned.

He let out a long sigh, his beer breath washing over me. "It was only after Fab died that I found out how much she loved him. They'd been seeing each other off and on for a year. A year! She never let on while he was alive, dammit. Once he passed, she was inconsolable."

"Oh?"

"Cried day and night. I wish I'd never introduced the two of 'em. She was totally swept away by his charm. Him and me were like total opposites. I actually thought he was a pretty decent guy when I first met him. I didn't mind her havin' a bit of fun, you know? I have my own fun and all. But then he did something I didn't like. Found that out after he died, too."

"What was that?"

"Took naked photos of Crystal. She told me, and asked me to try and find those pictures. Apparently, he dug that sort of thing. I draw the line at that kind of stuff, you know. Seems ill-advised. Anyone could get ahold of them and it could ruin her future job chances."

"So true. And I'm sorry," I said. And I was. Still, I didn't fully believe his story. Not yet. It seemed flimsy and illogical.

"Can you tell me who you were with that night? So, I can check it out?"

"Damn girl, you're more thorough than the cops."

I shrugged. "I try."

"I'm sure you can figure it out on your own. Ain't that many restaurants that serve gator around here. But don't you go telling that chief on me, okay? I've heard you two are tight. Not that he'd know what to do with alligator hunters, being a city boy from Tampa and all."

"Thanks," I said, standing up. "I hope you patch things up with Crystal. You seem like you really love her and want what's best for her." Maybe I'd been all wrong about Gary.

"I do. We have our issues, but I love her like crazy."

When I got outside, I spotted storm clouds on the western horizon, and thunder boomed in the distance. It sounded close, yet I knew it was far in the distance. Much like solving Fab's death.

* * *

Since I was a native of Devil's Beach, I knew three things about the Square Grouper.

One: It had the best grouper sandwich on the island. Flaky and succulent, it was almost a crime to put it between two pieces of bread. Sometimes I ordered it without the bun. The fish was fresh because the restaurant sourced directly from the fishing docks on Devil's Beach. Some restaurants didn't do that—it had been a big scandal some years ago when a food magazine revealed that many popular Florida restaurants used tilapia instead of grouper.

Not the Square Grouper, though. They were authentic.

Two: It had the best sunset view of any restaurant on the island. Proposals, weddings, retirement parties, birthdays. Everyone celebrated at the Square Grouper.

Three: It was opened in the mid-seventies by a retired New York mobster named Salvatore "The Chin" Rizzo. Sal thought it would be hilarious to name a restaurant after his old pastime—trafficking drugs. Tourists think the name quirky, but few know that the definition of a Square Grouper is actually a brick of marijuana, usually found floating in the Gulf or near the Keys after a trafficking boat throws it overboard when pursued by the feds.

Somehow Sal never went to prison, and lived the second half of his life as a jolly and law-abiding restaurant owner. That's what my dad claims, anyway. Sal died about ten years ago. and his son Josh took over the restaurant. As far as I knew, Josh wasn't a mobster. I'd gone to high school with him. He'd been a skinny, quiet guy, and my only real recollection of him was when the two of us were in a band together. He played clarinet, I marched in back with the cymbals.

Yeah, the mobster's son was a band geek. No one dared pick on Josh, though. He'd always had a crush on me in high school, and I was going to use that to my advantage today. Or try to.

I strutted in, channeling my inner Brittany. The blonde hostess with the plunging, black V-neck T-shirt glanced up. "Welcome to the Square Grouper," she said brightly. "Are you meeting someone?"

"I was wondering if Josh was here. I'm an old friend and wanted to say hi."

"Of course," she purred. "I think he's behind the bar."

That was the other thing about the Grouper. Sal, and now Josh, always tended bar. I assumed it was some holdover from Sal's mafia days when he was hanging out in smoke-filled private clubs in New York.

"Thanks," I said, strolling to the empty bar. It was only four in the afternoon, and while the tourists had gone, locals hadn't quite arrived for happy hour yet. Although I expected they would soon.

Josh was polishing a glass when I slid into a seat. "Hey there," I said, trying to mimic the hostess' purr. I sounded more like a frog.

Josh turned his head. "Lana Lewis? Long time no see."

He grinned. Surprisingly, time had been kind to him. He was handsome, in a nerdy way. Thick black hipster glasses, a shock of red hair. His skinny frame had turned lithe and muscular. Quirky. Not exactly my type. Tattoos ran up his arms.

"Right? Jeez, Josh, you look a lot different than you did in high school."

"Look at you. My old partner in crime from the marching band." He came around the bar and we hugged, then he sat in the chair next to me.

"How you doin'?" Somehow even though he'd lived on Devil's Beach his entire life, he had the New York accent of his dad.

I grinned. "I'm all right. Getting used to island life after more than ten years away."

"I heard about your divorce. Saw your dad at the hardware store and he told me all about it. I've been meaning to come by to the café and say hi. But this place keeps me so busy."

Thanks, Dad. I nodded.

"You know how it is," he shook his head. "Being a small business owner yourself now."

"Sure am. Trying to." I blew out a breath, thinking of the gas leak. "Listen, I'm sure you're going to be swamped soon, so I wanted to ask you something before the dinner rush."

"Sure. Anything, Lana."

"It's about a guy named Gary Leon Knowles."

His smile faded. "What about him?" His voice was both cautious and slightly threatening. Or maybe that was his New York accent. It came out as one, long word. *Whaddabout'im?*

"Listen. I'm here because of my own curiosity. Whatever you tell me will stay with me."

His eyes narrowed.

"I'm a reporter and I know how to keep my sources secret." I could tell he wasn't entirely convinced. "Right now, I'm doing a story for the *Devil's Beach Beacon.*"

He held up his hands like I was robbing him. "Oh hell no, Lana. No way."

"No, no, no," I waved my hands in response. "I don't care what you were doing. I don't want to write about you at all. I want to confirm what someone told me. That's all. I'm trying to figure out what really happened to my employee, Fab. The Italian guy."

"Right. Heard about him. Sad news." I wished Josh would blink, because his intense stare was extremely unsettling. "But I don't think I can help you."

I plowed on. During my time as a reporter in Miami, I'd learned to ask questions until someone slammed a door in my face. "There's some evidence that ties Gary to Fab's death. But Gary told me he was selling gator and playing cards when Fab died. He didn't divulge who he was selling to, but I figured it out, since you're the only restaurant with gator on the menu."

Josh rubbed his lips together. He paused. Then after an excruciating thirty seconds, he nodded. "This won't go in the paper? And you're not going to tell the cops?"

"Swear to God, no. This is only fact checking."

Josh sighed. "Gary was with me. We've got a bit of a side hustle together. Let's leave it at that. Fab also helped a couple of times."

Only in Florida would people describe alligator poaching as a *side hustle*, but that wasn't my concern right now. I nodded. "Thank you. That's all I needed to know."

"Gary wouldn't hurt a fly, you know. I mean. He might hunt or something, but he wouldn't hurt a person. He knew about Crystal and Fab. There was something a little more going on there. Like he encouraged Crystal to be with Fab, if you know what I mean."

I blinked. "Uh, I don't."

Josh rolled his eyes. "Gary's into that. He gets off on his girl being with another man. They've got a whole game. He tried to get me to do her but—"

I held up my hand and winced. I didn't need to know any more about Crystal and Gary's weird sex escapades. Apparently, I was the only one on Devil's Beach who wasn't into kinky stuff. "Say no more."

"I'm not that kinda guy, so I didn't pry. I'm aiming for one good woman, you know. Being single around here sucks." He eyed me.

"Can't argue with that." *Please don't ask me out.*

I didn't want to dash his hopes again, like I had in high school. So, I pivoted. "Hey, I think I might know a nice woman for you."

His face brightened. "Oh yeah?"

"Have you heard about the barista championship this weekend? If you come by, you can meet her. She's on my team. Her name's Erica. Gorgeous. Kinda mysterious. She's like poetry in motion when she makes espresso."

His face brightened. "Sounds intriguing. I'm all for a woman who can make a decent cup of coffee."

I scribbled the details of the competition on a napkin. Hopefully by Saturday I'd have written my article, set Erica up with a quirky hipster geek who trafficked in alligators, and was lip-locking with a handsome police chief—and not embarrassed myself or my business at the competition.

All seemed possible. Probable, even. But one thing was left hanging: solving Fab's death.

Chapter Twenty-Three

B y the time I arrived home, I was pretty dejected. Erica and Dad had dropped Stanley off, and he was thrilled to see me.

His puppy enthusiasm boosted my spirits for about an hour. We'd been working on playing fetch, which for him meant running around the living room with the ball in his mouth. Afterward, he tried to bite my ankles in an overstimulated, overtired, finale.

"We've got to get you into puppy school." I shook my leg free of his miniscule but needle-like teeth.

He snatched the undersized tennis ball in his inch-long jaws, then stared longingly at the sofa until I picked him up and put him on his favorite cushion.

I melted next to him, wondering what the heck I was doing. It felt like spinning my wheels.

All my life, I'd wanted to succeed at something. Probably because when I was growing up, so much was expected of me. Dad was a successful real-estate agent, beloved by everyone on the island. Mom was even more revered, as a swashbuckling coffee buyer then as the owner of a popular café that became the island's social hub.

In Miami, I thought I'd fulfilled my legacy by achieving it all—great job, awards, successful husband. All that came crashing down and then I'd returned to Devil's Beach. Tried to revive the café that had lagged after Mom's death.

For weeks, it had hummed along. Until Fab died. The cloud of Fab's death, and how I'd been nasty to him on the last day of his life, hung over me and Perkatory like a slow-moving tropical storm. Agreeing to write the article was a bad idea, too. I didn't have many interesting interviews yet, just a lot of disjointed quotes.

My deadline loomed like a guillotine. This wasn't turning out to be the triumphant return to journalism that I'd hoped.

Stanley snuggled into my side. As I petted his soft fur, I mentally went through both the possible suspects for Fab's death and the sources for my article. At this point, they were almost one and the same.

Gary Leon Knowles was in the clear because he'd been selling illegal alligator meat and playing cards. Crystal had been working, and she'd been too enamored with Fab to kill him. She also was at the strip club the night he died.

Could Paige have killed him for having other lovers? Possibly, but it seemed unlikely, because he was finally doing what she wanted and spending more time with her. Paige's father? Why would he hire Fab and kill him the same day he started? Made no sense. Plus, Noah said they had an alibi off island. I wondered if either of them could have hired someone to kill Fab.

Lex? What of that business on the boat? And yet, he too had an alibi with his shark bite. Although I hadn't verified with the hospital that he'd been there all night. This I could do tomorrow.

Perhaps there were other women, or other angry husbands. Or, another possibility, one that was officially endorsed by Noah: Fab jumped off the roof. Or was drunk, lost his balance, and tumbled to his death.

I drifted off to sleep there on the sofa, Stanley by my side. Nightmares of falling from a great height plagued me, and in one version, I fell and landed in the bathwater-temperature Gulf. Dark blue water surrounded me, and as I struggled to swim to the surface, a creature came at me. It was a dead mermaid, something out of a horror movie.

I woke with a start, my scalp slick with perspiration. Stanley was curled against me. I reached for my phone to check the time. It was five in the morning. I flicked to check social media and some headlines, then glanced at my photos. The picture Noah had texted me of the mesh bra found near Fab's body was the last picture I'd saved.

In the dark, I stared at the glowing screen for several minutes.

* * *

I waited until seven to text Noah. He hadn't come into the café yet this morning, and I was impatient to share my new theory.

Good morning. I think I have an idea on Fab's case.

He called right away. "Lana," he sighed, although it sounded more like a sexy growl.

"Noah, I think you should check out Brittany, the mermaid tail maker."

"Who?" I heard the shuffling of papers.

"Brittany Yates. She was a friend of Fab's from New York and moved here not too long ago. She was supposed to hang out with him the night he died. She says she was in her studio, sewing. But was she?"

"Sewing what?"

"Mermaid tails. I think I saw some fabric similar to that mesh bra found near Fab's body."

Another sigh. "Lana. All signs point to suicide. Or an accident. I think it's time you accepted it and moved on."

I chewed on my inner cheek. Fine. I'd have to do more sleuthing on my own. "You're probably right, Noah."

"We still on for Saturday at my house?"

"Absolutely." Although now I wasn't exactly sure I wanted to spend time with someone who didn't take my theories seriously. But he was a cop, and this was business for him. I understood he couldn't drop everything to interview everyone simply because I had a hunch.

Which definitely meant I'd double down on my efforts. I wasn't letting this go. He'd have to read about my conclusions in the paper. All I needed was to make a few connections, and that required more interviews.

After I hung up with Noah, I texted Brittany. I was certain she could fill in some gaps.

Hey, want to hang out tonight at the café? I reconsidered the barista spot. Sorry about the last minute change of plans. We can talk about our strategy. And, I wanted to ask you more questions for my article!

Sounds good? How about eight? I have an appointment with a client until about seven thirty.

See you there!

* * *

In the hour before Brittany was supposed to show up, I drank three espressos, wiped down all the tables, and paced around the coffee shop. I had my entire speech planned out—I'd been rehearsing all day—and had even baked some mermaid-themed cupcakes, hoping that would help win her trust. Okay, they were from a mix, and I'd purchased mermaid tail gummies from a candy shop downtown and stuck them in the pre-made frosting.

267

"I don't know. Just because you had a dream about a sea creature, doesn't mean she's a suspect." Erica leaned on the broom.

"She knows more than she's letting on. She knew Fab from New York. That counts for something, doesn't it? She might not be a suspect but she could lead me to the information I need."

Erica hummed and hung the broom on a hook, near the stock room door. "Maybe. Maybe not. You want me to hang out while you interview her?"

"I don't think she'll open up if you're here, given the little dustup you two had."

"All I know is that she has terrible taste in coffee. You and I both know flax milk is not acceptable," she sniffed.

I bit back a smile. Erica was a coffee purist through and through. "I know."

"Maybe I should be nearby in case you need me. She had a wild look in her eye the day she demanded the flax milk. I don't trust her. Why don't I go down to the Blue Bottle and check in every fifteen minutes by text?"

I thought about this for a few seconds. "Seems reasonable."

"Can you try to record the interview? Even secretly? In case she says something incriminating? Then hand the recording to Noah?"

I pondered this for a moment. "No. Under Florida law, all parties have to be aware of the recording."

"So much for that idea. Text me so I know you're alive." Erica grabbed her messenger bag and paused. "You want me to take Stanley with me?"

Dad had dropped Stanley off after the café closed. I glanced at the puppy, who was sacked out on the floor in the middle of the café. "Nah, he's pretty exhausted after his dog yoga with Dad.

Let's let him sleep. I'll text you and then come down to the bar for a debrief. Wait. I've got an idea."

"What?"

"I'll call you and leave the line open. That way you can listen in and know what's going on. On the off chance she says anything sketchy, get Noah to come down to the café. I'll text you his number now." I went to my phone and sent Noah's contact info.

"Cool. See you later." She strolled out.

Fifteen minutes later, there was a knock on the glass café door. I jumped, and Stanley woofed softly. He padded after me as I went to unlock the door.

"Hey girl," Brittany said in a cheery voice. Or was it fake cheer? Everything she did and said would be under scrutiny now. She was dressed in pale pink today, yoga pants and matching crop top, like she'd just come from class.

"Heyyy," I tried to mimic her tone. "You do yoga?"

"Sometimes. I usually like a more strenuous workout."

"Gotcha. Me too." That was a bit of an exaggeration, but I was trying to find common ground.

Brittany squatted to pet Stanley on the head. He turned and wandered away, which raised my suspicion about her even more. Stanley loved everyone.

"Yeah, I'd been thinking about Raina's retreat in Costa Rica. Actually, Fab and I had talked about going together."

I pulled open a Tupperware container, my skin prickling with awareness. "Oh yeah?"

"When I first came to the island, Fab took me to a hot yoga class at her studio next door."

"Hm. Interesting. Mind if I include that in my article?"

She stood. "I guess not."

"Have a seat." I pointed to a table in the middle of the room. "I made some cupcakes inspired by you. Check these out."

"Mermaid tails!" She squealed over the blue-green frosting of the cupcakes and set her purse down on a table.

"Latte?" I asked casually.

"Absolutely. You want me to do it? So, I can show you my qualifications?"

"Nah. Not now. Let's sit and chat for a few. I have some questions for you. Hang on."

I went behind the counter and made the coffee. My hands trembled a little as I pulled the espresso and perfectly frothed the heart. I did a little fist pump. Perhaps like when I was a journalist, deadline pressure was good for creativity. I ducked below the counter, pretending to arrange the milk in the fridge. In reality, I dialed Erica's number on my cell and slipped the phone in the pocket of my black barista apron.

"Here you go," I trilled.

I set the mug with the aromatic espresso and frothed milk in front of her, and she blinked three times, her brow wrinkling. "You're not having one?"

"I'm drinking black coffee tonight." I pointed to my mug that was already on the table.

"Gotcha." She took a sip. "Perfect."

I murmured a thanks.

"So, about the contest," she burbled, sweeping her long ponytail behind her.

"Yes, about the contest. Before we talk about that, I wanted to ask you something else."

"Right! Of course. The article." A grimace of annoyance crossed her face for a millisecond.

"Yes. The article. I wanted to know more about your relationship with Fab. I'm curious. Were you two dating? Did you date in New York?"

Her lip curled. "Why is that relevant?"

"I like to get my facts straight."

"We did sleep together back in New York. And we went out a couple of times here on the island. Until I found out that his girlfriend was pregnant." She snorted.

I made a clicking noise with my tongue. "Men. Same thing happened to me with my ex in Miami. He dumped me for a younger woman."

"Men," she muttered.

"But what I can't understand," I paused as I tapped my fingernails on my coffee mug, "is why Fab would kill himself, or how he could accidentally fall from the roof. The police chief said it was either a suicide or an accident. I just can't get behind that theory."

She swallowed.

"He didn't seem the type. Wouldn't you agree?"

She tapped her long, pink fingernails on the coffee cup.

"What do you think happened to him?" she finally asked.

Her blue eyes met mine, challenging. Mocking. There was no sadness in her expression tonight, which made me want to ask more pointed questions. "I think he was pushed. And I suspect you know more than you're letting on."

She rolled her eyes. "What are you, a detective?"

"No. But I do know that a mesh bra that looks similar to the one in your shop was found near his body. I'm planning on putting that in the article, and wanted to get comment from you."

She visibly blanched. "I don't have to answer."

"You don't. But we're printing the facts, regardless." Of course, I wasn't sure what Mike would print, but for now, I'd bluff my way through that minor detail. "I know you were supposed to hang out with Fab that night. Why don't you tell me what really happened?"

She snorted and rose, reaching for her bag. Crap. I needed to get her to talk, not leave.

"Okay, okay." I held up my hands. "Don't leave. Let's keep chatting. What if you tell me all you know about Fab? Kill my curiosity."

I winced at my terrible choice of words.

She reached into her handbag and pulled out a small pistol with a pink camouflage handle. It seemed almost comical, but the fury in her eyes told me it was a real, and deadly, weapon. And that I was in some deep doo-doo.

"I'll kill something else," she said, glancing at the sleeping Stanley.

Chapter Twenty-Four

"Stay away from the puppy." I tried to sound menacing, but my voice quivered.

Her gaze returned to me. We stared at each other for an excruciating few seconds, until the contents of my stomach curdled like spoiled milk in a latte.

There were pluses and minuses to this situation. In the plus column: I'd definitely solved Fab's death.

In the minus column, it seemed that my own death was also a possibility. Not cool at all. I needed to diffuse this situation immediately. Which was difficult because I felt like vomiting all over her pristine white sneakers.

"Let's not get crazy, Brittany." I stood up, shoving the chair back with such force that it clattered to the ground. Stanley skittered under the table, his fluffy tail between his legs. I couldn't let her hurt him.

"Want to see what I did the night Fab died? I'll sate your curiosity. Let's go to the roof."

A chill flowed through me. "I'd rather not, thanks."

She smirked. "You don't have much choice, thanks." Motioning with her free hand, she pointed at the back door leading to the stairs. "Get going. Now."

With dread flowing through my veins, I slowly took a few steps, hoping she'd at least forget about Stanley. Hoping Erica was listening to everything. Was the phone in my apron pocket still connected to hers? Had she heard everything? Did she know enough to call Noah?

"You won't get away with this," I said in a loud voice. Figuring I had nothing to lose, I slipped my phone out of the apron pocket but stupidly fumbled because I was trembling so much. Brittany jabbed me in the kidney with the snub-nosed barrel of the ridiculous pink gun.

Right before the cell hit the ground, I noticed the home screen—not the screen that was usually visible when a call was live.

The call had somehow disconnected. But when? *Crap.*

"What are you doing? Posting a social media update? Calling the cops? Let's go. Move it," she boomed.

I went to the back door, the one that led to the stairs. She followed, and I noticed that she pushed the door all the way to the wall, so it would stay open. Clearly, she had a better thought out plan than I did, and somehow knew that if this door shut behind us, it would automatically lock.

I snuck a glance at my watch. How long would it take Erica to get here? A cold sweat made my skin itchy with anxiety.

"Up the stairs," Brittany hissed.

I began marching, desperately thinking of ways to get out of this situation.

Erica would call Noah if the call was disconnected. They'd unlock the door and find the back door to the stairwell open. Would they know to come to the top of the building?

I was out of breath by the time we got to the stairs leading to the roof. "I think it's locked," I lied.

"Like hell. Fab said it's always unlocked. Move."

I pushed open the door and the humid night air slapped me in the face. It was just after sunset, and the sky was still ablaze with orange hues that were fading to the dark night sky.

It had been years since I'd been up here, and I'd forgotten how I could see the top of my own house, just a couple of streets over. My mouth grew moist, as if I was on the verge of vomiting. I moved to the middle of the roof. There was a table and chairs set up near the edge, just as Fab had described to me when we first started working together.

While keeping the gun pointed at me, she walked through the door but didn't shut it. I thought it had been on a spring; evidently not. Maybe I could make a run for it? She stalked up to me, her mouth in a hard slant.

"That night, I came over to visit Fab. We slept together in his apartment. He was an amazing lover, you know."

"Actually, I didn't know. Had no interest in him in that way." I was shaking now, trying to ignore the waist-high wall that separated the roof from the abyss below.

"Of course you didn't. He wasn't your type. And you weren't his type."

"Had I been, he'd probably still be alive," I muttered.

"After we made love, we came up here to drink wine and stare at the moon. That's when he told me that Paige was pregnant. He said that he wanted to keep me on the side. Said he was going to work for her father, but wanted to keep sleeping with me."

"Well, that was a jerk move on his part." I was sincere about this.

"Oh, there's more. He wanted me to also go to these swingers' parties with him. Apparently, he didn't want his actual girlfriend going now that she was pregnant with his child. So, I was his slutty substitute."

I groaned, a genuine sound. "What a pig. Truly. It's understandable why you were angry."

"I'll show you where he was sitting. Get up."

I shook my head and clutched my stomach. "Can't. I'm not feeling well."

She mimicked my speech. "I'm not feeling well. Get the hell over there."

I sucked in a breath and doubled over. My vision swam from dizziness. I shook my head again, and she came closer with the gun. "Move."

She prodded my neck with the gun, and I edged a few feet closer to the wall. Then she shoved me with one hand, and I almost lost my balance. My hand found the lip of the wall and I clutched at the stone.

"He liked to sit up there. Made him feel all strong and sexy. He was drinking his wine and sitting there when he told me. I was wearing only a mesh bra that I'd made. And a pair of shorts, of course. When he tumbled off the ledge, he reached for me. Grabbed my top and it ripped right off."

Well, that solves the mystery of the mesh bra found near his body. Great. Too bad I probably wouldn't get to tell Noah about that particular clue. "Listen, I'm really sorry. Let's forget I asked about this, okay?"

"Sorry. Can't. I knew you were about to figure me out. Which is one reason why I tried to cut the gas lines at the café."

What a little witch. "You did that?"

"Yeah. I'd stolen the keys to the café the night I pushed Fab. I figured you'd eventually figure out I was responsible for his death."

Stall. I needed to buy more time so Erica could save me. "You said one reason you cut the gas lines. Was there another?"

"Fab took photos of me. Like he did with lots of women. That last night we were together, he said he stashed them somewhere. In some drawer. I didn't find them in his apartment the night he died, and figured he might have left them in the café. He could be stupid like that. I didn't have time to look that night, though, because I wanted to get out of here. I had to get behind the counter as a barista so I could find the photos. I didn't want anyone seeing them."

"And when I didn't add you to the competition team, you decided to try to blow up the entire building? Well, that makes sense. Not."

"It made perfect sense. To me. Never found the photos, though. Not that it matters now."

A spike of anger hit my gut. She could've hurt, even killed, so many innocent people. "So how did you do it, anyway? How did you push him? He was quite a bit bigger than you. And stronger."

Now she was trembling, an expression of pure fury on her face. "I didn't mean to." Her voice was almost a scream now. "He was sitting there with that arrogant smirk. He'd told me how excited he was to be a father, but he didn't want it to interfere with his fun. Our fun. And then he said he wanted to share me."

A fat tear rolled down her pretty face, and I'd have had all the sympathy in the world had it not been for the gun—and the fact I was close to the edge of the four-story building.

"But why kill him? Why not just leave him?" My back was against the ledge, pressing into the small of my spine.

"I told you, I didn't mean to. He was so smug that I ran and pushed him with all my strength. And he fell. Down there. Look over the edge so you can see."

"That's okay, I get the visual."

"No. Do it." She waved the gun. "In fact, sit on the ledge."

She stepped closer, and I seriously contemplated whether it would be better to be shot in the chest than sit on the ledge. If I sat, I might be able to ask more questions. If I didn't, I might not survive a gunshot at close range. So, I gingerly lifted myself up, trying not to peer over. The ledge was about a foot and a half wide, but it felt like an inch.

Rivers of sweat poured down the backs of my legs.

"There. He was right there. And I pushed him." She pantomimed a pushing motion with her hands, and I winced, still gripping the lip of the ledge. My entire body was taut, tense, at the thought of what was below.

"Poof. He went over the edge."

"How did that feel?"

"How do you think it felt? Powerful. He was using me for sex. Just like he used me back in New York. I got him back for hurting me."

"You didn't run downstairs to check on him? To see if he was still alive?"

"No. I was too angry. Angry at everything he'd put me through, both here and in New York. I wanted him dead."

"Tell me about that. Your relationship in New York." I tried to press my bottom hard against the cold stone, as if that would somehow glue me to the ledge.

"None of your business. Do you think I'm going to fall for this? You're stalling."

"C'mon," I pleaded. "The least you can do is satisfy my curiosity. Tell me how it all went down."

She grimaced, and when she paused, I thought she was going to shoot. My limbs started trembling all on their own rhythm, and

I clenched the ledge, squeezing the stone so hard I could feel the rough texture against my palms.

"There's nothing to tell. He used me and I let him use me again when we ran into each other here on Devil's Beach. He was like my drug, and I had to kill him to stop the addiction. And now I'm going to kill you in the same way, then go downstairs to grab my photos. People will think you committed suicide because you were mourning Fab. Or because you were so guilt ridden about killing him," she ranted. "Do you want a push, or do you want to jump on your own? How much of a coward are you?"

My jaw dropped. Was this happening? Was this how I'd die, at the age of thirty? At the hands of a crazy woman who owned a pink gun and made mermaid tails for a living? It seemed ridiculous and absurd.

"You might live if you jump yourself. It's only four stories. Some people live at that height. You'll be seriously injured, though. Or you might get lucky? Why don't you look down?" She laughed.

I shook my head. "N-no. I won't do it."

"Look down," she hollered, inching forward.

Out the corner of my eye came a golden flash. A comet of fur. It was low to the ground and headed right for Brittany.

Stanley.

He clamped his tiny mouth around her bare ankle, probably wanting to play. He was so fast that it caught her off guard just enough that she lowered the gun.

I dove at her, and the two of us, along with Stanley, were a frenzy of arms, legs, and paws. Stanley growled like I'd never heard, a bit like a tiny wolf. I wrenched the gun from her grip and got the upper hand. While she was still on the ground, my hands clamped around the pink handle and I jumped to my feet.

"Stanley, down," I said in a stern voice, aiming the gun at Brittany. He galloped away, tongue lolling, thinking this was all a game. "And you, Brittany. Don't move."

She rolled to one side, into a fetal position. Stanley backed off and ran to the door—right in time for Erica to peek her glossy blue-and-brunette head out.

"Hey, kids, what's going on—whoa!"

Chapter
Twenty-Five

I t was well after midnight when all the detectives, crime scene techs, and other officers finally left Perkatory. Brittany had shot me a final, nasty glare as she was escorted away in handcuffs. She was booked into the county jail on the mainland on second-degree murder charges.

The only ones who remained behind in the café were Noah, Dad, Erica, and me.

"Anyone for a nightcap?" I asked, my voice gravelly from talking so much—I'd given my story to not only Noah, but two detectives. And to Mike, who came here personally to write a breaking news article since none of his reporters were answering their phones this late at night.

My body still buzzed with adrenaline, and I wasn't ready to go home. "How about a boozy iced coffee?"

Erica groaned, and Dad shook his head.

"All I want is to crash after all this excitement. Don't want any more stress on my adrenals." Dad pressed a hand to his chest.

"Man, same. I'm beat." Erica stretched and eyeballed me, then Noah. "You good? I'm gonna take off."

I squeezed her shoulder, grateful that she'd heard just enough of the conversation between Brittany and me to be alarmed. When

Brittany had uttered the words "I'll kill something else," Erica had immediately hung up, dialed Noah, and then rushed to the coffeehouse. He had arrived about a minute after Erica.

She and Dad stood up. "You need a ride?" he asked her.

"Nah, I have my scooter. Bought it the other day with my first paycheck."

"Cool beans," Dad said, sliding his arm around me. "LeLa, you need me to stay?"

"Nah. I'm good. I'm going to clean up here a bit, have a drink to calm down, then head home with Stanley."

"I'll make sure she gets home safe, sir." Noah's deep voice cut through the air conditioner's hum. He was sitting at a far table, typing a report on a laptop.

Erica snickered. "Have a good night."

She and Dad and I all embraced. "You two are awesome," I said, tears springing to my eyes. We broke apart and they walked out. Wiping my eyes, I turned to Noah and he snapped his computer shut.

"About that boozy latte," he said.

My eyebrows shot up. "Yeah? You want one? Really?"

"Are you having one?"

"Is there caffeine in coffee?"

"Then I'll join you."

I went behind the counter and got to work. After the events of the night, it felt good to do something other than talk. Or think. Into two medium glasses, I poured from a pitcher of cold brew I'd started the previous day—it seemed like years—then added shots of Frangelico, whole milk and a dash of vanilla stevia. After stirring well, I topped the drinks with a squirt of whipped cream, then stuck straws in each glass.

Noah grinned when I set the drinks on the table.

"When was the last time you had coffee?" I held up my glass.

"Years. Can't remember."

"Well, I'm honored that you're breaking your coffee fast for me."

We touched glasses.

"To reporters who don't take no for an answer. I owe you a thank you."

I laughed. "To police chiefs and new friends who arrive on the scene in time."

We both sipped. I stared at him expectantly. "Well? Thoughts?"

"It's much better than I remember."

I dabbed my mouth with a napkin and laughed. "That's the best you can do?"

"It's excellent, Lana. Thank you."

We sipped in comfortable silence and then he set his glass on the table. He stirred the drink with his straw. "You could've been hurt tonight, you know. What you did was dangerous."

I swallowed hard. "I know. It was kind of stupid. I got caught up in proving everything for the story. Instead, I became the story."

"You still writing that article on Fab?"

I sighed. "Mike said I couldn't. And I understand. It's one thing to write a first-person, New Yorker-style profile of someone for the features section. It's another thing altogether when you're the victim of a crime involving the perp. We'll see. He said we'd talk next week about freelancing other articles for the paper."

"You miss it, don't you?"

"Journalism? Heck, yeah." I paused. "You know, I was sure Fab's killer was Gary. Or even Lex. Both are really shady individuals."

"Lana, about that . . ." his voice trailed off and he rolled the glass between his fingers. "I'd advise you to stay away from Lex Bradstreet."

"Why? Because he was involved with the Mafia in Tampa? I read all about it. Is that why? Did you know him up there?"

Noah's dark eyes bore into mine. "I did. And let's just say that Lex isn't what he appears to be."

I scowled. "What's that supposed to mean?"

He shook his head.

"Not fair. You can't tease me with a detail like that. Oh. Wait!" I drummed my fingers on my chin in thought. "Is he some kind of police informant? That would explain why he's running around, free."

Noah took a deep breath. "I cannot confirm or deny that."

"Wouldn't he have a different name if he was an informant or in the witness protection program?" I smirked.

He didn't say a word.

I sucked the rest of my drink down. Noah did the same.

"Hey, do you think Fab was really the father of Paige's baby? Or is Lex the father?"

Noah tilted his head. "From what I know about Lex, my guess is on Fab."

"So, you do know more than you're letting on." I looked at him through my lashes.

"That's what investigators do, Lana." The look on his face told me that he wasn't going to give up any more details about Lex. "You must be exhausted. I'll walk you home."

We gathered our things and left through the front door. I carefully checked each lock at the front and back door three times, even though there was nothing to worry about. Fab's killer was behind bars. Devil's Beach would return to its normal, quirky, sleepy self.

Noah and I slowly strolled down the street to my house. I held Stanley's leash, and he tottered on sleepy legs. My little canine lifesaver.

The air was slightly humid, with a hint of a welcome ocean breeze. A screech of crickets sliced through the air as we made our way up the walk to my front door. We paused under the wan yellow glow of the porch light. Noah was as handsome as ever, his long, sooty lashes framing those dark eyes. No glasses tonight.

His broad shoulders filled out his uniform, still crisp after hours of police work.

Maybe it was time to take another chance on a man. After all, Noah wasn't Miles. Not by a long shot. It didn't matter if he was older. He was a true gentleman.

"Thanks for walking with me. And thanks for taking Erica's call. And for coming to rescue me, and—" He was staring at me with the cutest grin. "What?"

"You're pretty wonderful, Lana Lewis."

I bit my lip. For once, I was speechless.

"I'd kiss you goodnight, but since I don't usually end investigations with crime victims that way. So, I'll save it for Saturday."

"Okay, that sounds good," I squeaked. "Um, how about a hug?"

His strong arms went around me, and we hugged for several long and pleasurable seconds. How he smelled so incredible, like spicy cinnamon and limes, after such a long night was the real mystery. When we finally released each other, we were both grinning.

"See you Saturday," I said, unlocking the door. Stanley bounded inside.

"Night."

He waited on the porch until I was inside. "Make sure you lock the top and bottom," he called through the door.

I did, then pumped the air with my fist.

* * *

The first annual Sunshine State Barista Championship was held at the Devil's Beach Recreation Center, an alabaster-colored Art Deco building erected in the twenties, only steps away from Sunset Beach, one of the island's popular strips of sand. For decades it had been a dance hall, hosting Big Band greats such as Louis Armstrong and Ella Fitzgerald.

In the 1970s and early '80s, the building fell into disrepair, and then the city purchased the place. After millions of dollars in renovations, it became a top destination for weddings and conventions.

And now, several hundred coffee aficionados.

There were twenty teams in all, from across Florida. I feared the team I knew best: Paige Dotson and her father Mickey representing Island Brewnette.

I spotted him shaking hands with a group of island officials, while Paige stood alone near an empty row of chairs. Her pregnancy was evident, and my sympathetic side took over. Sure, she'd been nasty to me in high school. And recently.

But she'd suffered that awful loss, and probably felt humiliated when news of Brittany's arrest was splashed on the front page of *the Devil's Beach Beacon* this morning.

Come to think of it, why was she even here? How stressful for her. Was her father making her compete? *Probably.* Jerk.

I nudged Erica's arm with my elbow. "I'm going to make nice with Paige."

As I turned to walk away, Erica reached for me, making a clicking noise with her tongue. "Make nice afterward. I don't want her to psych you out. We've gotta focus here."

"Good point. Right."

Just then, Mickey caught my eye. He strode over with an expression that resembled a smirking bulldog. Erica swore under her breath.

"Good to see you showed up," he boomed.

"Wouldn't miss it for the world," I replied coolly.

"Guess we'll finally know which coffee shop makes the best lattes, won't we, Lana?"

Erica snorted.

I drew myself up to my full height of five feet two and a quarter inches. "I think we know which coffee shop is the best. Now we'll just make it official."

He harrumphed and glanced over my shoulder, then walked away.

"He is the worst," Erica said. "Forget about him."

Nodding, I immediately sized up our main off-island competition: two gorgeous women with flaxen hair from a café on South Beach in Miami, and two hipster-looking dudes with identical handlebar moustaches from St. Petersburg. I'd read about both teams in a coffee trade publication; they were known for being Instagram famous. Like Fab had been.

If only he could have had the satisfaction of competing against them . . .

A wave of grief percolated inside me, and I inhaled deep to steady my mood. I had to shove memories of Fab in the recess of my mind because the mayor was on stage and the event was about to begin. He thanked everyone for coming, and was going to act as the emcee, explaining how the contest would unfold.

Everyone in the competition had eight minutes to make espressos, then another eight minutes to make a milk beverage. There were four judges, and we would be assessed on both our technical skills such as tamping, extraction and steaming, and on our sensory skills—crema, taste, and texture.

The machines were provided by the sponsor, a large coffee distributor. We were allowed to bring our own beans, and I hoped our carefully curated selection would push Erica and I over the top.

Hours later, we'd run through the espresso round, and were now on the milk beverage portion of the contest. Erica and I were almost up. My heartbeat was beating like a bongo drum.

"We've got this," Erica murmured as we watched the hipsters with the mustaches froth their milk. "Look. Their timing is off."

We watched as they served the judges slightly watery lattes. To the average coffee-drinker, the beverages would have been perfect. But to judges like these—people who worked in the coffee industry, some of whom I recognized from my days traveling with Mom—the hipsters' drinks were subpar.

"Lana Lewis and Erica Penmark of Perkatory, you're next," the head judge called out.

We stepped up to the two white, enamel espresso machines that had been placed on heavy wood tables. And then Erica and I started our ballet, grinding and pulling shots and frothing milk. The air was heavy with the aroma of the coffee we'd selected for our drinks—beans from Guatemala, with notes of golden raisin, brown sugar, and rum. It paired well with our locally sourced whole milk.

Our plan was for Erica to serve a detailed, pretty unicorn latte. I was going the traditional route, with a heart. My hands were steady as I removed the stainless-steel milk pitcher from the wand, and when I held the espresso in one hand, I felt inspired. And confident.

Carefully, I poured a thin stream of milk into the espresso until I spotted a halo of white foam collecting on the top of the coffee. That was my cue to gently rock the pitcher from side to side. Once I reached the top of the cup, the only thing left was the piece de resistance: the rosetta stem.

I backed up on my pour while moving the milk stream forward, toward my thumb. The motion was similar to dragging a knife through chocolate and vanilla cake batter to create a marbled effect.

"There," I whispered, putting the cup on its saucer. While holding my breath, I carried it to the judges.

Then I made three more.

When we were finished, Erica and I sat on a row of bleachers reserved for the contestants. I was eager to watch the final team, and a ball of nerves grew in my stomach. I knew we'd nailed our presentation.

But Mickey and Paige were next.

Mickey worked flawlessly, but Paige was slow. She pulled an espresso and fumbled when she frothed the milk, almost dropping it. Mickey barked something in a low voice at her, but I couldn't hear what he'd said because the room was cavernous and echoey.

She shot daggers at her father, and I stood up to get a better look. We were about twenty feet away, and from my slightly elevated vantage point, I caught an eyeful. My eyebrows shot up and I eased myself back onto the bench.

Erica leaned into me and hissed, "Did something go wrong?"

"Dead shot, it looked like," I murmured. A dead shot was when the crema dissipates on the top of the espresso, and it's an indicator of the quality and freshness of the roasted beans.

Erica pursed her lips.

We watched, rapt, as the judges tasted their concoctions. As they had with all the teams, their faces might as well have been etched out of granite. Poker players had nothing on these people.

As the judges tallied the scores, the conversational roar in the place grew louder. I turned to Erica.

"You did amazing," I said.

"No, you were amazing. Seriously. Don't doubt yourself so much, okay? You worked hard for this. Maybe you need to consider the possibility that you're as good of a coffee shop owner as you were a journalist. It's okay to be two things in a lifetime, you know. Or more."

"Hmm."

The inside of my mouth turned to sandpaper. I pondered Erica's words while I studied the judges. If we placed in the top three, I'd be over the moon. It wouldn't take much to make me feel accomplished, this being a new direction for me and all.

Maybe Perkatory truly was a new beginning. It was something I hadn't honestly considered when I was laid off and returned to Devil's Beach. Coming home somehow seemed like a second-best option, but perhaps it wasn't.

My heart sped up when the mayor walked to the stage at the front of the room. He told all of the contestants to "come on down" to the stage, in a voice reminiscent of a certain game show host. Erica and I stood on the side, way in back.

We held hands, and I noticed that hers were just as clammy as mine.

From the floor, the head judge handed up a piece of paper to the mayor. Erica's fingers squeezed mine.

"And now for our second runners up," the mayor said.

He announced the names of the women from Miami, and they strutted to accept their certificates. A team from Jacksonville were the first runners up, and they high-fived each other.

"For the grand prize champion barista team, I'd like a drumroll, please," the mayor said. "Of course, there are no drums, so let's have a few seconds of awkward silence."

The crowd tittered. I let out a low grunt and crushed Erica's hand in a death grip. A pool of sweat had formed on my tailbone, and I hadn't taken a full, deep breath in what seemed like hours.

"And the winners of the inaugural Sunshine State Barista Championships are . . ." the announcer's voice echoed through the rec center, "The team from Perkatory!"

"No way," I murmured. Everyone on stage turned to stare at us, and the audience clapped and hooted. My feet felt like they were encased in asphalt.

"Way. We did it!" Erica shouted, pulling me toward the front. The head judge, a woman who was an executive at a famous coffee brand from Miami, beamed while handing each of us trophies. They were golden espresso cups atop a square wood block.

I swept Erica up in an embrace, and we hugged and jumped and made squealing noises while clutching our trophies.

"I can't believe it," I cried.

"See? Told you." Then she cleared her throat. "Uh, I think your nemesis wants a word with you."

Paige stood about five feet away, staring at us. She looked like her father when she smiled.

"I'll catch up with you later," I said to Erica, then spotted my dad waving at us. Holding up my trophy, I winked at him and Erica bounded in his direction.

I took a few steps toward Paige. As I got closer, I noticed her eyes were rimmed with red. "Hey," I said in a soothing voice, as if talking to a feral raccoon.

"Hey. Congratulations. You two were excellent."

"Thank you. You and your dad were great, too. Everyone was great. Great contest. Great stuff. Just great." Oh lord, I was babbling.

A muscle in her jaw ticked. "I wanted to apologize. Obviously, I was wrong about you and Fabrizio. He put me through a lot, and

I'm just coming to terms with it. I'm sorry for my outburst that day in the grocery store."

I had to admit, I was impressed by her self-awareness. "There's no need to apologize at all. You've been through a lot." The image of Lex rubbing her feet popped in my mind. "Do what you need to grieve. If you ever want to talk, maybe we could—"

She cut me off, tossing her ponytail over her shoulder. "Yeah. Maybe we can have a cup of coffee. Well, you can. I'll have herbal tea." She patted her stomach.

"I'd like that."

She smiled, this time genuine and relaxed. "Anyway. Congrats. You and Erica really do make great coffee."

She melted away into the crowd. I was almost as shocked at Paige's grace as winning the competition. This was turning out to be quite the day. My gaze landed on one very handsome man dressed in a police uniform.

Noah.

He stood below the stage, holding his hat in hand. He was smiling up at me, a little shimmer of something that looked like admiration in his deep brown eyes.

"Let me come down there. Don't move." I wound my way through a few groups of people, down three stairs and found Noah on the rec center floor.

"That was incredible. Quite suspenseful at the end. Congratulations."

"How much of the contest did you see?" I asked.

"I saw about the last half hour. Enough to watch you make a perfect latte. Super impressive, cupcake. Were you nervous? I saw you watching the Dotsons as they made their coffees. You looked pretty intense there on the bleachers, winding one of your curls around your finger."

"Nah, I was cool as a cucumber." I paused, then glanced at the trophy in my hand, glowing. "Wrong. Yeah, I was super nervous. I didn't think we'd make it."

"Well, you did. Add champion barista to your already impressive resume." When he grinned, his dimples emerged.

"You're working today? On Saturday? Don't you ever get a day off?" I teased.

"Not really. We had another tourist-monkey skirmish today. Had to call in the state wildlife officers. I still have some paperwork left, but it shouldn't take me long. Walk me outside?"

Still clutching the trophy, I followed him out of the community center, down a concrete sidewalk that led to the beach, passing bathing-suit clad families and hipsters on beach cruisers, who pedaled while drinking cocktails. The smell of suntan lotion was thick and sweet compared to the earthy scent of coffee I'd inhaled all afternoon.

We stopped at a bench flanked by two enormous sea grape bushes and a sign that said. DEVIL'S BEACH: LIFE IS DIFFERENT HERE.

In the distance, the Gulf of Mexico shimmered a bright blue, the color of the sky. It was late in the afternoon, probably around five. I turned to Noah. "I'm about to head home and shower, then I should be over at seven-thirty or eight. Sound good to you? We are still on for tonight, aren't we?"

"We absolutely are still on for tonight. Sounds perfect," Noah said. I was mesmerized by how the late-day sunshine made his brown eyes glitter.

A warm breeze kicked up and blew a strand of my hair into my face. Without saying a word, Noah swept it away with his index finger, then tucked it behind my ear. My whole body sparkled like the water a few dozen yards away.

"I'll see you in a while. By the time you get to my house, I'll have the grill all fired up," he murmured. "Congratulations on your win."

I was already fired up, just standing next to him. Between the win and our date, I was almost giddy. "Thanks. I've already made dessert for tonight, by the way. Want to know what it is?"

He shook his head. "Surprise me." Grinning, he took a few steps back, while I sank onto the bench. I'd been standing for hours, and my feet ached.

"You going back inside?" he called out, pointing at the rec center.

"Not right now. I'm going to stay out here to get a breath of air."

"Okay. Talk soon." He turned to walk away, and I couldn't stop grinning.

Suddenly, both my heart and my life felt full, as if it could burst from happiness. Something I hadn't felt in quite a long time.

I stared at the trophy in my hands, then at the sign near the bench. I started to giggle.

Devil's Beach: life is different here.

THE END

Acknowledgments

I have many to thank for this novel. Kat Faitour, Erin Novotny, Jessica Cline, Jocelyn Cole and Brikitta Hairston were all invaluable early readers, and I'm forever grateful for your time and attention to detail.

To my agent, Amanda Leuck: thank you for always standing by me.

The Crooked Lane Books team has been amazing—thank you for helping me with my first mystery. Lou Malcangi created a beautiful cover.

Brendan Smith of the St. Pete Coffee Tour was generous and helpful with both his knowledge and his tasty beverages.

And last, but certainly not least, my husband. He gave me the space to travel in 2019, which led to me sitting alone in a coffee shop in Quebec City and plotting this book. I love you, Marco.